A Plum Jewel

Cenarth Fox

Dedicated to these courageous and caring people:
The Reverend Doctor Donald Caskie
Doctor George and Fanny Rodocanachi
Pastor André and Magda Trocmé

*'How wonderful it is that nobody need wait a single moment
before starting to improve the world.'*
Anne Frank

Chapter 1

Berlin, Germany 1938

The brick shattered the shop window. Glass fragments flew inside. Rachel Roth served a customer buying a special gift for his parents. He wore a thick coat, scarf and hat, and those garments saved him from nasty injuries. In turn, his body protected the jeweller's wife.

Benjamin Roth ran from the back of his shop. If asked, God would describe him as a good man. His jewellery business, in a small street near the Boulevard Unter den Linden, attracted Berliners because of the quality of its merchandise, and the friendliness and expertise of the owner and his wife.

Their young daughters, Miriam and Sura, were 6 and 4, and cared for at home by Herr Roth's widowed mother, Gerda known as Bubbie. Her mother was French and Bubbie spent time teaching her two granddaughters to speak the language.

It was late afternoon when the brick smashed the window. Various witnesses all suffered an attack of blindness as the criminals struck then fled. Calling the Polizei was pointless, and Herr Roth's already extortionate insurance premium would increase again.

'Rachel?' gasped Benjamin holding his terrified wife.

'I'm all right but Herr Rickard's been hurt.'

Roth moved around the counter to assist the confused customer.

'Don't touch me,' he snapped, and for a moment Benjamin thought the man blamed him for the terrorism. 'I'm sure I have glass on my clothes. You may be cut if you touch me.'

'Thank you for your consideration, Herr Rickard, but are you in pain?'

'No, I feel no pain.'

Benjamin examined the customer's back. 'There is glass on your coat, Herr Rickard, and on your scarf and hat. Thank God it is cold and you are dressed appropriately. Let me remove these fragments.'

'Be careful, Bennie,' said his worried wife fighting hard not to cry.

Outside the damaged shop people gathered and stared. Violence against Jewish traders happened every day in Germany thanks to the Nazis. Many of Chancellor Hitler's speeches claimed the country's economic woes were caused by the world's Jewry with Germany a prime example of the Jewish curse.

Using gloves and tweezers, Benjamin extracted splinters of glass as his wife held a small pan, and bit by bit they removed the debris.

'There, all done, Herr Rickard,' said Benjamin.

'Excellent, thank you, Herr Roth,' said the customer.

'Please send any cleaning bill to me, Herr Rickard, and I will deliver the finished gift to your home tomorrow evening. There will be a genuine reduction in the cost.'

'Thank you, Herr Roth but I will pay the price we previously agreed and will have the exact money when you call. Good evening.'

'Good evening,' said the husband and wife. Benjamin locked the door and flipped the *Closed* sign. The couple looked at one another, at the mess in the shop, and at the people outside staring in.

Benjamin began collecting items. 'Everything to the safe, my dear.'

Without speaking, they stripped the displays and drawers, and placed the rings, watches, necklaces and other items in the safe in the rear of the shop. With the main lights killed and the doors locked, Rachel made coffee, and Benjamin sat in the workroom and, for the first time in ages, couldn't stop tears sliding down his cheeks.

He sat in the dim light, silent; no howling, moaning or sobs. Rachel saw his tears and continued making coffee. She too wanted to cry but knew her husband needed support. A strong wife might be the only person to stop him doing something terrible. Their daughters were young. To lose their father would be tragic and disastrous.

Under huge pressure for years, this attack became the straw that broke the camel's back. Roth's suffering exploded. Being born Jewish meant he offended the government; to them he was less than human.

Anti-Semitism dominated. For Jews it was a triple whammy. The Government enacted laws to punish them, encouraged people to abuse them, and denied Jews even a semblance of justice and redress; for the Jews it was a lose-lose-lose situation.

Rachel put the coffee on the bench beside her devastated husband. He wiped his eyes and took strength from her love.

'Thank you,' he whispered without making eye contact.

She paused, hating to say what needed to be said. 'It's time, Bennie. We have delayed too long already.' He knew that and agreed. 'Sell as much as you can for as much as you can.'

'I know,' he replied, 'but we need a different approach.' She stared at him, worried he would procrastinate yet again. 'You take the girls and Bubbie and go to Paris for a holiday.'

'No,' snapped Rachel, wanting to force his hand.

He shook his head. 'Not a real holiday because you will not return.' That killed her protest. 'A family without the father is less likely to be seen as escaping. Take few possessions, buy return tickets, and make it appear as if you will come back in two weeks.'

'And you?'

'I will pretend to have the shop window fixed, and put trinkets in the front. The authorities and vandals will think I plan to stay. The hoodlums will plan to smash the window again and the authorities will encourage them. I will plan to escape indirectly from Switzerland. Soon I will join you in Paris and we will start again, free from this terror.'

A worried Rachel agreed to do as he suggested. At least this time he proposed a plan. Rachel told Gerda, her mother-in-law, but naturally said nothing to the children. Two days later all four females boarded the train for a short holiday to visit Rachel's cousin in Paris.

Benjamin didn't rush to repair his shop. He knew if he replaced the glass as soon as possible, it would be smashed as soon as possible. He fixed a board to cover the broken glass and placed a sign facing the street. *Closed for Renovations. Re-Opening soon.* The thugs gloated and planned their next attack.

Benjamin made house calls fulfilling every order and maintained the fiction about the shop being repaired and re-opening soon.

He gathered stock, as much as he could carry without appearing suspicious, and by day travelled in taxis and trams on crowded streets. He called on wholesalers and retailers offering his stock for sale. They knew his situation and offered ridiculously low prices.

Desperate, Benjamin sold what he could but kept his finest diamonds and gold. He faced two problems. Could he escape to France? Could he smuggle his gold and best diamonds with him?

Rachel, Gerda and the girls left for Paris. As the train approached the German border, officials entered demanding papers. Aryans were given scant regard but those of Jewish extraction copped the full treatment. Rachel and Bubbie were thoroughly searched including their coats and hats.

Small amounts of cash were taken as, "it is illegal to remove German currency from das Vaterland".

Both women were smart enough to never complain and to avoid eye contact with their "masters". Relief overwhelmed them when they crossed into France and eventually arrived in Paris.

In Rachel's cousin's two-bedroom flat, the four extra bodies found life tight but gloriously safe. With her daughters asleep on the floor, Rachel took the doll and teddy bear carried from Germany by the little girls, and unpicked the stitching she made in Berlin.

From within each beloved toy, Rachel removed the diamonds and gold sewn inside. Jews 1, Nazis 0.

Back in Berlin, Benjamin pondered purchasing additional toys for his children as a way of doing what his wife did to smuggle valuables. His sewing skills dissuaded him. He planned to never return to Germany until the scourge of anti-Semitic hatred died. Right now, such a prospect seemed impossible.

He sent two packages to a friend in Berne. One was expertly wrapped and sent with Benjamin's Berlin business address displayed prominently. The second was poorly packaged with a return address of a rundown area with the Berne address written in a sloppy hand.

Soon after his family reached Paris, Benjamin began a circuitous route to leave the land of his birth. He pretended his shop was being repaired. He locked his empty safe with a note inside; *Help yourself.*

He caught a train to Hamburg and then another to Dortmund. He stayed in cheap hotels. He caught more trains getting out at each city, going into the business heart before returning to the station and moving again. He sold nothing. In Munich he caught a train to Berne in Switzerland, his first real test.

Approaching the Swiss border, German officials demanded his papers. Benjamin made sure he carried a bit of cash and a small collection of poor quality diamonds. He thought about offering them to the officials as a bribe. He chose instead to let the cash and stones be confiscated. They were.

He showed his collection of tickets used during the last few days.

'I have important business within Germany and Switzerland,' he pleaded. 'I have been to all these cities and tomorrow I return to Stuttgart before finally returning home to Berlin.'

Having "collected" his now depleted possessions, they let him through. For the second time in ages, Benjamin cried, this time when he alighted at Berne Station.

Both parcels posted in Berlin arrived at his friend's address. The expertly packed parcel contained low quality diamonds. They were missing. The three books in the poorly packed parcel arrived. That parcel too was examined but not well enough. Precious stones and gold were secreted in the spine of the books. Benjamin rejoiced. From Switzerland he took a train to France. Jews 2, Nazis 0.

Paris, France

When Benjamin arrived in Paris, his family celebrated with much joy. Within a week, the Roth family from Berlin found their own apartment in the 6th Arrondissement, and Benjamin went in search of a business in need of an expert jeweller. He soon found work.

The Roths had mixed feelings. Being safe in France brought relief but letters from friends back in Germany spread fear and distress. Benjamin read one letter to his wife.

'Jews are forbidden from working in certain professions, from entering certain shops and more than half have emigrated.'

Rachel sewed, refusing to look at her husband. Deep down she believed the future for Jews would be misery and premature death.

Her premonition came true in November when, in their homeland, mobs attacked Jewish businesses and synagogues in what became known as Kristallnacht, the night of broken glass.

Many Jews were murdered and many more committed suicide. 30,000 Jews were arrested and 7,000 Jewish businesses destroyed. For Jews, Germany became a full-blooded lawless country with authorities ignoring the mayhem, and failing to protect Jews or prosecute criminals.

Benjamin spoke quietly to his wife. 'We must move again.'

'And go where?' she asked.

'To America; the land where Jews are treated as human beings.'

'What about your mother? She may want to stay.'

'Why? War is coming and all of Europe will be swamped. I'll sell most of our gold and diamonds and visit the American consulate tomorrow to apply for entry to the United States.'

Rachel's face turned blank. Her heart ached and would ache even more when their troubles multiplied in the morning.

The principal of daughter Miriam's school telephoned the Roth home.

'Can you come to the school, Madame Roth?'

'What has happened?' asked the shaken mother.

'Miriam is asking for her mother.'

'I will come immediately,' said Rachel.

The child couldn't hide her distress. Seeing her mother, Miriam ran and clung so tight it made Rachel's fear explode. She whispered to her daughter but stared at the principal seeking information.

'There was an unfortunate incident in the playground, Madame. A few of Marian's classmates behaved appallingly.'

The child sobbed as her mother stroked her head and kissed it.

'I think you should take Miriam home and we can discuss the matter tomorrow. I assure you the children involved will be punished and the parents informed and warned about this behaviour.'

Rachel took her miserable daughter home. When the 6 year-old Miriam explained how classmates taunted her, called her a Jew and then spat on her, Marian suffered despair more than anger. When Benjamin came home and heard the story he raged.

'I know the Germans are racist pigs but the French? And today the tormentors are children, *French* children. Miriam is never to return to that school and we are to leave Europe, now, before it explodes.'

Rachel knew he didn't mean today, but she agreed. Jews in Europe in 1938 were destined for annihilation.

Leaving Europe would not be easy for Benjamin Roth and his family. Eighteen months later they still resided in the French capital.

Chapter 2

Paris, France 1940

Donald Caskie worked as the minister of the Church of Scotland in the unusual location of Paris, a long way from his home on Islay, part of the Inner Hebrides off the coast of Scotland. His congregation consisted mainly of Scots whose accent gave them away. Caskie spoke fluent French and English and could dazzle with a touch of the Gaelic. His fellow believers loved and admired him.

Their Kirk in Rue Bayard sat slap bang in the middle of the City of Light, a wee caber toss from the Champs-Élysées.

In the summer of 1940, Paris hid its usual lively self due to the new world war. Many Parisians remembered the last one, some 20 years ago.

Caskie 37, single, and devoted to his flock, was worried. When, not if, war came to Paris, where would he go and how? Many of his flock were elderly and he took their spiritual and worldly wellbeing to heart. Who would care for them when the Nazis hit town?

Fifth columnists were a part of war and one already attended Caskie's church. This stranger sat in a pew taking notes as the parson preached. No-one in the congregation knew the man's identity, what he wrote or for whom, but it was easy to guess his politics.

Caskie spoke his mind. From the pulpit, the crofter's son attacked German injustice and brutality. Castigating the Chancellor, the dictator seemed like a death wish. But such was the character of the reverend laddie and yes, his remarks were noted.

Then the Nazis arrived. Germany won the Battle of France and marched into Paris. Elsewhere in the city, a young Englishwoman using the name, Juliette Beauchamp, worked as an active agent for the Secret Intelligence Service. She'd never heard of Donald Caskie who packed his socks, underpants and kilt and prepared to leave town.

Before the Nazis settled in Paris, Parisians fled. More than two million residents of the capital departed. Mothers wheeled the family bicycle with parcels and a child or children perched on board. Lucky car owners had the roof of their vehicle laden with goods. A group of nuns sat jammed in the back of a lorry. Thousands of pairs of walking shoes were given away to assist the mass of refugees on foot. If you had a cart but no horse, you hitched an ox and got going. Some could not bear to part with their beloved pet meaning their dog joined the exodus. Prams for babies were filled with food, photos and a toddler. Even Belgian and Dutch refugees were part of the French farewell.

The stranger in the Scottish kirk, the one taking notes during the Reverend Caskie's sermons, prepared to snitch to the Gestapo once they opened for business in Paris. It was time to scarper, Jock.

Sad and frustrated, Caskie went to visit each member of his congregation, believing his exit meant letting them down, especially the old and frail. Tears were shed and promises of prayer made until, with few possessions, the clergyman set off. As mad as it sounds, he planned to walk south, yes, on foot, find a port and from there sail home to Britain. He was not alone. Huge lines of Parisians joined him. Most walked.

Catching a train proved impossible. Few ran and, if they did, for every seat there were ten, no twenty would-be passengers.

How you left the city was not as important as *when* you left. Remaining in Paris after the Nazis arrived meant dicing with death. If you were Jewish, to stay was insane.

Joining this flood of refugees were Allied soldiers who missed the last boat or ship departing Dunkirk. Sitting on the beaches while Germans strafed them didn't appeal. After the disastrous Battle of France and missing a ride home, these soldiers headed south. They were hungry, sick, sore, sorry, even wounded and, like Caskie, most walked. Happiness and good health were in short supply.

The garrulous by nature Caskie changed, meaning he travelled alone and spoke little. He suspected a fifth columnist could well be the next person he spoke to. The warm weather became hotter and the future unknown. Forget about plans for the next day, week or month; let's just make it through the next hour.

The masses travelled on the roads until a military or some sort of official vehicle came along forcing humans to scatter. It became every Parisian and especially every Jew for him or herself.

Benjamin Roth, his mother, wife and two young daughters were in this mass of humanity. His attempts to secure passage to America more than a year ago came to nothing. Once war kicked off, Benjamin tried everything including begging and bribery but failed.

When the French army and others were routed, the Roth Plan B was simple—flee south. Buying a car proved impossible but a baker's horse and cart with an enclosed area behind the driver sold for an extortionate fee. In the back, Rachel made her mother-in-law comfortable and sat with her two young daughters, who were excited about this unusual vehicle and trip. Papa rode up front as the driver.

This was no happy adventure. As they went clip-clopping through the Parisian suburbs, many desperate people frightened the children, refugees shouting for a ride. Several attempted to climb aboard. Their threatening behaviour made the little girls cry.

Gerda took control. 'Come along you two, let's play a game.'

As a brilliant watchmaker, Benjamin made a lousy driver. During his 39 years on Earth, this became his most wretched moment, totally lacking in hope. He felt great pressure to protect his family but with no fighting skills, weapon or knowledge of escaping through a foreign country, he felt lost. He now owned a horse and cart. What food do you give a horse? When do you feed it? How far should I make it pull the cart before it needs a rest? Life offered nothing but problems and questions without answers. He tried to remain calm.

He was not alone in a state of despair. Thousands like him with as many issues and problems headed south. Complaining was useless.

Then the heavens opened with steady rain at first and nobody took shelter. Those without protective clothing were soaked. Heads down, they concentrated on putting one foot in front of the other.

Benjamin's younger daughter wanted to pee. 'Can we stop, Bennie?' asked his wife.

He looked back in the cart. The safety of the family he loved rested in his hands. France might have been overrun but Benjamin's biggest problem was his 5 year-old daughter's bladder.

He kept driving feeling despondent for the horse. To his wife, he said, 'We're in the countryside. There is no lavatory and even if there was, she'd be drenched and catch a cold. Find a bucket or a pan, anything.'

He tried to block out the mixture of sounds of crying and soothing words in the cart behind him. He wanted to weep and prayed silently for a change in fortune. His relationship with the Almighty was tenuous at best. The reply from above produced more and heavier rain. It whipped the horse and the humans. Benjamin called out to the horse. 'As soon as we find shelter, I will stop, I promise.'

The horse nodded. Benjamin didn't know if that meant thanks because the beast had been nodding its head ever since they left Paris.

After twenty minutes, half an hour, who knows? Who keeps time when your life is hanging by a thread? The rain eased and stopped. The sun shone giving warmth. People stopped for a break and steam rose from their soaked clothing. Life felt better, not remotely good or pleasant mind, just less traumatic.

But then the refugees would have considered the episode of pelting rain to be glorious compared to what followed. A new disaster appeared out of nowhere. A German plane, a dive-bombing Stuka, sounded loud because it flew so low, and its wind-driven siren ramped up the terror. Its two 7.9 millimetre machine guns provided an indiscriminate massacre. Yes, there were straggling, unarmed soldiers within the column of refugees, but did that justify the pilot firing at the mass of humanity below? Silly question; and anyway, who did write the rules of war?

Elderly people like Gerda Roth and her young granddaughters, Miriam and Sura, were not exactly a threat to the invading German army. Bullets smashed into people, animals and property. The scream of the plane drowned out the screams of the people and animals.

The attack lasted seconds but its impact a lifetime.

Who decides where the bullets will go? How does the pilot feel as he wheels away from his latest courageous act of mass slaughter?

Benjamin reacted once the sound of the plane arrived. His instincts took over. He yanked the reins to the right heading towards the trees at the side of the road. People ran beside and in front of the horse. Where else could they go? What else could Benjamin do?

A ditch beside the road lay unseen amidst the panic. The horse stepped over the channel but the right hand wheel of the cart dropped tipping the vehicle on its side. Disaster.

Benjamin fell off the seat onto the ground in the forest. The horse cried out in fear and fell on its side. The females inside the cart were tossed around as the cart crashed on its side. Poor little Sura copped the contents of her saucepan of pee. Fear ran rampant.

'Give me your hand, Monsieur,' said a kind voice. Donald Caskie bent beside Benjamin and helped him to stand.

'It's my family,' he panicked pointing to the overturned cart.

The men scrambled to the rear and peered inside. Rachel helped her daughters towards their father and the stranger. The girls, in shock and too afraid to scream or even cry, were lifted out and placed on the ground.

Benjamin reached in for his wife. 'Take my hand, my dear. I'll fetch Gerda.' Rachel hesitated. 'Come on, before the cart moves again.'

Rachel spoke softly. 'Gerda is dead.'

Benjamin felt an arrow pierce his heart. His mother, the woman he automatically loved, had never stopped loving, breathed a minute ago. She moved house to live with her son's family when Benjamin's father died. A brilliant grandmother, she enabled the Roth husband and wife to work hard in the family business. Gerda kept good health, excellent for a woman of her age. How could she be dead? The bullets from the plane missed the Roth family and its vehicle.

'Allow me,' said Caskie. Benjamin's expressionless face announced his grief and shock. The Scottish cleric helped Rachel climb out before he climbed in to examine the blood-free, unmarked body. With no medical training, even Donald could see the poor woman's neck was broken.

He closed her eyes and gaping mouth, found a towel and covered her upper body.

Benjamin stared into the cart. Caskie studied the grief-stricken man, grimaced and shook his head. 'I'm sorry,' he whispered and crawled out to join the Roth family.

Finally a cloud with a silver lining appeared as two bedraggled British soldiers stopped and spoke in English.

'Do you need a hand?' asked the Londoner.

'Indeed,' said Caskie in English with his Scottish lilt.

The soldiers were taken aside and Caskie explained the body inside. The second soldier, a farmer from Lincolnshire, attended to the horse. With the animal tethered, and Rachel and her girls settled in the woods, the soldiers with Caskie and Benjamin heaved and shoved trying to get the cart upright. They made it.

Then someone needed to make a decision. With his limited English, Benjamin insisted on taking the three helpers with him. But what about his dead mother?

In his fluent French, Donald introduced himself as a man of the cloth from the Church of Scotland, and offered to conduct a service.

Benjamin encountered grief, relief then worry. 'Oh Father,' he whined, 'I am Jewish and we are not a religious family.'

'Your faith is one thing, sir, said Caskie, 'but respect for the dead is universal. Allow me to conduct a service for your dear mother.'

Benjamin couldn't handle this response. Someone, anyone being kind proved too much. His tears ran free. Caskie embraced him and Benjamin's head rested on the minister's shoulder.

When the tears stopped, Caskie made a suggestion. 'Why don't we make her comfortable in the front of the cart and your family can sit in the rear. When you reach the next village, you can find the priest and give your dear mother the burial she deserves.'

The Londoner understood. 'Good on you, Padre; damn good idea.'

Benjamin recovered. He didn't want his wife and children to see him like this. He wasn't ashamed but rather was desperate to set an example as a strong husband and father.

The soldiers hopped in the cart and placed Gerda in the front and covered her with a blanket. They made a sort of wall using suitcases and bags.

'All set, Guv'nor,' said the Londoner indicating the rearranged interior. He whispered. 'The kiddies can't see nuffink.'

The Lincolnshire soldier attended to the horse. Benjamin hugged the Cockney. 'You and your friend must ride with us. This is the least I can do to repay you.' He turned to the clergyman. 'And you too, Padre. I insist.'

'Most kind,' said Caskie although I think you should consider your horse. If you give the beast too hard a task, you will have lost your transport. And, unlike me, these fighting men, need help.'

And so this tiny portion of the mass of humanity continued on their journey. The Roths moved steadily to the next village with the Lincolnshire farmer up front guiding the horse, the Tommy from London beside the driver. In the back, Benjamin and his family hugged each other. They waved to the Reverend Caskie as he faded into the mass of refugees. He and they continued to travel without hopes and dreams.

Donald felt warm inside. Preaching the gospel was his calling, but feeding the hungry and clothing the naked ranked just as high on his list of priorities. Righting an upturned cart and attending to the dead and to a helpless family were close behind.

The Roths and the soldiers were the first people he spoke to since leaving Paris. A fear of spies in the ranks pushed him to silence. But he always enjoyed chatting to fellow humans.

He reached the next village by nightfall but saw no sign of the cart and its occupants. Hunger pangs annoyed him, and finding food and a bath would equate to Paradise. He thought about finding the local Catholic priest for news on a burial but instead went in search of sustenance.

Moving out of the village, he spied a vineyard and despite being well aware of the 7th commandment, his hunger pangs led him to a bunch, no, two bunches of grapes. Their juice slaked his thirst and their fruit lined the sides of his stomach. The thieving Padre moved to the edge of the vineyard, climbed over a wall and fell asleep.

Chapter 3

Vichy France 1940

Once the Germans conquered France, the country split in two with a puppet French government established in the south in the spa town of Vichy. The WW1 hero, Marshall Phillipe Petain became its leader.

The Roths finally fell on better times as they headed towards Vichy France. Two British soldiers on the run helped, if not saved the Jewish family. The priest in the next village agreed to bury Gerda Roth and refused payment. Benjamin left details for a simple nameplate. You did such things in wartime.

As the group headed south, the horse enjoyed good care, and food and shelter were found, and although slow, they made progress.

The British soldiers chatted and reckoned they'd be better off alone. The family was holding back the soldiers who fancied catching a train to Bordeaux, Toulouse or Marseille. They took Benjamin aside. Their French and his English made for a tricky conversation.

'You 'ave to make your own decision, Guv'na,' said the Cockney. 'We 'eard the Germans and the new French government down 'ere, are tryin' to catch Jews.'

Benjamin understood. He'd been persecuted for years.

'You have advice for me, gentlemen?' he asked.

The farmer pointed. 'If you head east, you'll come to Switzerland. They're neutral. No fighting and no persecution of Jews. The Red Cross will care for you and you can ride out the war in peace.'

Benjamin studied the soldiers.

'I agree wiv' 'im, Guv'na,' said the Cockney.

'But where will you go?' asked Roth, concerned for the welfare of the men whose efforts helped the Roth family survive.

'We'll head south, reach a port and catch a ship back to England.'

Roth nodded. 'We wish to go to England. Do you know London?'

The Cockney smiled. 'East End born 'n bred, Guv'na. When you get there, ask for Tommy at the *Bricklayers' Arms*. I'll stand you a pint.'

The men shook hands and Benjamin told his family about the parting of the ways. There were hugs all round. The Cockney produced two rolled pieces of brown paper used to wrap parcels, and handed one to each daughter.

'A little present for you, ladies, somefing to remember us by.'

The girls opened the papers, each with a portrait in charcoal, one of Miriam, the other of Sura; a magnificent likeness. Joy shone on the girls' faces. Their parents choked with emotion. The art, created by the Londoner, an untrained, brilliant artist, delighted the family.

The Lincolnshire farmer checked the horse, gave it his last apple and beckoned to Benjamin. With the German by his side, the farmer lifted the front off-side leg of the horse and pointed to the shoe.

'Next village, Monsieur, have the farrier change this shoe. See here.' Roth nodded. 'You need a new one before Switzerland.'

Benjamin surprised even himself when he hugged both Tommys. In a land where death and misery impacted everyone, the milk of human kindness gave massive relief. Tears were shed as the soldiers kissed all the females then set off on foot. They turned to wave at the first bend in the road. All four members of the Roth family were waving—hands, handkerchiefs, even rolled up portraits.

They were alone again and took the advice of the soldiers. 'All aboard,' said Benjamin. 'Next stop Switzerland.'

The Roths were Germans in a conquered foreign land, passing through, trying to escape. Benjamin pointed the horse east and set off. They came to a village where an old man sat in front of a shop.

'Bonjour, Monsieur,' said Benjamin. 'My horse needs a new shoe. Is there anyone nearby who could help me?'

'Next village, twenty kilometres,' he said puffing his pipe.

Rachel poked her head through the hole in the panel behind the driver's seat. 'The girls are tired. We are tired. The horse is tired.'

Benjamin understood but felt unsafe staying where people could see and report them. Cooking, eating and washing outdoors became easier but staying safe was key.

'We will stop soon,' he said urging the horse forward.

Not far out of town they passed a farm. Smoke rose from a chimney in the simple house. He told the horse to stop, tied the reins to the side of the cart, told Rachel of his plan then walked to the house. She called in a soft voice. 'Be careful.'

His heart raced. His wife's heart raced faster. He knocked on a door and a woman appeared. Rachel watched dreading an awful reaction. Benjamin turned back and pointed. The woman looked at the cart then spoke to Roth. He returned to the cart faster than before. Rachel worried. *Has he been threatened?*

Benjamin untied the reins. Rachel asked. 'What happened?'

'She has invited us to stay the night.'

'What? But we are strangers and Jews. It could be a trap.'

'Perhaps, or maybe there are French people who have sympathy for refugees. I told her we would pay.'

Rachel groaned softly believing her husband to be too trusting. Out here in the countryside they could be robbed, killed or worse, betrayed. But her fears disappeared as the couple welcomed the family with open arms.

They provided food and shelter. The nourishing meal tasted great. The old and leaky bathtub mattered little once the girls hopped in together and soap and hot water felt wonderful, while the straw mattresses in the barn were soft, ticklish and perfect for hours of sleep. So, not everyone hates Jews.

In the morning Benjamin woke, wandered into the yard and found the farmer working on the Roth horse. The farmer explained.

'Pardon, Monsieur, but your horse it needs a new shoe.'

Benjamin collapsed. He dropped to his knees, and shook his head, speechless. The farmer worried. 'You do not want this, Monsieur?'

The visitor struggled and started blubbing his thanks. After years of persecution, some friendship, kindness and decency from one human being to another proved overwhelming.

The Roths enjoyed the best breakfast—ever. The wife wrapped bread, cheese and ham in a towel and gave it to Rachel who found it hard to express her gratitude. The girls gave the childless wife a long hug. She felt a pang of sadness not having been able to conceive.

Away from the others, the farmer took Benjamin aside.

'You are Jewish, are you not, Monsieur?' asked the farmer. Benjamin nodded. 'The stories we have heard about your people being sent to camps is truly evil. Not all French citizens will try to help you. You must be careful.'

'I cannot express how much your kindness means to me and my family. You must allow me to offer you a small payment.'

Stressed by this and determined, the farmer shook his head. 'Please, do not even think of that. It is the least we can do and if our roles were reversed, you would do the same for me.'

Benjamin grasped the farmer's hands and squeezed them so hard, the sunburnt, gnarled fingers of the man of the land felt pain.

The Roths climbed aboard their cart and with their newly-shod horse set off with everyone waving. The children didn't stop until the farmer and his wife were out of sight. In all their misery and grief, this ray of sunshine gave the family a glimmer of hope.

Although relatively young and fit, Donald Caskie reckoned walking pretty much the length of France, and in wartime, was ridiculous. He reached a village and nearby, met a farmer who gave him a feed, and offered his barn as "the room at the inn".

Donald slept beside a cow whose mooing, as opposed to Caskie's snoring, proved soothing. In the morning, the clergyman spotted an old bicycle in a corner of the barn and, for a small fee; Donald forsook walking and cycled through the country famous for its bike race.

He wasn't pedalling a racing bike or one in great condition but he travelled with speed and with ease on the flat. His mind relaxed. With a fair wind he could make Bordeaux within, well, before Christmas.

He rode into a village and saw many faces watching the stranger. Despite this being unoccupied France, while the Germans dominated the north of the country, locals were wary. Surely the Germans will move south soon, and before then, spies will ride into town to check out the lie of the land. Is this man a German spy? Hardly.

Donald pulled up in the main street to be surrounded by curious and suspicious locals.

With his excellent French and a broad smile, he spoke, 'Bonjour.'

'Look!' yelled a local pointing at the back of the bicycle. Others pushed to see. The crowd jeered. They grabbed Donald and frog marched him and his machine to the police station, the visitor having no idea why.

Events were explained to the senior officer who immediately suspected Donald of being a German spy.

'Monsieur, do not think you can fool us. We hate the Germans, defeated them in the last war and will defeat them again.'

The audience, their number swelling, gave strong vocal support to their local gendarme. Donald worried. He knew they were wrong but not why they were convinced he was an enemy of France.

'Messieurs, please hear my story.' He noticed a subdued hubbub begin with no-one ready to believe this stranger danger.

'I am indeed a foreigner in your land but I am British.' The mob hesitated. 'I am the minister of the Church of Scotland in Rue Bayard in Paris.' A buzz began. He is a priest from Scotland? Surely not.

'I fled the capital with, it seems, most of Paris. I spent the night in a farm near La Rochette and the kind farmer sold me this bicycle.'

The policeman challenged Donald although with less venom. 'You have a German bicycle.' He pointed. 'See!'

The bicycle was turned around and there on the back below the seat was a Nazi sticker, small but easily recognised. Donald was as shocked as the locals. How it got there was a mystery. The clergyman stood tall.

'I never saw this bicycle until yesterday. If I am a spy, why would I advertise my German sympathies? Surely I would keep my true identity a secret. Messieurs, I am British and trying to find a way to return to my homeland to help liberate your country. Vive le France!'

He spoke with passion and so much so the policeman believed him, pumped his hand and the visitor received more pats of encouragement and apologies than he could count.

Donald ripped the Nazi emblem from his bike, accepted one of the offers of accommodation, and the next day set off for Montpellier.

The Roth family headed south. The driver, with no map and no sense of direction, thought they were going east but they were heading to the Mediterranean. At their speed, it was light years away.

The young girls grew restless wanting to know when they would reach their new home, longing for a bathroom with a lavatory, a bedroom with clean sheets, and meals like Grandma used to make. The mention of Gerda, now lying in a Catholic graveyard in a French village, brought pain to their parents.

They made camp for the night beside a river. As the girls played, Benjamin tended to the horse. Rachel prepared the meal using their dwindling food supply and was the one to broach the subject.

'We can't go on like this.'

He knew she spoke the truth and felt his body ache twice over. First, it was from the physical effort of travelling as they were, and then from fearing he would be unable to protect his family. He was the man, the breadwinner, the patriarch, and he it was who must provide for and protect his wife and children. Already his beloved mother was dead.

They ate in silence and Rachel put the girls to bed. When she stepped outside, her husband was deathly silent. She knew he was doing his best but distraught. She hugged him and whispered.

'Life will be better in the morning. You are doing a brilliant job.'

She was wrong about life getting better. Disaster struck. The horse was gone. Benjamin despaired, blaming himself. Talk about the last straw. He tethered the animal but apparently incorrectly. Could he do anything right? He ran forward, the way they planned to travel, calling, searching while fighting back tears. He saw nothing.

He returned remembering last night's discussion with Rachel and her words. 'Whatever happens, Bennie, we must remain calm and positive. If the girls see us defeated, they will be frightened.'

He put on a brave face. 'The horse might have gone back the way we came. I'll go and find it.' He set off the way they came but again saw or heard nothing. His heart ached. He fought to hold back tears. *What will I do? What can I do? I am a failure.*

He remembered the people walking out of Paris, pushing prams or carts even wheelbarrows. He was lucky having a horse and cart. Now, without a horse, he could not provide for his wife and children.

Rachel watched for him but knew they'd lost the horse. It wasn't Benjamin's fault. In the night, an opportunist thief silently led the animal to the river and walked it away in a cruel act of robbery.

'Where's our horse, Daddy?' called Miriam. 'Did he run away?'

'I think he did,' said her father.

'Will you pull the cart, Daddy?' asked little Sura.

As ridiculous as it sounded, Benjamin agreed. 'All by myself,' he said and the others laughed.

'Let's have breakfast,' said Rachel, and the change of subject brought some relief to the parents, especially the patriarch. Inside, his heart was on fire.

Benjamin took his wife aside. 'Pack a bag with the food we have and extra clothes for the girls and hide it in the woods.'

'Where are you going?'

'If anyone comes along, take the girls and hide in the woods. If they steal the cart, at least you will have the basics.'

'Benjamin, I'm scared.'

'I'll go in the direction we would have taken. There has to be a farm or village. I'll find help and come back as quick as I can.'

'But it could be ...'

'Don't argue, Rachel. Do as I say. Tell the girls I'll be back soon.'

He kissed his wife, turned and hurried away not wanting his daughters to see him go. His mind exploded with sadness.

Will this be the last they'll see of their father?

He walked as fast as he could, scanning the countryside for any sign of habitation. The weather was warm. He removed his jacket, licked his parched lips, and ignored the sweat on his face and neck.

It seemed like he'd walked for miles. Then he heard a sound. He stopped. It came from behind him. The road twisted and he could only see about a hundred metres. It was a truck, something a farmer might use to take produce and livestock to the market. The sound grew louder and Benjamin panicked.

If he flagged it down and the driver or his passengers were German or Vichy sympathisers, as a Jew he was dead. His family would have no-one to help or protect them. He would have failed.

The truck appeared. It was old and battered. Roth needed to decide. It might be his best, his only chance to save his family but if he hailed the driver, he could be signing his own death warrant.

In two minds, at the last moment he ducked into the trees and hid. His heart accelerated as the truck slowed. Why? *They saw me.* The truck horn blared. Terrified, Roth crouched and prayed, which was twice in a week now for the non-believer.

Oh no! The truck stopped. The horn sounded again. Roth froze expecting shots but couldn't believe the sound he heard.

'Daddy!' cried his daughters. He rose and stared. From the window of the truck's cab, Miriam and Sura waved and called. His heart rate exploded as he staggered forward not able to understand.

The driver, needing a shave and a wash, more a scrub, smiled.

'Your taxi, Monsieur Roth. Please, do come aboard.'

From despair to delight, Benjamin saw his grinning wife and daughters seated inside the cab beside the French farmer.

'There is room in the back, Monsieur, if you don't mind the pig poo.' He didn't. 'You should hide if a vehicle is coming or going.'

He'd hide, fly or climb mountains if it meant saving his family. He clambered in the back where their possessions from the cart were stowed, and saw his daughters laughing through the back of the cab. The driver was right about the faecal droppings. Some were rusted on, some deposited today. Benjamin happily sat in the shit.

The truck bounced along passing or being passed by the occasional vehicle. Benjamin stayed low. All was well for an hour or more until the truck slowed. He worried. The truck stopped and he heard his wife and daughters getting out.

'Come on, Daddy,' they called. He climbed down. Rachel used her head to indicate the driver. Benjamin approached him.

'Sorry about the crap, Monsieur,' said the driver.

'Please do not apologise,' said Benjamin gazing at his saviour. 'Thank you from the bottom of my heart.'

'I told your wife about a village where you will be safe. It's a fair walk and uphill but they'll see you right.' He revved his engine. 'Must go; pigs to feed.' He tooted and waved. The Roths all waved back.

Benjamin joined Rachel and his daughters wanting to hug them all but stopped when Miriam spoke.

She held her nose. 'Oh Daddy, you stink.'

'Oh Daddy,' added little Sura, 'there's poo on your clothes.'

The parents exchanged glances and the hint of a smile. Rachel pointed. 'There's the road,' she said. 'It's not far but is uphill.'

'Come on you lot,' said Benjamin picking up the suitcase and the heavier of the three bags. 'Let's go.'

And that was how the family Roth from Berlin, and then Paris, eventually made their way to the village of Le Chambon-sur-Lignon somewhere in the south of France.

Chapter 4

Marseille 1940

Donald Caskie made it to Marseille, a port on the Mediterranean on the south coast of France. He travelled by foot, bicycle, and car and when he arrived, was offered a berth on the last ship sailing for England. He declined. Yes, after all that travel, he chose to stay.

'I have a duty to help folk here,' he said. 'I will stay and do God's work in Marseille.' The American consulate officials thought him mad and tried to persuade him to leave. One official lost his temper and cursed the man of the cloth.

The ship sailed without the clergyman. He fronted the local authorities with his offer to work. They agreed he could take over the old and empty Seamen's Mission at 46 Rue de Forbin by the docks.

'But be warned, Padre. Refugees and sailors only may enter your establishment. If we find even one POW escapee or downed air crew member on your premises, it will be closed, they will be arrested, and you will be locked up and the key thrown away. Do you understand?'

'Perfectly,' replied the man from Islay, who lied with sincerity and cared not a jot for Vichy punishment. He sought ways to ignore rules.

He scrubbed the old double-storey building making it ready for anyone wanting a bed and a feed. His "home" became the biggest safe house in France. In time he helped hundreds of British and Allied fighting men flee France and cross into neutral Spain. There were more than 30,000 refugees who made the trek. Caskie knew he was playing with fire but as the war weary made it to Marseille, he found ways to harbour then help them escape.

But what a challenge escapees faced. Many Vichy police were pro-Nazi and loved hunting POWs on the run and in particular, Jewish refugees. The Gestapo and Abwehr loitered in the shadows.

For all escapees, avoiding capture was but part of the challenge; first they had to cross a vast mountain range. It intimidated everyone. Climbing the Pyrenees in good weather was tough. Even fit and able-bodied adults found it a challenge. Throw in bad weather, elderly refugees and children, and the task screamed impossible.

Even if you could obtain the right clothing, footwear and supplies, you needed an expert guide to lead you up into the clouds and back down again in another country—Spain.

If you bumped into a Vichy patrol or a traitor it meant death. Some guides, called passeurs, would betray the trekkers for 30 pieces of silver. A few did. Who could you trust?

Refugees, escapees, and evaders made their way south with many reaching Marseille. Some came alone while others were guided, some from as far as Paris, even Belgium.

Donald Caskie took them in. He knew the risks. He promised he would never help escaped POWs. He lied. He promised he would shun air crews who were shot down but they were welcomed and hidden. They needed accommodation, clothes, supplies and guides. Caskie raised money from wealthy sympathisers. He served his God by saving the desperate and, in so doing, saved lives, countless lives.

Le Chambon-sur-Lignon, France

The pig farmer spoke the truth. The small town of a few thousand people was a good hike distant, and the walk uphill. The Roth family struggled to get there, the girls in particular. When they reached the outskirts of Le Chambon, they stared at the town. It seemed God had picked up the houses and placed them on a plateau surrounded by mountains and forests, kilometres from anywhere. Again the family faced uncertainty with begging their main, their only hope of survival.

To give it its full name, Le Chambon-sur-Lignon built a reputation where many of its residents, Huguenots, chose to help rather than hinder refugees, most of whom were Jews.

Huguenots were French Protestants who understood persecution. In 1572, after a royal wedding, thousands of Huguenots were massacred by Catholics in and around Paris. It provided a shining example of brotherly love, of doing unto others what you would have them do unto you. Why have heathens as enemies when fellow

Christians are there for the killing? The Huguenots never recovered and only ever made up a small percentage of Christians in Catholic France.

In 1940, a churchman in Le Chambon-sur-Lignon, Pastor André Trocmé, supported by his wife, Magda, preached forgiveness and love, and urged their congregation to give shelter to those he called "the people of the Bible". Other churches did the same. News spread. Refugees, and especially Jews and children, were made welcome.

Thousands came. Refugees were hidden in cellars and attics, farms and houses, and even in hotels and schools. International bodies sent money to pay for food. Many Jewish children received their primary education living there. The Roth family knew nothing of this as they waited on the side of the road seated on their suitcase and bags.

A man on a horse came along and stopped. 'Are you coming or going?' he asked.

'Coming,' said Benjamin, 'we've just arrived.'

'Wait there. I'll tell the Pastor,' he said then nudged the beast and continued into the village.

Half an hour later a man and a woman arrived seated on a cart pulled by two horses. 'Welcome,' said the man. 'I'm Pastor André Trocmé and this is my wife, Magda.'

Benjamin introduced himself and his family. They were helped onto the cart which made a graceful turn and headed into town. That night, with their daughters asleep, Benjamin and Rachel cuddled in their umpteenth bed in recent times and pondered their situation.

'I always knew you would take care of your family,' said Rachel.

Benjamin sighed. 'Liar,' he said and squeezed her tighter.

For the next days, then weeks, the Roth family found somewhere safe to stay. They discovered new ways to live. To maintain their status as locals, they went to Sunday services in a Protestant church. Now that was something rare—Jewish Huguenots. And when word spread about an approaching Vichy patrol, the Roths with all the other Jews were led into the forest.

An hour later, the refugees heard singing in the village and long-time incomers explained.

'When the villagers start singing, it means the Vichy police have gone and it's safe to return. The authorities often ask the Pastor about

Jews in his town and he replies, "We do not know what a Jew is. We only know men".'

Benjamin shook his head in amazement. 'What a place,' he said to his wife as they strolled back to their new home. Their growing daughters went to one of the local schools and thrived. Benjamin found work as a baker and Rachel as a seamstress. They moved to the back of an old hotel. Cramped, yes, but the peppercorn rent and donated furniture made it feel like home. No, it *was* home. The next thing they knew, Christmas approached, another first for the Roth family, and Miriam and Sura loved the present giving.

Apart from the friendship and generosity from these Gentiles, the one amazing fact about Le Chambon-sur-Lignon was its lack of snitches. Not every resident in town supported the refugees but no-one became a traitor; no-one contacted the Vichy police.

Being safe and respected brought wonderful peace but as the months rolled by, Benjamin worried their good fortune could not last. The threat from the enemy seemed ever present. After about a year, he went to discuss things with Pastor Trocmé.

'You're welcome to stay for as long as you like, Benjamin.'

'I know, and cannot thank you enough, Pastor, but I feel as if we are a burden on your hospitality.'

'Nonsense, man, you are working at an honest job, your children are happy, being educated, and most of all, we, the people of the village want you to stay.'

Benjamin struggled with such kindness. 'I still can't believe you are doing all this for so many Jews; there must be hundreds.'

'We are doing God's will, helping people regardless of their faith including, like your good self, those with an absence of faith.'

'I cannot shrug off the feeling I am totally dependent on you and often think we should move on.'

'And go where? This war may get much worse before it's over.'

'My ideal goal is to sail to America.'

The priest stared at him. 'I admire you, Benjamin. At times I wonder if Jews are glad God named the Israelites his chosen people.'

'It's not something I've thought about.'

Pastor Trocmé quoted. "The Lord your God has chosen you out of all the peoples on the face of the Earth to be his people".'

'I'll take your word for it, Monsieur.'

'And yet you face so many pogroms, so much persecution; I mean, do Jews really thank God for giving them His blessing?'

Benjamin shrugged. 'You're asking the wrong man, Pastor. I believe in family and hard work.' Their philosophical discussion began to run out of steam. 'Although in the last year I have met three Christian holy men who have given me help unstintingly while steadfastly refusing any form of payment. When escaping from Paris, a Scottish priest helped us when my mother died.'

'I'm sorry.'

'And a Catholic priest buried her willingly while also refusing any payment. Then you and your wife have literally saved my family. There must be something to this Christianity where, without judgement or asking anything in return, you help those in need.'

André smiled. 'You might be right.'

'So, for my family to find a ship and sail to America, Pastor, what do you recommend?'

'Sleep on it. Weigh up everything. If you wish to leave, I will do all I can to help. But if I were you, I would be content knowing my wife and children are happy, safe and free from persecution.'

Benjamin admired the man of the cloth and held out a hand.

'If I ever become a believer, Pastor, I will tell the Almighty about a Frenchman in a small town in the French countryside who went out of his way to help others. Again, I thank you.' They shook hands.

Benjamin went home and told his wife they were staying, at least for the time being. She said nothing but her heart sang for joy.

Chapter 5

Lyon, France 1941

Louise Beatrice Wellesley, known at different times as Sister Claudine or Plum, walked away from Lyon. The bishop in the magnificent cathedral had just tried to murder her. She escaped after the religious toppled from the cathedral's balcony smashing into a solid oak pew, decorating it and the floor with his blood, brains and crucifix. Pity the cleaner involved with that lot.

But the bishop's demise formed only part of Louise's exploits in this city and its surrounds. In the local prison, she stabbed a guard in the heart, cut the throat of a Gestapo officer, stopped and delayed a German troop train by blowing up a railway track, and plunged a knife in the posterior of the leader of a local Resistance cell in order to prevent him from raping her. And all this happened while she lived as a nun in the nearby enclosed Carmelite order. Not bad going for a Sister and bride of Christ.

A local priest, Father Flory, told her to leave town. The Wehrmacht, Gestapo, Resistance, Vichy police, and even the Holy Roman Catholic Church all wanted a chat with this now nun on the run.

Louise listed two goals. Escape from France anyway she could, and return to London to uncover the traitor in the SOE. No-one in London knew what she knew. She confronted two spies in the crypt of the cathedral. Both were now dead. She made Father Flory have the radio operator she rescued tell London she was missing presumed dead. She reckoned being dead gave her the best chance to uncover the spy at SOE HQ in Baker Street.

On a sunny and warm morning outside Lyon, Louise's worries about being caught pushed her hunger, thirst, and weary bones from her thinking. Flory gave her specific instructions. She followed them and outside the city, off a track in the forest, found the small hut.

She inspected the inside and decided it would be safer to wait outside. Louise moved into the forest and from an elevated position sat with her back to a tree and waited.

She dozed but snapped awake when she heard a sound. Someone approached along the track. Louise watched. A man, no, a boy about 16 stopped near the hut and called softly, 'Sister? Sister Plum?'

Louise threw a stick which landed behind the visitor. He spun around and went searching in that direction but saw no-one.

'Hello?' he called again with a soft voice. He went to call again but froze when he felt something hard on his spine. A low voice growled.

'Move and I shoot.'

The young man raised his hands and begged for mercy.

'Please do not shoot. I am a woodcutter looking for my dog.'

Louise stepped back and spoke in her normal voice. 'What, your dog is called Sister Plum?'

Hearing the unthreatening female voice helped the teenager relax and turn. He faced Louise who held a stick from the forest. She tossed it aside.

'Oh Sister, thank God I found you.'

'Who sent you?'

'Father Flory.'

Louise studied the boy and thought him almost young enough to be her son. 'Let's go in the hut.'

Apart from a wooden bed frame with slats, the hut stood empty. They sat. He took off a bag slung across his shoulder and gave it to her. Inside were bread, sausage, and cheese. She thanked him then went to stuff the food inside her jumper.

'Take the bag,' he said. She did and took control.

'Thank you. Now, the less we tell one another, the less you can tell the Germans if you are captured.'

'I know.'

'I need you to help me reach the south coast, and then guide me over the Pyrenees into France.'

He gasped. 'But Sister, I can't possibly do what you ask.'

It was her turn to be shocked. 'I thought you were my guide.'

'Yes, to the next safe house.' Louise sat stunned. 'This is how we help escaping British airmen and POWs. We take them to the one safe house we know, and then someone does the same to the next safe house and so on. It's all I know.'

'I'm sorry, I should have known.' She stared at him. 'May I ask how old you are?'

He tried but failed to puff out his chest. 'I turned 14 last month.'

She nodded. 'Right, I shall call you 14. So what happens now?'

'If you are ready, Sister, I will take you to your safe house.'

Louise stared at him, smiled and stood. 'Then lead on ... 14.'

Through the forest they went always listening for other humans. This part of the world all appeared the same to Louise and the prospect of stumbling upon a certain group of Resistance fighters, some of whom were after her blood, made her skin crawl.

They reached the crest of a hill. The boy stopped and pointed. 'Drop down through the trees and cross that river. You will have wet feet, Sister, but once across, turn left and walk along the bank for two kilometres. The first farm you come to is on your right. You will be among friends.'

She smiled at him, leant forward, and kissed his cheeks.

'Thank you, 14, and make sure you get home safely.'

She skipped down the hill dodging the trees as she went.

Once across the river, Louise moved into the forest, sat and ate. She remembered her SOE training about survival on the run. Ration your rations, rest where possible, assume nothing and, night travel is best.

She set off keeping the river in sight. Moving through a forest creates sound. She avoided twigs and dodged branches. Without warning, a strange sound exploded behind her. She ducked, turned and was relieved to see a large bird flap away.

A mooing cow told her the farm was close. Questions bounced inside her head. *Are they expecting me? How will I approach them?*

Through the trees Louise saw the cleared land and animals, and a house; solid, old, and in need of repair. A shed with hay and ancient farm implements stood nearby. *Where are the people?* She waited, watching for humans. Louise didn't want to frighten them and racked her brain to remember training sessions on approaching people. She remembered how to do so in the street. Was this the same?

Louise crept closer, crouching behind a ramshackle fence and weeds. A dog raced out of the old shed heading straight for the visitor. Its bark exploded. Louise froze, not so much from fear, as to make herself a small target.

The canine knew the stranger lay hidden and told her repeatedly to vamoose. Louise whispered trying to calm the savage beast. He refused her entreaties.

The back door of the house opened and a woman called. 'Dreyfus! Come here!' More barking came from the canine. The woman wandered towards the dog and the unseen interloper. She was intrigued and the dog determined. Louise decided to make a move.

'Help!' she called. The woman stopped, the dog didn't.

'Who's there?' called the woman.

Louise stood setting off the canine who now barked at its owner.

'Bonjour, Madame. I believe this is a safe house.'

The elderly woman stared at the young woman with the rough appearance, disheveled even, but behaving in a polite manner. Yes, this was indeed a safe house for friends of France, but for escaping POWs and downed airmen on the run, all of whom were male.

'It is,' she said, still uncertain. 'Please come inside.'

Louise hesitated as Dreyfus ignored the order to Stand Down.

'Dreyfus,' snapped the woman and the dog understood. Louise hopped over the fence and held out her hand to the woman. They smiled, gave no names, and went inside. Dreyfus followed, curious.

The rustic, rural kitchen, the engine-room of the house, played host to cooking, eating, washing and more. Lived-in best described it.

'My husband will be home this evening, Mademoiselle. Would you like food?'

'Thank you, Madame, I have eaten but if you have water ...'

'Would you like coffee?'

Louise's smile told all. For her, coffee was a luxury. The woman fussed and Louise relaxed for the first time in a long time.

Secrecy would be her salvation. The infamous deeds of the Carmelite nun in Lyon put Louise at the top of the Most Wanted List. Telling anyone her identity would be playing with fire. She remembered her SOE training and concocted a new ID.

'My name is Helene, Madame. I am a nurse helping brave soldiers. As the Germans drove our army south, I fled with them. I became separated, and now I need to reach the coast where I can help our escaped POWs and those brave pilots who have crashed in France. I met Resistance fighters who told me your house is safe. If you can help me, I will be most grateful.'

'But of course, Mademoiselle.'

Louise sipped coffee in a remote French farmhouse wondering how she could travel further south, and join the escaping Allied men and refugees fleeing from France to Spain. She hoped the absent husband would have the ideas and the means.

She felt dirty. Late nights killing Germans, destroying railway lines and fighting fifth columnists left her emotionally exhausted and in need of a bath. Her hostess read her mind.

'Would you care for a bath, Mademoiselle?'

Louise wanted to hug the old woman.

From the yard they fetched a tin bath then tipped several pots of boiling water therein. They topped this with water from the pump in the yard and when the temperature settled, Louise prepared to strip.

'Give me your clothes, Mademoiselle and I will wash them while you bathe.'

They struck the deal. Louise scrubbed herself from top to toe. The feeling proved sensational. 'I think you like your bath,' said the woman and Louise laughed with happiness. 'I will hang your clothes on the line and the sun will dry them in no time at all.'

'Thank you, Madame, you are most kind,' said Louise and lay back amongst the suds and warm water. *This is heaven*; she thought then panicked when a loud male voice sounded.

'Elsa.'

'Shit,' said Louise, softly, and tried to hide beneath the water.

The door opened and the husband entered. 'Mother of God,' he said imitating a pillar of salt.

There is no diary account stating when Renato, husband of Elsa, last saw a naked woman, but it is true to say it was a fair while ago.

Time stood still for both the naked and dressed occupant until Elsa entered from the yard with fury to burn.

'Get out!' she bellowed at her husband. 'How dare you enter while our guest is taking a bath? Go!'

The husband skedaddled without a backward glance. As much as he wanted to gaze at their visitor, the shock and his wife's bluster drove him away.

'I am so sorry, Mademoiselle. My husband has no manners and I will deal with him when you have gone. Now, here is a towel to dry yourself, and a nightdress to wear until your clothes are dry.'

Louise took the towel and dried herself. 'Thank you, Madame. Please don't be angry. Your husband did nothing wrong.'

She snorted and started to prepare a meal. Louise slipped on the nightdress. It throttled her neck and covered her toes and would never feature in any fashion magazine. Her wet hair clung to her face and neck. She used the towel to make a turban.

'Excellent,' said the woman and then yelled. 'Now you can enter.'

Renato took his time. He opened the door a little and peeked inside. His wife gave him a blunt message.

'You said you would not be home till dark.' He entered and impersonated Mr Humble. 'First you must apologise.'

'I am very sorry, my dear.'

'Not to me, you turkey, to our guest.'

Renato apologised. 'Please forgive me, Mademoiselle.'

Louise said she wasn't offended, and they discussed her visit. When she repeated her story about Helene, the nurse, he still doubted her. All previous visitors they entertained were male. To Renato, a woman on the run seemed incredible. She wore no military uniform, looked so young and, well, beautiful. He struggled.

They dined. Louise told as much as she dared. 'I need to avoid the Germans and reach the coast so I can continue to help our soldiers and their allies. Can you help?'

Renato shook his head. 'We can help you reach another safe house, Mademoiselle, but nothing else. We do what we can. We know nothing of the people who are sent to us.'

'I understand. But can you tell me how long it will take for me to reach the coast?'

'Walking?' She nodded. 'Months, Mademoiselle, going from safe house to safe house is dangerous and also time-consuming.'

'Are there cars or bicycles I could use? I need to move fast.'

The couple felt bad. They were poor with little knowledge of the war, the Resistance or the Vichy administration.

'There are trains, Mademoiselle, but you would need tickets and identity papers, and there are checks everywhere. You could be stopped, arrested, and deported or killed.'

'What about Phillipe?' asked Elsa. 'He can help.'

Renato agreed with his wife. 'Yes, he does know people.'

Louise felt better, not excited but hope flickered in her breast beneath the tent she wore.

'Can we meet Phillipe tonight?' she asked.

Renato nodded. Elsa disagreed. 'I think Mademoiselle Helene should remain here. It is too dangerous for her to go into the village.'

Louise gave Renato a certain stare. He decided. 'I will ask about papers and train tickets. After, we will make plans.'

'What is the nearest train station?' asked Louise.

'Lyon,' said the couple together and Louise felt sick.

Right now, half the city of Lyon wants my blood. How can I wander the platform and hop aboard any train? I'll never make it.

Then Elsa became excited. 'If you go by train, Mademoiselle, you must go in disguise.' They watched her reaction. 'I have clothes, even some of my late mother's clothes. You must become an old woman like me.' The others reacted. She tackled her husband. 'When you see Phillipe, ask about a wig.'

'A wig?' he asked, confused.

'Yes, one for an old woman like your wife.'

Chapter 6

64 Baker Street, London 1941

Where is Sister Claudine? Is she alive? Is she in jail? Who would know? These and other questions were discussed in the F Section of the SOE. 'The last message is pretty clear,' said Jermain Attard, a Frenchman and desperate to see his country free again. 'Sister Claudine is missing presumed dead. She's gone and so we move on.'

'Presumed dead is not the same as being dead,' argued Vera Atkins, a Romanian, highly educated and dedicated to defeating Nazi Germany. 'It's like Missing in Action. She may still be alive.'

Maurice Buckmaster, in a senior position in the French Section, didn't take failure well. 'If she's alive, why hasn't she made contact?'

Royston Black gave his boss a serve of sarcasm. 'Buck, it's a little bit tricky to whip off a Morse message if you're shackled to a wall in a filthy Gestapo cell.' He and Buckmaster were fellow students at Eton during the previous war. They endured an abrasive relationship. Buckmaster recommended Black for the SOE, but Black reckoned he would make a better leader and coveted his boss's job.

The discussion bogged down in petty claims and questions.

'We can be sure about certain facts,' said Atkins wanting to make progress. 'Claudine arrived in Lyon. She discovered this Father Flory is on our side, and we know radio operator Alfie is alive and making contact. The question, gentlemen, is how do we find out if *she's* alive?'

Silence. Buckmaster argued. 'Sending in another agent to find her is throwing good money after bad. She's trained. She's resourceful. Let's continue to make contact with Father Flory and agent Alfie and respond to their reports.' He observed the other three. 'Agreed?'

Atkins and Attard nodded, Black didn't. 'I disagree. She knows a lot about our set-up. She joined the SIS before she joined us. There are rumours she's pals with the Royals. If the Gestapo grabs her and discovers her social standing with the Palace, she's a serious liability.'

"

'Or trump card,' said Atkins.

The others stared at Black. He oozed a steely determination, his eyes gleaming.

'What are you suggesting?' asked Buckmaster.

Black paused. 'We need to send someone to southern France to see if she's still alive.'

'And if she is alive, what then?' asked Atkins. 'Do we ask her why she hasn't made contact? Do we ask her to continue operating as an SOE agent, as a nun? Should she maintain her religious vows?' Vera's sarcasm pushed the room temperature up a degree or three.

Black spoke calmly. 'Anyone'd think I'm suggesting we kill her.'

The atmosphere simmered approaching boiling point. Attard with his charming French accent made a suggestion. 'I can contact my Resistance friends in the area and see what they know.'

Buckmaster nodded. 'Okay, do it. In the meantime, we assume she's captured or dead. Now moving on, what's happening with those new special effects at the Museum?'

Elstree Studios, near London

The movie business took off in the 1930s with silent films giving way to the talkies. In Britain, studios cranked up productions meaning skilled behind-the-scenes people were in high demand. Set designers, builders and set dressers were always needed but now technical crew people who knew about microphones, lighting, cameras and special effects, all became super important.

One of the major film facilities was located at Elstree about 15 miles north-west of London.

When WW2 kicked off and intelligence units were formed or boosted, experts working behind-the-scenes on movies in studios such as at Elstree, joined the SOE using their technical know-how to work on bomb-making, map-making, and other secret devices for use by SOE agents.

Obviously the boffins needed a place to work, and one location they used was the British Museum (Natural History) in South Kensington. Whole rooms were cleared to allow damn clever technicians, scientists and tradesmen to design and build new devices.

Hailing from Elstree, one technical expert was Harry Williams, who became a leading light in the SOE nasty tricks department. In a room next to a giant dinosaur, Harry and other chaps became the SOE agents' back-up team. They dreamt up ideas to turn simple everyday items into dangerous, lethal weapons.

One bright idea involved stuffing a dead rat with explosives. SOE agents then placed said rodent in a building, occupied by Germans, with a furnace for heating Fritz and his friends. Pop the dead rat in the corner by the coal where the stoker would find it, hate it, and do the sensible thing by tossing the rodent in the flames. Ka-boom!

These SOE scientists produced all manner of gadgets. Maps made of silk so they didn't rustle and give you away, shoes that left an imprint of a bare foot, a compass in a lipstick container, and arguably the most terrifying, TNT made to look like bits of wood or coal or even horse manure; exploding horse poo! Here in the most unlikely of settings, Mr Churchill's baby operated at all hours to help SOE agents cause Jerry as much confusion and pain as possible.

Not all inventions in the so-called toy shop were meant to be harmful. Harry and his mates came up with such things as radios hidden in petrol cans, and food disguised as driftwood. This unusual laboratory in the heart of London enabled countless SOE agents to succeed in hurting Hitler. The general public never knew about these men and their machines buried in the British Museum.

The boffins even created a folding motorbike, which could be ready to ride in 11 seconds; a sort of Blitzkrieg for beginner bikers.

Chapter 7

Vichy France 1941

As the crow flies, Lyon to Marseilles is about 300 kilometres. The simplest and fastest mode of travel in war torn France was by train. Louise knew she needed to vacate Lyon. She was not so much on top of the Nazi's most wanted list; she starred having her own poster.

The next day Renato brought Phillipe back to the farm to meet Louise. He didn't fill her with confidence. Like Renato, Phillipe struggled to believe in a female POW or pilot, and became skeptical about one without identification or uniform. These farmers had only helped British escapees. Who is this French woman and why is she escaping?

One problem for Louise involved secrecy, never mentioning her Carmelite nun role and achievements. *Trust no-one* became her one defining rule. Revealing her SOE ID invited death. The grapevine would hum. Many would love to kill her and for money; others would love to capture her. And if word got out she was alive, the traitor in the SOE in London would be tipped off.

She told Phillipe the same Helene nurse story she told the couple. He agreed to help. 'I can obtain for you top quality identification papers, Mademoiselle but what is this about an old wig?'

'She must go in disguise,' said Elsa. 'A young woman travelling alone will attract attention. An old crone like me will be ignored.'

The men nodded with both thinking Helene's beauty would alone be enough to attract attention from friend and foe alike.

'It will take a day or two to get what you require,' said Phillipe. 'I suggest you stay here and out of sight.'

Louise agreed but itched to move, wanting to leave today.

She could offer little support to help the elderly couple on their smallholding with chickens for eggs, a cow for milk, and a horse for transport. The shed roof sported multiple holes but her carpentry skills were non-existent. She needed to move as the waiting around doing nothing made her nervous. Rather than get under their feet, she decided to go for a walk.

'No, no, no, Mademoiselle,' said Elsa. 'It is far too dangerous. You are a stranger and that alone makes you suspicious.'

'Only to the river, Madame,' said Louise, 'no further I promise.' She managed to win reluctant permission.

The couple worried. If Helene was caught, massive trouble would follow. For any French person helping an enemy of the Fatherland, the penalty was death, shot on sight. The Germans hated trials.

'Go after her,' said the wife. 'Don't let her see you but be ready to help if there is trouble.'

Renato peered through the kitchen window, last washed in 1936, and waited till Helene disappeared. He followed.

Louise reached the river. The surrounding dense forest stood quiet and peaceful with birdsong and a gurgle of water the only sounds. The steep bank and an exposed tree root offered a sort of cave like space. She slid down the bank then climbed underneath the tree, removed her shoes, trousers and shirt, stored them and slid into the river. Bliss. The cold water made her feel alive. The stillness of her surrounds seemed incongruous with the war and evil and misery in the next valley.

She was drifting with the current when she heard voices. Panic. With limited cover, she swam silently towards the bank. Who were they? Where are they? They were on her side of the river.

She ducked below the water. The voices were muted but seemed close. Under water she pushed herself upstream back to her hidden clothes. Air, she needed air.

Close to the bank, she broke surface and gasped as quietly as possible. The voices were louder, obviously closer. She glanced upstream. The exposed tree root was about five metres away. She took a deep breath, dropped below the surface and swam.

Because the water was clear, she saw the roots. Slipping under them, she surfaced, again in silence. Then she saw the humans, well their legs and feet. Two men sat on the bank above her, smoking and chatting. How long would they stay there? Could they see her pressed hard against the bank amongst the tree roots? She remained still but privy to their conversation. After a few sentences she died. They were talking about her.

'For a girl to abseil down a sheer cliff and know about explosives sounds bloody amazing but she was a nun.'

'Why do you reckon she stabbed the boss?'

'Because he tried to have his wicked way with her.'

'No! He tried to seduce a nun?'

'Seduce is too kind. And why else would she stab him? She stopped the train, saved us from the Bosch, and he says thanks by abusing her.'

The second fighter paused. 'So where do you reckon she is now?'

'Could be anywhere. I heard a rumour she killed a bishop in Lyon.'

'What? No. A nun killed a bishop?'

'That's the gossip in Lyon.'

'Jesus, how many Hail Mary's is that worth?'

The first man laughed and Louise sensed movement. She dared not look up and was glad she didn't as a stream of urine flowed from above splashing into the river.

The men left and Louise waited. The sounds of nature returned and still she waited. Feeling cool in the shade, she grabbed her clothes and shoes and carefully climbed out of her hiding place. Not a human in sight. She scrambled up the bank and nearly died.

'Bonjour, Mademoiselle,' said Renato. 'Or should I say, Sister?'

For a second time he found her in a state of undress.

'Turn away,' she snapped.

He did and she dressed quickly, her wet underwear dampening her clothes. She approached him.

'You must say nothing, not even to your wife.'

He gave a half bow. 'Of course, Mademoiselle, and I suggest you go first. I will follow later and tell my wife I did not see you.'

She stared at him and, having no choice but to trust and believe him, she returned to the house.

In the evening, Phillipe arrived with gifts. 'I have your identity papers with your name Helene Smythe and your occupation as a nurse.'

'Thank goodness you have my real name.'

An awkward pause followed. 'And a train ticket,' he said and placed a parcel on the table. 'And here is your unusual request.'

Elsa opened the parcel and removed the straggly, old and definitely secondhand wig. Its greasy smell gave Louise visions of head lice and worse. The black hair mingled with streaks of gray. 'Try it on, Mademoiselle,' said the old woman.

Louise did and it changed her appearance dramatically. 'I will fetch the clothes,' said Elsa and left. Phillipe went over the paperwork with Louise who felt a rush of excitement.

Later, Renato walked Phillipe off the property, and Elsa helped Louise to dress. The result saw the old woman gasp with delight. 'This is excellent, Mademoiselle but there are two more steps.' She fetched a stick. 'You must walk with a limp and change your face.'

Louise sensed she'd joined an acting class with a director explaining her new role. An old pair of spectacles appeared. 'And you need a dirty face, Mademoiselle. Can you grow a wart and facial hair?'

Louise laughed as Renato returned. 'Voila!' said his wife indicating their visitor. He shook his head in amazement then gasped as Louise moved towards him.

Her walk proved mesmerising. She stooped then shuffled, leaning on her stick. She stopped in front of the man of the house and spoke in a deep, crackly and rural-sounding voice. 'Pardon Monsieur, but where is the railway station?'

Elsa clapped and Renato grinned. Both knew that Helene the nurse or nun or whatever would be a remarkable escapee. He couldn't believe the stunning young woman he saw climb out of the river in her underwear had become the sickly old crone standing before him.

Over the evening meal, they discussed how Helene would travel to Lyon to catch her train tomorrow. Elsa and Renato trusted no-one in Lyon. Dressed as a crone, with a one-way ticket to Marseille, and her new ID papers, Louise was on her own.

She slept fitfully thinking about any number of challenges. *Don't get caught. Reach Marseille. Find somewhere to live. Forget Helene or Louise and become, I don't know, Madame Defarge.*

The trip into Lyon brought back memories. When she dropped out of the sky one night not so long ago, and dressed in a nun's habit, she found her way to a farm. After a wonderful breakfast, the farmer drove her into the outskirts of Lyon on his cart. Life repeated itself.

She took an age to adjust her costume and hair and apply her make-up. Using an old cracked mirror, she was reminded of the ugly sisters when as Cinders in *Cinderella*, she performed at Windsor Castle. *Goodness, a lot of water has flowed under the Mathematical Bridge since then.*

Elsa gave Louise a powerful hug and kissed her cheeks. They even looked like sisters. The real old woman waved as the cart disappeared.

Renato took the long way to avoid being stopped. Getting closer to Lyon, Louise's nerves came alive and her chest grew tight. She kept her head bowed but peered from side to side watching for signs of danger. If forced to run, ditching her outer garments would be the first step.

Renato pulled into a side road. 'I think you should depart from here, Mademoiselle. The station is a busy place and it will be better if you approach on foot.' He smiled at her and she squeezed his hand.

'One day, I hope I can repay you and your wife for your kindness. Vive la France.' She went to move then thought better of it and whispered. 'You should be giving me a hand, Monsieur.'

He realised his error and hopped down to help the "old woman" from the cart. They glanced at one another before she left.

Renato's claim about a busy station proved correct. Louise limped, head down searching surreptitiously for her platform. She passed a group of Wehrmacht soldiers, not yet officially in Vichy France, and possibly men who were on the troop train halted by the old crone now walking past them.

On the correct platform, she moved slowly in search of her carriage. Stepping off the train were two men, Gestapo officers dressed immaculately. She stood in their way. One wanted to push the hag. If only they knew this smelly witch was the nun who slit the throat of their colleague in the Lyon jail only a few blocks away. She backpedalled and they went on their way.

Louise reached her carriage and compartment and, delighted, found it empty. She sat in a corner facing the locomotive and produced knitting given to her by Elsa. She remembered their conversation.

'I can't knit, Madame,' protested Louise.

'Pretend, Mademoiselle. Pretend you are a real Madame Defarge.'

Time passed slowly. People moved along the corridor and the platform. A loud whistle sounded. Steam hissed. An official called and then the train shuddered. It moved but backwards giving Louise a fright before it stopped then moved forward. She felt fantastic.

She panicked when she heard voices yelling. Five men raced along the platform, grabbed the railing beside the steps at the end of her carriage, and boarded the moving train. They burst into the corridor and her compartment and puffing, collapsed on the empty seats.

They were dressed as civilians but strangers to her, and Louise's training made her wary. They travelled with little luggage. She became suspicious. One leaned across to her and spoke slowly.

'Bonjour, Madame.'

Louise froze. She tried to give the impression she was deaf, not interested and afraid.

The man repeated his statement only louder. 'Bonjour, Madame.'

Again the old hag refused to respond. The men exchanged glances. The one who spoke to Louise now addressed his fellow travellers in a much softer voice. 'Quiet time, if you please, gentlemen; forty winks methinks.'

What he said and how he spoke gave Louise a serious jolt. He might well have come from Louise's hometown of Farnham in Surrey as he spoke perfect English with a Home Counties accent.

Chapter 8

Le Chambon-sur-Lignon 1941

The last 12 months were more than kind to Benjamin Roth, his wife and their daughters. Miriam now 8 and Sura 6 were excellent students in a local school, their French as good as their native German. Their parents were calm, quietly contented Jews living in a Protestant hideaway village in Catholic France now conquered by Nazi Germany.

One afternoon Benjamin arrived home upset. Rachel asked why and his face said it all.

'There's trouble in town. Vichy officials were again asking about Jews. Pastor Trocmé defied them. No longer do we scurry into the forest. We are considered residents of Le Chambon. The locals say we have a right to be here.'

'And we do,' replied Rachel. 'The Pastor will always keep us safe.'

'Not if he's arrested. What if they take him away? Last month the young man who refused to reveal the names of the Jewish youths in his care, left for a concentration camp. He's never come home.'

Rachel worried. 'It might be dangerous but it is dangerous everywhere.'

The Roth family enjoyed luck beyond measure living here for so long. But was it now time to move? And if so, where to?

'I will speak to the Pastor,' said Benjamin and did.

The Reverend Trocmé constantly smiled. 'Hello Benjamin; how is your family?'

The pleasantries ended as André saw Benjamin looked troubled.

'Is it true, Pastor, the Vichy threatened to arrest you?'

'Yes but they do so every time they come here. It makes them feel superior.'

'So you don't think living here is becoming more dangerous?'

André paused. He did think current times were more dangerous but always took the positive line. 'Benjamin, we do the will of God, not of men.'

The Jew struggled. 'And last month, did the Almighty approve the arrest of a young man who protected Jews here in this town?'

That sounded cruel and certainly unfair to a man who risked his life daily helping others. But André could see Benjamin's fear. The threats and visits from the Vichy were more frequent, and even André now expected to be arrested. Times had changed.

'I believe we should make a move, Pastor. I don't have the words to adequately express my admiration and gratitude for everything you and your wonderful wife have done for me and my family. You rescued us from disaster. My daughters have been educated. You've given us shelter, food, work and love, and most of all, hope.'

Benjamin found it natural to embrace the man of the cloth and hold the embrace.

'Right then,' said André breaking free, 'so what are your plans?'

'We wish to reach Marseille, and find a ship to America. What do you suggest?'

'Well, Marseille is about 250 kilometres due south and I'm sure you can't risk taking the train.'

'No, but is there someone with a car I can hire?'

'There is in the next village but he's not a generous man. He will charge you the Earth and more so, because you have a great need.'

'Can I walk to this village?'

'You could but I would not recommend it for your children. I will find someone to take you. If you are successful, then God speed. If not, you are always welcome to return.'

Benjamin choked. His throat and mouth froze. The kindness of the Pastor overwhelmed him. André squeezed his arm.

'You are a proud man, Benjamin Roth, and one who loves his family. I am glad to have met you and will pray for you all.'

Tears flowed leaving Benjamin unable to speak.

At night he told Rachel the news. She expressed reservations but saw how much it meant to her husband. He wanted them to live in a country where persecution, evil and injustice for Jews were no more.

Next morning, they told the girls they were off on another adventure. Both loved the people of Le Chambon and wanted to stay. Subtle promises of a brighter future helped persuade the children.

With fewer possessions, the Roth family went by horse and cart to a nearby village. Benjamin found the only car owner in town, and knocked on the door of the nicest house for miles around. In the driveway sat the nicest car for miles around. The owner appeared and sneered down his nose at the well-travelled Herr Roth.

'No beggars,' he said and closed the door.

'I have gold, Monsieur.'

Nothing happened and then the door re-opened. 'Show me.'

Benjamin always carried his supply in small lots. He hesitated then removed one amount. The man held out his hand. Benjamin saw a vision of having his gold snatched, the door slammed and his walk back to the family being the same as walking to the gallows.

'What do you want?' asked the man.

'I have a wife and two small daughters, Monsieur. We need to reach Marseille as soon as possible.'

'Marseille!' scoffed the car owner.

'I would like to hire you to drive us, please.'

'Do you know the price of petrol today?'

'I imagine it is expensive, Monsieur.'

'It's outrageous. I'll need twice this amount to even think about it.'

Benjamin panicked but jumped in feet first. 'I agree, Monsieur. I will pay half when we leave, and the other half when we arrive. But we must depart within the hour.'

Benjamin hated this situation and paying way over the odds but the life of his wife and children were in the balance. Haggling involved an ultimatum. If the driver wanted the money, he would need to make a decision there and then.

'Be here within the hour or I keep the gold and the trip is off.'

The door slammed and Benjamin froze. Shock glued his feet to the ground. Then he came alive and ran. It was 100 metres to the cart and Rachel saw her husband running. It must be good news.

He thanked the Huguenot driver, helped his family off the cart, and led them along the road. 'Hurry,' he urged them, 'we're leaving now.'

When he knocked on the huge door of the palatial house, the driver stood there shocked. 'We are here, Monsieur,' said Benjamin trying to control his rapid breathing.

'I will need extra petrol and we need to renegotiate the price.'

Benjamin didn't care. 'I agree to pay an extra ten per cent.'

'Twenty,' said the driver and Benjamin replied in an instant.

'Twenty if we leave in the next five minutes.'

The driver glared at Benjamin, hated the way the Jew kept adding his own demands, then stepped inside and slammed the door.

Benjamin hustled his family to the car and tied their suitcase to the rack on the boot. The driver walked from the side of the house. Benjamin went to introduce his wife.

'Get them in,' said the driver, 'but you and I need to talk.'

Benjamin helped Rachel and the girls into the back seat then walked to the driver. He held out a hand. Benjamin turned his back, retrieved an amount of gold and paid the man.

He checked it. 'The same again in Marseille,' he said. 'Agreed?' Benjamin nodded. The man got into his car and started the engine. Benjamin scrambled to sit in the front passenger seat. They left.

The car ran well. No conversation, only silence. The girls were told to remain silent; whispering only. The man drove on quiet roads and avoided main towns. Having settled his anxiety, Benjamin spoke.

'Thank you for this service, Monsieur. We are grateful for your kindness.' He turned to the back and encouraged his wife to speak.

'Indeed, we are most grateful, Monsieur,' said Rachel.

The driver grunted and they continued. After two hours, he pulled to the side of the road in the countryside. Benjamin panicked.

'Call of nature,' said the driver who removed the ignition key, hopped out and walked into the trees.

'Do you wish to share your plan with your family?' asked Rachel. Benjamin refused to turn back and she regretted asking her question.

'As we planned,' he said. 'Marseille, close to the sea where many of our people are gathered. Vessels to America are found in the port.'

The driver returned.

'Do you know how much further it is, Monsieur?' asked Roth.

'Two hours,' he said, driving again, 'or less.'

The afternoon shadows fell across the road and Benjamin rejoiced when he saw a sign, *Marseille 50 kms.*

The forest gave way to farms and then houses as they neared their goal. Benjamin couldn't stop tears brimming in his eyes. At last, at long last after his flight from anti-Semitic Berlin which began years ago, he'd brought his family so close to safety. Finding a ship to America would be the final, most wonderful step. His heart raced.

They entered the outer suburbs at dusk. They reached the outskirts of the city. Without warning, the driver pulled over.

'Monsieur, we need to be close to the hotels,' pleaded Benjamin.

'This is Marseille. Now, the fee,' he said with hand extended.

Benjamin thought about it. 'Certainly but please allow my family to get out first.' It seemed a small matter but to the patriarch, essential. The driver grunted his approval. Benjamin turned back to Rachel indicating the door with his head.

'Out girls,' said Rachel and she and the children stood by the side of the car. Benjamin wound down his window and called.

'Rachel, please take the suitcase off the car.' She went to do so.

'Okay,' said the now angry driver, 'enough of the delaying tactics. Give me the gold now.'

'As agreed,' said Benjamin who wanted his family and their meagre possessions free first.

The driver threatened. 'You do know the authorities are rounding up your people and sending them back to wherever you came from.' The tense mood broke free. Now, anything could happen. 'For an extra payment, I can make sure they do not hear about your family.'

The last three words were laced with evil.

Benjamin stared at him. 'Are you threatening me, Monsieur?'

'Call it what you like, but we both know you have more gold and if you want to be safe, you'll have to pay.'

Benjamin called to his wife. 'Hurry Rachel, collect the case.'

She called back. 'I can't untie the straps. You'll have to help me.'

Benjamin reached for the door handle but stopped when the driver produced a pistol and rammed it into the passenger's ribs. 'Don't move. Give me all your gold and we'll say no more.' Both men froze and stared at one another. Benjamin decided. He removed the gold he agreed to pay and offered it to the driver.

'This is what we agreed,' he said. 'Take it and we will go.'

The pistol hurt Benjamin's ribs. The driver snarled. 'Give me all your gold, Jew, or your family will be fatherless.' He pushed the pistol harder and tightened his finger on the trigger. 'Now!'

Rachel needed help and approached the driver's door. She couldn't see the weapon. 'The straps are too tight. I can't undo them.'

The driver turned to look at her; Rachel saw the gun and screamed distracting the driver. Benjamin grabbed the gun. The men fought, the driver exploded as did the weapon.

Silence. Rachel peered inside the car. Benjamin's face stared back, blank. She grabbed the driver's door and yanked it open. The driver fell out backwards with blood oozing from his open mouth. Rachel tried to scream but couldn't.

'Take the girls,' snapped Benjamin. Rachel hesitated. 'Now,' he hissed. She grabbed the sisters and led them away from the car. Benjamin hopped out, undid the straps and put the case on the ground. He went back to the driver's door, pushed the driver inside, felt through his pockets, and discovered the gold he'd already paid, and pinched it. His conscience hid behind a fence. He closed the door and hurried after his family. He and Rachel spoke with their eyes.

They turned a corner and saw commercial buildings ahead.

'This way, girls; Daddy promises you a special treat. Come on.'

Everyone struggled. The girls were hungry, irritable and unsure about what had happened in the car. Rachel kept distracting them by pointing to buildings and making comments.

My kingdom for a hotel, thought Benjamin. He approached an old man from behind. 'Pardon, Monsieur.' The man turned and Benjamin looked at the bearded face of a fellow Jew.

'Shalom. Can I be of assistance?'

Benjamin's roller-coaster ride of emotions took off yet again. 'My family and I are searching for a hotel. Do you know this area?'

'I do.' He smiled at Rachel and the girls. 'But there is a spare room in my flat. You are welcome to stay the night.'

Benjamin grabbed the old man's hand in two of his and kissed it. The family followed the compassionate stranger and spent the night in what they considered to be luxury. They were dry, hungry, but safe.

Yes, but for how much longer?

Chapter 9

Marseille 1941

When Benjamin and Rachel Roth and their two daughters arrived in Marseille a month ago, the parents panicked. They arrived by private car and once they stopped in a Marseille suburb, the driver died in his vehicle. He was shot in an act of self-defence. The adults lived in fear believing the body of the wealthy landowner, slumped in his car, would be linked to them. Were there witnesses in the nearby houses? If so, once caught and charged, any judge would hardly rule in Herr Roth's favour when it became known the man was a German Jew.

After a kindly old man put them up for the night, they found a cheap hotel and later a small flat by the waterfront. Benjamin still carried the gold and diamonds he smuggled all the way from Berlin.

He needed to find work, a school for his girls but above all else, a way out of France. A ship to America or England would be ideal. He possessed funds to bribe a passage for the whole family. But who could he trust as war raged in Vichy France? He lived on his nerves.

He found work as a night porter in a hotel and because he dressed well and treated guests with impeccable manners, the owner gave him black market food and promised him help if ever he needed it.

But what sort of help? Marseille became ever more dangerous. At one time, the authorities made a distinction between Jews from other countries and French Jews. The locals were treated better. But the Vichy attitude changed and even French Jews were being imprisoned.

Thanks to his time in Le Chambon, Benjamin obtained fake identity papers which disguised his German/Jewish roots. He became Monsieur Pierre Moreau from Grenoble. But would that save him?

When the girls were asleep, Benjamin told Rachel about his fears. 'Many Vichy police have become the French Gestapo. They hate Jews and finding and deporting them, us, is their life's mission. We really have to escape to America.'

She argued. 'But if you ask the wrong person about travel, we could be betrayed. There are French people who would shop their grandmother for money. You need to find someone you can trust.'

He breathed deeply. He found it hard to remember when he wasn't a fugitive. Protecting his family remained his raison d'être. He knew they must escape but not how. Who could help?

He finished his night porter shift around dawn and walked home alone in the Marseille streets as the sun crept above the horizon. He turned a corner and panicked as two men hurtled towards him. They were fifty metres away but closing fast. His mind raced. *Are they criminals running from the police? Are they Jews running from the Nazis?* He stepped back, hiding in a doorway. The men were only metres away and flying, fleeing for their lives. They searched for a particular place.

One stopped and called to the other in English. 'There,' he said and pointed to a building opposite to where Benjamin hid.

The other man ran back and they tried a door. It opened. They dived inside. Benjamin waited then, as quiet returned, headed home as a car roared around the corner coming straight towards him. He stopped in fear. The sleek car screamed Gestapo officers or Vichy police. It screeched to a halt.

Benjamin stopped breathing.

'Hey,' yelled an official. 'Did you see two men running in this street?'

'Do you mean this morning, sir?'

'Yes, you fool, just now.'

Benjamin swallowed. He knew all about harassment, to be hounded by officials with guns. 'I saw them,' he said and pointed. 'They ran down to the waterfront and turned left.'

The official offered no word of thanks and the car raced away. Benjamin wondered if they'd come back searching for him. He set off for home but froze when he heard a voice behind him.

'Pardon, Monsieur.'

Oh God, he thought. *A witness saw what happened and heard me lie.* Footsteps sounded as the speaker approached him. *I'll never see my wife and children again.*

The speaker stood right behind him. 'Monsieur,' he said. Benjamin clenched his fists in fear ready to punch and fight for his freedom, turned and stared into the eyes of the Reverend Donald Caskie.

Both men were shocked. Each remembered the other from their meeting in the summer of 1940 when the Germans entered Paris and millions of people fled the city. Benjamin's cart toppled over as a German plane attacked the helpless convoy of refugees.

This man and two British soldiers came to Benjamin's aid. The accident killed his mother, and this man gave him help and advice.

'Bonjour, Padre,' said Benjamin, relieved and actually smiling. 'It is lovely to see you again after all this time, and looking so well.

'And you, Monsieur,' replied Donald as they shook hands. 'I saw what you did with those men in the car.' Benjamin held his breath. 'God bless you. Please tell me your wife and children are safe and well.'

'Thank you, they are.'

'Excellent. But now over breakfast you must tell me of your escape through France.'

'You are most kind, Monsieur but ...'

Caskie took Benjamin's arm and led him across the road. 'This way and I believe you are in luck as we have fresh pastries.'

Benjamin entered the Seamen's Mission, a large barn of a building which housed an odd assortment of people. They nodded or smiled as he was introduced and Benjamin felt welcome.

'Please sit there,' said Caskie then announced to the others. 'This kind gentleman has just helped our two new friends escape.'

People buzzed their appreciation, applauded and thanked him. The two men who minutes ago were sprinting in the street outside, approached and offered their hands.

Both spoke with an English accent. 'Merci Monsieur, merci.'

Caskie interrupted. 'Now gentlemen, you know you are not allowed in here. We take refugees and sailors only. Away to your hidey hole if you please.'

They left giving Benjamin a thumbs up and a grin. A steaming cup of coffee settled before him with what smelt like heaven in the form of a freshly baked croissant.

'Please, Monsieur,' said Caskie indicating the breakfast and sitting beside the new arrival. 'So, you and your family have made it to

Marseille.' Benjamin nodded as he chewed. 'And what are your plans? Where do you go next?'

Benjamin's upbringing meant he could not speak with food in his mouth but even so, the clergyman's question shocked him into silence.

'You must know, Monsieur, Jews can be treated as wickedly here as in Paris. So what is your plan of escape?'

Benjamin coughed as food caught in his throat. Finally he spoke.

'All my hopes of finding a ship and sailing to America or England have come to nothing. I have heard so many cases of betrayal, I am afraid to ask for help. If I am discovered, I will be arrested and who will care for my family?'

Caskie understood and patted Benjamin's arm. 'Well, we have plenty of trust here, Monsieur. We deal mainly with military men who wish to return to England but there are far more civilian refugees like you hoping to do the same.'

Tears appeared in Benjamin's eyes. From despair came hope. Weeks of lying low and fearing the worst placed a massive burden on him. Every day he waited for that knock on his door. He wondered about his mental health, and possible insanity. Despite his forged papers, the Nazis and their partners found ways to find Jews.

Now, out of nowhere, out of nothing came a person he knew who was kind and peaceful, and who knew about people like Benjamin and his family desperate to escape.

'May I ask, Padre, ...'

'Please, call me Donald. I will call you Monsieur.' His smile told Benjamin his host provided confidence in anonymity.

'May I ask, Donald, how your guests manage to escape?'

'They walk away.'

Benjamin gasped. 'They walk?'

'Yes, they walk over the Pyrenees from France into neutral Spain, and from there they make their way to Gibraltar and sail or fly to England.'

This became too much for Benjamin. 'But is it not dangerous?'

'Extremely dangerous and there are those who have died or been captured. But to remain here is dangerous too as you just saw.'

'But I could not leave my wife and children, Donald. Escaping without them is not an option.'

'My dear Monsieur, of course you cannot abandon your family. Of course you must take them with you.'

The shock so overwhelmed Benjamin he couldn't speak.

'Hundreds, probably thousands of refugees from the elderly to children are making the trip. If you and your family want to do so, I can put you in touch with the right people. But beware, Monsieur, putting your trust in the wrong people is a recipe for disaster.'

Benjamin still couldn't speak. Just the idea of escaping was frightening in itself, but to do so by climbing the Pyrenees with small children scrambled his brain.

'Finish your breakfast, Monsieur,' said Donald, 'and I'll come and see you before you go.'

It rained as Benjamin left the Seamen's Mission. He ignored the moisture because his mind buzzed and his heart sang. He arrived home to find Rachel deep in worry at his late arrival and now because his clothes were soaked. She went to reprimand him but saw his face.

'What has happened?' she asked with anxiety shoving her blood pressure higher.

'We're going to Spain.'

Her face grew bigger. 'What?'

He told her everything.

Chapter 10

Vichy France 1941

The Lyon to Marseille train clickety-clacked its way through the French countryside. In one compartment of the second-last carriage were five British chaps, most of the crew of a downed bomber, and an old woman known variously as Louise Beatrice Wellesley, Sister Claudine, Plum, Helene Smythe or more recently, Madame Defarge.

She knew the men in her compartment were British and most likely on the run. They, like everyone else she'd met of late, didn't realise she was barely in her twenties, English to her plimsolls, a fake knitter, and currently an SOE agent trying to get the hell out of France and back to Blighty.

They were dog tired and drifted to sleep. Most likely they'd been travelling by night, sleeping rough, scrounging food and avoiding checkpoints. Beards were in and hairstyles non-existent.

Louise kept asking herself a question. *Should I reveal myself and if so, when?* Something told her to stay shtum.

About two hours into their journey, the door to their compartment opened and an official blocked the exit. 'Tickets,' he said. The men were awake and feeling pockets. They held out their tickets forcing the official to move into the compartment. All five tickets were in order. Only the gorgon in the corner remained.

'Madame, tickets,' he said.

'She is asleep,' said the one Englishman who spoke good French.

Louise worried. She needed to draw as little attention to herself as possible. The ticket in her hand would pass muster but would her young hand betray her? Her make-up and specs added longevity but were her youthful hands a giveaway? She groaned inside.

Using as much of her sleeve as possible, she poked out her ticket. It proved to be enough for the official who didn't fancy standing too close to the hag. He retreated but stopped in the doorway and glared at the five men. It was a glare full of anger. He left.

'Should we leave and spread out?' whispered one man.

'No. Our tickets are good.'

'But what about our papers?' asked another.

They hesitated, unsure about whether to stay or go.

Too late. A Vichy policeman appeared with pistol drawn.

'Shit,' said one of the men as the door flew open and the officer stood in the doorway with pointed gun.

'Show me your papers, all of you,' he barked, 'and one at a time.'

The Brits froze as the policeman appeared angry and worse, nervous. The gun gave him courage but the odds were scary. He couldn't shoot all of them if they came at him. He wanted them in a corner as far from him as possible.

He waved the pistol. 'In the corner, go.' One didn't need to speak French to understand. The two seated on the side beside Louise were made to move to the window end of the compartment.

'You, Madame, sit here.' He pointed to the seat closest to the corridor beside him. No sense in shooting the old biddy. She moved slowly because of her age and infirmity. He snapped at the men.

'Sit together—now!'

The escapees shuffled closer. They were confined at the far end making rushing the armed officer tricky, no suicidal. Louise glanced at their faces. She sensed fear and despair.

One of the men with head down whispered. 'Be ready to rush him.'

His mates were now afraid. They were so near with Marseille only an hour or so away. The Freedom Trails and neutral Spain beckoned.

'You,' said the officer pointing his pistol at the man who gave the whispered order to attack. 'Show me your papers.'

The atmosphere had tension to spare. The Englishman removed papers from his jacket and moved towards the cop.

'Stop,' spat the officer. 'Kneel.'

The man paused. 'Pardon?' he asked.

'On the floor, kneel.'

The Englishman knelt. 'Papers,' barked the officer holding out a hand. The papers were examined and found wanting.

'These are fake,' he screamed in anger so loud he shook with rage.

'No, his papers are good,' replied the French speaker.

'You lie,' said the policeman, stepping forward and pressing his pistol to the forehead of the terrified man. 'Confess or I shoot.'

The other four escapees were like a coiled spring. To save the life of their comrade they were set to leap forward. The tension crackled and as the men were about to spring, the old crone moved first.

She lashed out with a leg forcing the gun up. It exploded giving the carriage ceiling a bullet hole for Christmas. Everyone froze except the elderly passenger. She stood, chopped the throat of the officer and as he bent choking for air, she grabbed his head against her hip and snapped his neck. He dropped like a stone.

Her audience of five gaped in awe. Their speechless behaviour continued when the old witch spoke in Home Counties English. 'Let's have the window open, gentlemen, if you please.'

She bent to collect the deceased. The window rose bringing the outside sounds inside. 'Let me know when we're on a left hand curve.' One of the men poked his head out of the window. She handed the Vichy pistol to the nearest evader.

'Bloody good disguise, Miss,' said one.

'Bloody good unarmed combat skills,' said another.

The man with his head out of the window, pulled his head inside. 'We're starting on a left curve.'

Louise ran the show. 'Right, lend a hand, please.' She grabbed the back of the dead man's collar and the top of his trousers. She struggled until the once kneeling man gave a hand and the deceased Vichy policeman was prepared for a new journey. Louise directed.

'One, two, three,' she counted and the policeman went head first out of the window of the penultimate carriage on the stopping train from Lyon to Marseille. He suffered no pain on landing or rolling to his resting place, and provided food for local wildlife before his tatty uniformed remains were found many weeks later.

'Flight Lieutenant Andy Carstairs,' said the officer holding out his hand to Louise. She shook it.

'How do you do?' she said. 'We are definitely on the same side, sir, but alas I'm not at liberty to reveal anything further.'

'Understood and thank you for your brilliant work.' His colleagues gave warm and vociferous support.

'So any suggestions, Miss; not that we want you to break any orders or official secrets?'

'There's nothing secret, Flight Lieutenant. I'm alone heading to Marseille to escape to Spain, and have no contacts in France.'

'Then we're definitely on the same mission and you're most welcome to join us.' His colleagues couldn't say, 'Hear, hear,' quick enough. 'Our only contact in Marseille is a Scot by the name of Caskie, living in the Seamen's Mission by the docks.'

'Thank you and do you have any other tips or leads.'

'We heard the stationmaster and train driver are sympathetic to escapees and evaders. As we approach the Marseille station, if there are police or Gestapo there, we'll hear three blasts on the whistle.'

'And?' asked Louise.

'And we get off before the station.'

'Oh?' she asked wondering what he meant—exactly.

'There's a river and many chaps have taken a swim to avoid the authorities.' She pondered the comments. 'Can you swim, Miss?'

'I can,' she said, 'although not so well in my current outfit.'

All five males thought immediately how they might offer to assist her to disrobe. They sat as the train rattled closer to its destination.

'Next stop, Marseille,' cried one of the men spotting a signpost.

The passengers double-checked their footwear, possessions and for anything which might identify them as foreign.

Then they heard the sound; a long blast on the locomotive's whistle. Everyone froze. Silence. Then two short but definite blasts.

'That's it,' cried Carstairs opening the door. The others followed. Louise prepared to disrobe. She put her hands on her wig. The line of departing soldiers stopped and turned out of curiosity to see what the young woman really looked like. Off came the wig and glasses, and jaws dropped as a beautiful, feminine creature appeared.

'Move,' shouted one at the back of the line. They did while the last turned back. 'After you, Miss.'

'I'm fine, I'll catch you up.'

'Good luck,' he said. 'See you in Spain.'

He left and the men gathered on the steps at the end of the carriage. As the train hit the bridge they prepared to jump. They leapt aiming for the middle, and hopefully, the deepest part of the river.

They didn't see Louise. She stayed on board and replaced her wig and specs, choosing the dry route, and committed the words Caskie and Seamen's Mission to memory.

The train pulled into Marseille. Louise took time to adjust her disguise. With papers ready and stick in hand, she climbed down the steps and walked, hunched over and limping. *Not too much,* she reminded herself. *Overacting will draw attention.*

She headed to the ticket barrier, and by watching without watching, she examined the gathered officials. Vichy police searched for Jews. She allowed fitter, younger passengers to pass her.

Louise stood next in line. 'Papers,' snapped the official. They were examined without much care as an old woman struggling to walk didn't rate a second look.

'Pass,' said the man returning her papers. Feeling grand, she shuffled away to the streets of Marseille.

'Wait!' called a new voice, a cold, sharp and vindictive voice. Louise kept going. *It can't be me.* 'Old woman,' screamed the voice, and Louise died inside. A man moved to her and told her to wait. She heard footsteps and the officer who called arrived.

He stared. She thought her performance convincing so why stop me? He used a baton to point to her shoes.

'Unusual, Madame, for one so old' he said. He used his stick to lift the hem of Juliet's dress. 'Trousers, Madame, not a petticoat?'

Louise reckoned speaking was essential. 'I am old, Monsieur.'

'Major,' spat the man and Louise felt her head throb. This man sounded, even smelt like Gestapo. 'Where are you going, old woman?'

Her training prepared for such a conflict with her backstory down pat. 'I am to stay with my sister, Major.'

'Address?'

'Number 46 Rue des Docks. It is by the waterfront.'

'What is the nearest church?'

Louise fought hard to maintain her character. Her heart caught fire. 'I do not know, Monsieur Major. I am not religious.'

He exploded. 'And you are not old.' He grabbed her wig and yanked. It came away revealing messy but gorgeous hair. 'Seize her,' he shouted, and on the station at Marseille, Louise Beatrice Wellesley was arrested.

Chapter 11

Roth apartment, Marseille

'You want me and the girls to climb the Pyrenees?' gasped Rachel.

'Others have done it.' Benjamin pushed, Rachel resisted.

'Are you insane?' Her stunned, defensive and incredulous response hurt Benjamin whereas he buzzed with excited anticipation.

'This man I met is the man who helped us when the cart tipped over and Bubbie was killed. You must remember him.'

'Of course but how does that help two young children do something many adults cannot do?'

'He told me other Jews have made the trip with whole families making it to Spain. Please, at least can we explore the possibility?'

He begged. She saw pain in his eyes; it had lingered for years, in Germany and all through their time in various parts of France.

'What's this man's name?'

'Donald Caskie and he's a priest like Pastor André. We met again by chance. He runs a mission for refugees here in Marseille. Rachel, he is a good man and this could be our best chance to escape.'

She hesitated. They knew Vichy France had changed its attitude to Jews, and there were stories the Germans might invade the south and thus occupy the whole of France. Changing their name meant no guarantee of survival. Every week they heard of Jews in and around Marseille being arrested and put on trains to labour camps or worse.

'Be careful,' she said, her way of agreeing to him exploring the fantastic possibility. 'This Caskie man must be known to the authorities. They will be watching him and his mission.'

'Of course,' said Benjamin. 'But one step at a time, my dear.'

The authorities had long suspected Donald Caskie and were constantly watching him. Escapees and evaders long knew him as the man to see when trying to escape. They also knew he would be closed down in an instant if they gave him away. The five men who jumped from the train knew this and, having landed in a river, they swam ashore, hid and tried to dry their clothes awaiting nightfall. They were crew members of a Vickers Wellington Bomber shot down over France, and had no idea their aircraft was named after one Arthur Wellesley, a distant relative of the young woman who saved their lives.

'Did anyone see the girl?' asked Wireless Operator John Matthews.

'She didn't jump,' replied Navigator Alan Peters.

'I don't mind being wet and cold,' moaned Rear Gunner Gareth Owen, 'but I couldn't half murder a bacon sandwich.'

This prompted groans from the others trying desperately not to think of food.

'So what's the drill, Skipper?' asked Second Pilot Mark McKenzie.

'I wish I knew,' said Carstairs. 'We need the Seamen's Mission on the waterfront. But do we travel as a group or split up?' He held up the stolen pistol. 'At least we've got a weapon.'

'Why don't we hire a cab, sir?' asked Owen turning comedian.

'I suggest we split up,' said the leader. 'If we're unlucky, at least some of us may make it. Agreed?'

'Skip,' they said then decided on travelling companions.

Carstairs gave them some French vocabulary basics. The moon took a break and the men headed into town in two groups. They knew the Caskie destination but asking directions of the wrong person could be fatal.

'Pardon, Monsieur,' said Owen to a man he assumed to be a local and hopefully not sympathetic to the authorities. 'Waterfront, ships, s'il vous plaît?'

'Ah, Anglais,' he said and the two Brits nodded and prayed. 'Two kilometres,' he said pointing. They thanked him and set off. He spoke in English. 'Good luck, Tommy.'

They smiled and left always watching for anyone likely to arrest or report them. Families were at home, but individuals moved about. They thought they could see a ship so reckoned the waterfront must be close and tried to walk like a local.

As they approached an intersection, two men in uniform, possibly police officers, turned the corner and headed their way.

'Damn,' said Owen, who grabbed his mate and bundled him off the street through the closest door. They entered a small and dimly lit reception area. It didn't rate a second glance. They waited hoping like hell the two cops who might have seen them would disappear.

The evaders breathed deeply; their hearts sprinted. No response from the street. Then, from behind, someone spoke French.

'Bonsoir, Messieurs. Welcome to our humble abode.'

The nervous airmen turned and gawped at a middle-aged woman, plump, tarty, wearing the reddest lipstick, and enough rouge to plaster a small room.

'Bugger,' whispered Owen. 'It's a knocking shop.'

'What is your fancy? We have blonde, brunette and big Bertha.'

'What did she say?' muttered Wireless Operator John Matthews.

'English, Madame, vive la France,' said Owen.

She understood and spoke their tongue. 'Ah, English, welcome Tommy.'

Owen explained. 'Pardon, Madame, we want the Seamen's Mission.'

She inspected their damp clothes. 'But you are all wet. Take off your clothes and I will dry them by the fire.' The men stared at her.

Matthews panicked. 'Did I hear her correctly?'

'You did; she wants us to strip.'

'You will not need clothes where you are going, hey?' She cackled.

Owen pleaded. 'We would love to spend time in your magnificent establishment, Madame, but we have a most important meeting at the Seamen's Mission.'

'You want to see Donald?'

'Sorry?'

'You want to visit the padre from Paris?'

Owen understood. 'Yes, yes,' he replied, excited. 'Is he near here?'

She headed to the back of the brothel. 'This way.' They walked along a corridor with interesting sounds being produced behind doors they passed. She opened the rear door revealing a laneway. 'Go to the end, turn right and the Mission is 50 metres ahead.'

They kissed her hand. 'Merci, Madame, merci,' they gushed and hurried away.

She went back inside. 'Tight arse English, Vive la France indeed.'

They reached the Mission and knocked. Donald Caskie unlocked and opened the door and before the Brits could speak, the Scot let rip.

'What kept you?' The visitors were shocked. 'Come in, and be quick about it.'

They entered and their shock continued as their three comrades sat there, each draped in a blanket, drinking steaming mugs of tea.

'What happened to you two?' asked Carstairs.

Owen turned to his mate. 'You tell 'em and I'll kill you.'

All five were taken to the bowels of the Mission. All POWs or evading air crews were well hidden in case of a sudden raid. Caskie's business and his life were constantly in danger.

The men were fed, given dry clothes and then quizzed.

'We were once six, Padre,' said Carstairs.'

'Six? Where's the other chap?'

'He is a she who saved our lives.' Caskie listened, hooked, as the tale of the old woman in the carriage was told. He realised and became sad.

'Oh no, she's been arrested.'

'What?' said all five men together.

'I heard a Gestapo officer stopped her at the station, tore off her wig, and had her taken away. They must know her, and will kill her.'

'Can we rescue her?' almost demanded Carstairs.

Caskie shook his head. 'Not from the Gestapo HQ. It's an old warehouse with a rabbit warren of rooms they use as cells.'

'Where is it?' asked Carstairs having but one thought in mind.

Caskie explained, and the new arrivals put their heads together and produced a simple plan. They explained it to Caskie.

'This young woman fooled everyone with her disguise. We'll do the same. Where can we find Wehrmacht uniforms?'

'You're mad,' said the Scot, 'but you're more likely to find Vichy police uniforms than German. There is a police station nearby.'

'What about weapons?' asked McKenzie.

'They carry side arms but you'll run a tremendous risk if you attack them in the streets.'

Carstairs stared at Caskie with feeling as the pilot fingered the pistol he was handed on the train by the old crone. 'You organise the secret hidey-holes, Padre, and we'll sort out the Gestapo.'

Louise wanted to vomit but couldn't. She sat in the back of a swish automobile between two Gestapo agents with her hands tied behind her back. The tight tie hurt although the pain in her wrists was nothing to the pain in her guts.

They reached their destination and dragged Louise into an old rock solid building, a perfect air-raid shelter or, as in this case, a perfect torture chamber and killing factory.

She landed in a makeshift cell still with her hands tied. No furniture, little light and only a bowl which she wasn't sure was her water supply or lavatory. Crying didn't feel right or useful. She flopped on her side and tried not to think of her mother and brothers.

Failure hurt. Not being able to reach her cyanide pill, hidden in a button on her shirt, made her misery worse. She wasn't sure of the time but fell asleep.

The bellowing guards woke her, and being dragged to her feet made her nightmares real. She was taken upstairs to a room with a clean floor, a powerful low-hanging lamp, and a desk and chairs. The Gestapo officer from the train station lounged behind the desk. Another stood nearby, sneering. Louise slumped on a chair in front of the desk. The Nazi spoke perfect English with a hint of an accent.

'I am Sturmbannführer Reinhardt Kappler, Major to you, and charged with identifying enemies of the Reich here in Vichy France. You have been arrested and are well advised to answer my questions.' He paused. She remained silent. 'What is your name?'

Louise paused. 'You have my papers.'

He remained calm as if enjoying the conversation. He knew far more about her than she of him. 'What is your name?'

'Helene Smythe.'

He slapped the desk. 'Liar.' She remained still, determined to die with dignity trying to make the best of a terrible situation.

'Why were you travelling in disguise?'

'I am a French citizen. I did not wish to be arrested.'

He walked around the desk, leaned on it only two feet in front of Louise. 'If you tell me the truth, your punishment will be reduced.'

She met his eyes but spoke calmly. 'Come, Major, surely both of us are required to be honest. By punishment you mean torture.'

He fumed, moved in, and slapped her face. As they say, he put his back into it. The pain was sharp and the shock as bad. He roared in her face, his spittle the salt in the wound.

'You are an SOE agent pretending to be a nun. Your name is Louise Beatrice Wellesley, and your code name is Sister Claudine sometimes known as Plum.' He smirked. 'Am I right, Miss Wellesley?'

'Not exactly, Mein Herr.' She now knew the mole in the SOE was alive and still kicking goals for Germany.

He raged. 'Liar!'

'Plum is not my code name, it's a nickname created from the rules of cricket. Have you ever fielded in slips, Mein Herr, or at deep backward square leg, or have you ever bowled a maiden over?'

The truth of her words and his complete lack of understanding of the language of cricket made him pause. He recovered his rage.

'You are responsible for espionage and murder against the Third Reich. The punishment is death. If you confess we shall proceed straight to execution.'

'That's extremely generous of you, Major. Does the Gestapo always offer its victims a choice?'

Her answer stung him. He hated her and himself having revealed he knew so much about her. Apart from evil gratification, his use of torture was now less important. Before he continued, Louise spoke.

'It would appear, Sturmbannführer, we are in the same boat.'

He laughed. 'Ah, the so-called British sense of humour.'

She remained calm. 'You know a great deal about me, and I know a great deal about you.'

He stopped laughing. What did she mean? 'Apart from my name and rank, you know nothing about me, nothing.'

'Au contraire, Mein Herr; I and the world know you are a racist, a bully, a coward and a murderer.' His glare became electric. 'And you are a liar informing your people that concentration camps are Jewish holiday resorts with fun for all.' She paused. 'Barbarity becomes you.'

'Enough,' he shouted and came close to frothing at the mouth.

She nodded at his uncontrollable rage. 'I rest my case.'

He smirked. 'Enjoy your diatribe, bitch. You'll be dead in an hour.'

'An hour? Why, that's extraordinarily civil of you, Major.' Her approach was simple. If I'm going to die, I might as well give the bastard a piece of my mind. 'Tell me, Sturmbannführer, what is it about the Jewish population which you Nazis find so repugnant?'

'Ah, playing the ignorance card, Miss Wellesley. We both know they control your London banks as they do the banks of the world.'

'But surely you must be selective in your mass extermination. Not every Jew is a banker. Much of what Jews have done down the millennia has benefitted Aryans. National Socialists live longer and better lives from the medicine, education, and justice concepts introduced by Jews. Why, their attention to the Sabbath even gave Germans their weekend. Music, literature, and art created by Jews is adored even by many rabid Nazis. So, surely killing every Jew is cutting off your nose to spite your Aryan face.'

The Nazi fumed. 'Tell me your contacts here in Marseille, the people you were to meet once you left the railway station?'

'Why? It all seems a bit pointless if your threats are real.'

'Oh, they're real all right. I'm the best with the white-hot iron and pincers.' She died inside.

'But if I'm dead within the hour—your words, Mein Herr—why would I squeal? I've been trained to endure torture for 65 minutes.'

Now, she was goading him, scared witless mind, but with nothing to lose, Louise gave him sarcasm and scorn in spades.

He watched her, fascinated, as he'd never faced a prisoner like her. Most were terrified and many talk in the hope of being killed quickly or with the faint hope of release. Not this woman. She used irony and sarcasm to taunt and belittle him. Her wit and courage gleamed despite both knowing he could kill her and slowly. But first he wanted her contacts in this part of the world.

Hundreds of Allied soldiers and airmen were moving through France from north to south. They were crossing from France into neutral Spain. Who helped them? Who ran these so-called Freedom Trails? SOE agent Louise Wellesley would know. To make her talk, Kappler became desperate.

She talked tough but surely ripping off a fingernail or three would loosen her tongue. No harm in trying. He glanced at his comrade.

'Prepare the prisoner for examination.'

Louise understood the euphemism. Her plan was to keep Kappler talking and delay the torture for as long as possible. She tried to remember her training about being interrogated and tortured.

The other Gestapo officer placed a case on the desk and from it produced what seemed to Louise to be scientific equipment.

'What I don't understand,' she said, 'is German stupidity.' Both men wanted to growl. 'One of your lot gets killed, so you execute 10 innocent civilians as a reprisal. Surely you must see that is counter-productive. Hatred of the German invader grows exponentially. Millions of locals, even old people, feeble of body even, are now more determined than ever to hurt, harass and kill Nazis.'

'Words, only words,' scoffed Kappler. 'We speak with action.'

'Our job is to force Germany to have its men spend their time trying to control enraged locals. You're helping us. You shoot civilians and shoot yourselves in the foot. Are you really that stupid?'

He fumed inside as she outpointed him with her accurate comments and fearless taunting. He reckoned she would fight to not give up her contacts, which made his torturing her all the more important. He must not let her win. He must have the last say. Her last word would be a scream. He felt better thinking, *Let's see how brave the bitch is when the pain kicks in.*

The assistant pulled down Louise's jumper and ripped open her shirt. The cyanide pill in the shirt button was now further away, but with hands tied, she couldn't reach it anyway. Her chest was exposed with only her brassiere in place; for now. The Nazis used nakedness as a weapon. Louise forgot how to pray.

'Gentlemen, for your sake, I hope Germany wins the war.'

'Oh, we will,' scoffed Kappler, rolling up his sleeves.

'Certain, Mein Herr? Your invasion of my country has stalled because, despite Germany having four times the number of aircraft, you lost the Battle of Britain.'

'As you British would say, a hiccup.' He picked up a knife and Louise tried to psyche herself into believing she would not scream.

'Because if the Allies win, it will be your turn to be exposed, only you will have nowhere to hide, and when governments stop hunting you, if you're still running, the families of those you have slaughtered will begin the hunt. Work hard to win the war, gentlemen, because if you lose, your hell will make God's Hell seem like heaven.'

Enraged, the Major slashed the straps of her brassiere.

Chapter 12

Marseille

Carstairs was champing at the bit. 'Where can we find these Vichy police?' he asked.

Caskie wanted to help rescue anyone captured by the Germans or by local police, and with a woman involved, he became doubly keen. He was naturally anxious believing war was no place for a woman. But the survival of the Mission and his ability to help people flee France depended on him not falling foul of the authorities. Attacking Vichy police had danger written all over it.

'Should I ask about your plan, gentlemen?'

Carstairs smiled. 'We'll leave you and your Mission well out of it, sir. But that amazing young woman saved all our lives and the least we can do is try and return the favour.' His comrades agreed.

'You do know you may have to do the exact opposite.' He confused the visitors so explained. 'You may face the appalling prospect of having to kill her yourselves.' This shocked the evaders. They stared at the serious Caskie. He explained. 'If she's been tortured and disfigured, and is horribly wounded, sometimes death is the kindest option. Will she thank you if she returns to her previous life looking like a freak, or unable to feed herself or wipe her own bottom?'

They knew of stories of Nazi brutality but didn't want to even think about the possibility of killing one of their own.

Caskie gave the men the location of the Gestapo HQ as well as the address of the nearest police station. 'I have no firearms, gentlemen, and at the risk of ruining your plan to rescue this brave woman, if you kill any Vichy police officer, and especially someone in the Gestapo, they will exact revenge like you wouldn't believe. If they trace the killings back to this place, you will do untold damage to our work here helping the likes of you to escape to Spain. In other words, you'll shoot yourselves in the foot, and that's after you've cut off your nose to spite your face.'

His words hurt. These evaders desperately wanted to help the young woman disguised as an old woman. But they now faced the prospect that saving her could ruin their own escape as well as unknown comrades who followed them.

'What do you suggest, Padre?' asked Carstairs.

'Everything we do is a risk,' he replied, 'but a wise man once said, "All that is required for evil to triumph is for good men to do nothing." I'll leave you to your thoughts, gentlemen, and pray for your success.' He left the room.

'We know the risks, lads,' said Carstairs, 'but for me, doing nothing isn't an option.' The others agreed with feeling. They spread a map of Marseille on the table.

They slipped out of the rear of the Mission into the dark streets with hope and a plan. Anything could happen and delay was their enemy.

They scattered. Two led, two followed 30 metres behind, and Rear Gunner Owen, brought up the rear. Two carried kitchen knives, two held large forks used to carve the Sunday roast, and Carstairs had the pistol stolen on the train thanks to the old crone they hoped to find alive and rescue. They pinched some of the Reverend Caskie's rope and tea-towels, and went gendarme hunting.

There were plenty of shadows in the narrow streets. The police station was close. They hunted one, preferably two Vichy officers.

At the intersection where the police building stood, the first two evaders stopped, peered around the corner and saw nothing. They hated hanging around. It reeked of suspicion.

A cry made them turn. The Brit on his own, Gareth Owen, was sprung by two local Vichy policemen. Owen protested speaking unintelligible French about being an Italian sailor.

The others quietly moved to the fracas. Carstairs and McKenzie crossed the road to swing around behind the trio. The middle two, Matthews and Peters, went towards Owen. They waited for Carstairs and McKenzie to get in position, and once there, launched the two-pronged attack. Actually it became three-pronged because when the police turned to be confronted by the four vagabonds, Owen banged the officers' heads together.

The police were punched with force, threatened with a knife and large fork, overpowered and dragged into a darkened side street. Their pistols were pinched giving the Brits three weapons.

At gunpoint, the police were frog-marched to a small park. In bushes they were soon in their underclothes then gagged with tea-towels and tied together either side of a large bush.

Carstairs, with his French linguistic skills, would be the first choice as one of the new police officers, but being tall and thick set, the stolen uniforms were way too small. The new gendarmes were McKenzie and Owen. Neither spoke French, and McKenzie sounded like an inebriated Scot which he often was. En route to the Gestapo HQ, Carstairs distributed the weapons and gave final instructions.

The Gestapo perfected the art of stealing. They took people, possessions and property. They stole their Marseille HQ, a former warehouse. The two fake Vichy policemen stood outside the front door either side of Carstairs their fake prisoner. The other two gang members were flat against the wall either side of the door.

'Good luck,' whispered Carstairs and Owen gave the door a heavy knock. Nothing, no response. 'Again and louder.'

The fake police officers were quietly shitting themselves. Dressing up and pretending to be French while confronting the Gestapo wasn't covered during bomb aiming lectures and parachute drops.

'Someone's coming,' hissed Owen. The door stayed shut.

A voice called in French but sounded German. 'What do you want?'

Carstairs, with his head down, did the talking. 'Police. We have a prisoner, a pilot from the RAF.'

The door was opened by a Gestapo officer whose recent evening meal tasted delicious. He considered the French police and their prisoner, then stepped out only to be seriously assaulted. Carstairs punched the German so hard his recently consumed food—sausage and potatoes—stopped dead on its journey to the stomach.

The helpless Nazi smelt death as a pistol burrowed into his eye as he was "helped" indoors. One of the back-up Brits closed the door.

'Make a sound and you die,' hissed Carstairs. The German froze, petrified. 'Where is the female prisoner? Tell me,' snarled Carstairs.

'Upstairs, turn left, end of corridor.'

Peters became the designated guard and, armed with a knife, he and Matthews bundled the prisoner into a small room. On the floor with hands tied behind his back, his feet bound, and a tea-towel in his mouth, the German was going nowhere.

Matthews joined the trio heading upstairs. They saw no-one, turned left and set off. Halfway there, with hearts racing, they panicked when a door opened and, wiping his hands, an officer came out of a lavatory, his shock greater than that of the four Brits combined. He shouted. 'Hey!' but nothing more as Carstairs' right fist smashed his mouth leaving the enemy in excruciating pain. He couldn't shout as to do so while gargling teeth proved impossible.

The quartet became a trio as Matthews secured the enemy. Carstairs, Owen and McKenzie hurried to the end of the corridor. They were about five metres away when they heard a woman scream.

The men sprinted and with guns drawn, threw open the door and burst inside.

Ten minutes earlier, Reinhardt Kappler fumed. The woman he arrested was an SOE agent with knowledge he wanted. His threats of torture not only didn't appear to weaken her resolve, they made her stronger. He knew he might not succeed in making her talk but would lose face if he didn't torture her. Besides, he enjoyed inflicting pain.

Some people believe that imagining the pain you are about to receive is as bad, even worse, than the actual agony. Louise battled to remember her training and the lectures on being tortured. Her cyanide pill lay hidden in a button of her shirt now tossed on the floor. Since her arrest at the railway station and with her hands tied behind her back, the pill stayed there. With her upper body naked, her brain got busy.

'I'm willing to talk,' she said in a calm, businesslike way.

Kappler baulked. 'Short on courage are we, Miss Wellesley?'

'Not at all and I know I'll be tortured and killed.' Shock hit the Gestapo men. 'But the longer you take to extract information, the better the chance my contacts have to flee.'

She made sense. He took the bait. 'Then talk,' he said, 'but if you lie or omit anything, the treatment will commence and continue for a very long time.'

'I agree to tell you everything about all my contacts but only after you truthfully answer my questions.'

Kappler raged. 'You think you can make demands. You will soon be dead. Escape is impossible. You are in no position to bargain, you conniving English bitch.'

Louise remained calm on the outside but internally her heart prepared to explode. 'Well it's your choice. Torture me for hours and I may tell you nothing, and if I die, you'll *have* nothing. But if you agree to my proposal, you'll have your contacts within five minutes.' She ran rings around the Nazis. 'So, do you want my contacts or not?'

The Gestapo agents glanced at one another. Sturmann Max Flesch, although new to the caper, urged his superior to accept her offer. Kappler hated giving in to a prisoner and worse, a woman.

'Be careful, Miss Wellesley, if this is a pathetic game or trick, we will commence the treatment immediately.'

'Treatment, you call it treatment? What happened to being truthful? The word, Herren, is torture.'

Kappler smirked. 'You are incorrect again, Miss Wellesley. By treatment I mean torture and rape.' He turned to Flesch. 'I think it's my turn to go first today.' They grinned.

'Thank you for clearing that up,' she said leaving them uncertain. No-one ever spoke to them like Louise or proposed such a deal. 'Do we have a deal?' They glared; their silence prompted her to start. 'My first question; why do you claim the Aryan race is superior?'

The Nazis were shocked and it showed. They didn't know what to expect, but it wasn't that.

'Because it *is* superior,' replied the smug Kappler.

His agitation contrasted with her calm demeanor. 'Now you would not accept an incomplete list of my contacts, Mein Herr. Nor will I accept your incomplete answer.'

He so wanted to strike her. Then he thought he would win the argument, collect her details and then torture her anyway.

'We are the perfection of beauty; tall, long-limbed and slim.'

'Really? Well, if that is true, where does the obese Reich Marshal Göring or the short and deformed Herr Goebbels fit in your manual?'

'Your smug semantics destroy your pathetic argument.'

She smiled. 'So, tell me, why do you persecute Jews?'

He scoffed. 'Surely that is not your best question?'

'It is an honest question to which I expect an honest answer.'

Kappler regurgitated Nazi propaganda. 'We all know they rule the world through greed and economic domination. They have caused great harm. They murdered the Son of God, and their habits are disgusting.'

'And all Jews are the same, and according to National Socialism, all must receive the same treatment. Do you agree?'

'Of course. The world will be a much better place when the Jewish curse is removed.'

'Are there any exceptions? I mean what about Jews such as Albert Einstein and Sigmund Freud?' The Gestapo brutes remained silent. 'Aryan scientists, doctors and philosophers have gained enormous benefits from the work of these and other Jews. Do you agree?'

'I agree nothing. Now, it is your turn to answer my questions.'

'One more, Mein Herr, please.' He fumed. 'Please answer either yes or no. It's my final question and whichever answer you give, I will keep my promise and give you all my contacts.'

She paused, and he hated her more. The Nazis were hooked. 'You must answer yes or no. Once you answer, I promise to reveal the details of all my contacts. Ja oder nein, bitte Mein Herr.'

She paused. The Nazis stood fascinated as she asked her final question.

'Would you like your family to suffer the same treatment as the Nazis have inflicted on the Jews?'

Kappler was trapped. Both Nazis were. Either answer would condemn them. Kappler refused to answer. 'Stop this; no more; your pointless game is over. We will proceed as planned.'

'Yes or no?' she yelled at him. He slapped her. 'Coward,' she whispered as both men moved in to do their worst.

By stripping Louise, they added indignity to her misery. With her hands tied, they found it tricky to remove her clothes but used a knife where necessary. Her footwear was thrown aside. With her shirt tossed away, the cyanide pill was well out of reach. Mentally she wanted to die. It was time for the denouement, the physical pain. It's easy to act brave beforehand, but how do you react once the nervous system explodes and roars inside your brain? What sort of pain comes from burning flesh or a needle prick in your eye?

The Germans left her naked. She remained on a wooden chair with her hands tied behind her back. She could see a branding iron placed in a small brazier of glowing coal generating ferocious heat.

During his sessions, Kappler preferred to have a relative of the victim present. By torturing the spouse, parent, or child of the victim, especially a child, the suffering of the loved one often made the prisoner confess. Louise's loved ones were far away, and she never felt more alone.

Kappler milked the moment. Making the victim wait increased the pressure. Let them see the apparatus. Let their mind play tricks. And always speak quietly in a polite manner. Kappler's aim was to give the impression he was about to say, "This is going to hurt me more than it will hurt you." Of course, it was yet another Nazi lie.

He dipped a small brush in a pot of red paint, moved close to Louise and drew a circle on her left breast around the nipple.

'I like to be precise, Miss Wellesley. It means my assistant knows exactly what to do and where.' He stared into her eyes and saw fear. 'I tell him when.' Then Kappler turned on a pfennig. 'Oh, I do apologise. I should have reminded you that all this rigmarole is unnecessary if you simply provide details of the people helping the Allied escapees setting off from Marseille.' He paused and studied her again. 'No?'

She seemed fearless and taunted him. 'You threw away your chance to learn everything in a minute, all my contacts in one fell swoop, but by refusing to answer one simple yes or no question, you will now have to hope your barbaric behaviour works. And even if it does, it's only a pyrrhic victory, Herren. What fools you Aryans are.'

His eyes glowed with rage. She spoke the truth but her tactic failed. She closed her mouth and willed herself not to weep.

'I think you're all talk, Miss Wellesley. I wager you'll sing like a robin red breast.' He spat on her now red breast and spoke to his colleague. 'Pincers, Flesch.' The assistant went to the case.

Kappler leant in close to Louise's ear and whispered. 'I find the old methods work best.' She dared not look at him. She dared not speak. 'I will make it easier for you, Miss Wellesley.' He produced a blindfold and covered her eyes. She could see nothing. This became exquisite torture. You know what is coming but not when. There is no warning.

Louise felt the cold metal of the pincers on her left breast. They pressed lightly and moved up and down. These Gestapo bastards were trying to caress her before inflicting appalling torture. The pincers froze but rested gently on a nipple.

Seconds ticked by. How much fear could the woman take? Would she blurt out the names of her contacts as the pain ripped her body?

She heard the rusty pincers being opened; at least the sound convinced her that is what happened. Then she felt them gently grip her nipple. She clenched her teeth so hard it hurt.

The inactivity continued before the shock became worse than the pain. Then the pain hit her. One officer—does it matter which one?—using the glowing branding iron touched the tip of her right big toe.

The surprise plus the pain helped her to scream. Fearing irreparable harm to her breast only for her toe to be burnt, lit her nervous system. Her scream generated such volume it covered the sound of the door being flung open as three RAF chaps on the move, with two dressed as Vichy policemen, exploded into the room.

The Gestapo officers suffered a major surprise. Surprise, yes but fear too, naked fear. They didn't think, they *knew* the pain and misery they doled out was about to be returned and with interest. All three visitors were armed. What could the Nazis do? They backpedalled dropping the pincers and branding iron.

McKenzie rushed to Louise and cut the tie binding her hands. She removed the blindfold, hopped up, grabbed her damaged clothes and dressed in record time despite the pain from her scalded big toe.

'Good evening, gentlemen,' said Carstairs in impeccable English while being threatening enough to frighten God. 'May one ask which International Rule Book you are following in this particular exercise?'

Kappler recovered. 'We surrender and under the terms of the Geneva Convention demand the rights of wartime prisoners.'

Carstairs glanced at Louise. 'Are you okay, Miss?'

'Much better thank you, and good evening, gentlemen.'

All three visitors spoke as one. 'Good evening, Miss.'

Carstairs turned back to the cowering Kappler. 'I'm sorry, old chap; I missed that last bit, although I thought I heard the word *demand*. Now, whoever said you Germans have no sense of humour?'

Kappler produced perspiration to bath in and spoke. 'The Geneva Convention states that belligerents treat prisoners of war humanely.'

'Really?' replied Carstairs. 'The Geneva Convention you say?'

'Yes,' squeaked Kappler.

Carstairs remained calm. 'I'm sorry, gentlemen. I well know you bastards are good at reprisals, and I want to avoid any of the locals being harmed, but in this case I really do believe a Kangaroo Court with a spot of rough justice is absolutely the right way to go.' He addressed his colleagues. 'What do you reckon, chaps?'

'The rougher the better, sir' said McKenzie.

'Absolutely, Skip,' said Owen and Kappler lost it.

'Nein,' he screamed. 'Hilfe, hilfe!' he yelled trying to warn his colleagues both currently trussed as Christmas turkeys. Kappler stopped screaming when Carstairs shot him in the thigh. It hurt.

The Flight Lieutenant turned to his colleagues. 'You two help the young lady and pop along,' he said. 'I'll have a chat with these chaps about the Geneva Convention.' The others hesitated. 'Get her out of here,' snapped Carstairs, and Louise and her helpers disappeared.

As the door closed, Flesch grabbed the pincers and hurled them at the Englishman. He swerved but copped a glancing blow on the side of his head drawing blood. Carstairs sensed pain and distraction.

Flesch snatched the branding iron and rushed at the enemy as Kappler forced himself up to grab his holstered gun on the table. From a metre away, Carstairs shot Flesch in the middle of his heart. Handy because, as the Nazi landed, the branding iron, still glowing, fell on his crotch and he died dressed in smoldering trousers; totally incorrect for uniform-precise Gestapo officers. Kappler struggled to withdraw his pistol. Carstairs fired and hit the Nazi in the shoulder. Now sporting two wounds, he collapsed still clutching his weapon.

Carstairs moved quickly to Kappler and stood on his gun. The Nazi gazed pathetically at his foe. 'Geneva Convention my arse,' said the Englishman, and shot the Gestapo agent between the eyes.

When Carstairs opened the door, the trio was disappearing down the corridor. He checked with Matthews and double tied the Nazi.

On the ground floor, they secured the doorman and then all five men and their rescued SOE agent fled. Louise couldn't stop crying as her rescuers took it in turns to carry her through the back streets of Marseille and into the Seamen's Mission. Nothing much shocked Donald Caskie, but when the striking but messy Louise Wellesley entered being carried by two evaders, he stared then smiled.

'How do you do, Miss? I'm Donald.'

Chapter 13

Marseille

The Roths spoke constantly about their possible escape over the Pyrenees with Rachel becoming less aggressive in her opposition to the idea. Both were nervous. Stories filtered through to Marseille. Jews remaining in Paris were under shocking pressure from the resident Nazis. And now, in the south of France, German pressure meant Vichy officials became less tolerant of Jews. People saw the change. There were now local concentration camps for Jews. What next; the ovens of the Third Reich in Montpellier?

The issue for the Roths was their girls. Now nearly 9 and 7, they'd led a sheltered childhood. They were kept indoors for obvious reasons. People could not be trusted. For money, spite or politics, certain locals reported Jews.

Benjamin's chest felt tight. If it was difficult and dangerous for adults, how could young Jewish girls who rarely played outside in the rough and tumble of a busy childhood, climb the Pyrenees? But if they stayed in Marseille, even God couldn't guarantee their safety.

He stared at Rachel and made a final pitch. 'That priest who helped us near Paris says he can obtain the papers we need for Spain. From there we go to Lisbon or Gibraltar and catch a ship to America or England.'

What a terrible choice for the parents; watch their children die on a dangerous mountainside, or stay here and be shoved aboard a train, a cattle car en route to a concentration camp and the gas chambers.

Benjamin ran out of arguments and when Rachel spoke his frustration turned to shock. 'I've changed my mind,' she said.

He stared at her. 'What?' His mind exploded. 'What did you say?'

'I agree with you. We have to go.'

He sat with mouth open. His face asked for an explanation. 'To Spain?' She nodded. 'Over the mountains?' More nodding. 'But why?' he gasped. 'What's made you change your mind?'

'This morning, Frau Weismann told me the entire Schmidt family left to cross the Pyrenees.'

'What?' gasped Benjamin. 'But they have four children.'

'Five,' said Rachel, 'and she knows other families who are preparing to go. I now agree with you. We have to escape.'

Benjamin stuttered. He knew life was dangerous but to discover other Jews were thinking of going or had already left the city, came as a real shock. He spent time talking to men who knew government officials and discovered nothing. Rachel spoke to their neighbours and discovered what was happening in the real world.

'Thank you,' he said and hugged her, both becoming teary.

Their older child, Miriam, wandered into the room and complained. 'Mutti, I can't sleep.'

Benjamin smiled at his daughter, and Rachel took the child's hand and led her back to bed. Younger sister Sura slept.

When Rachel returned, she made coffee and when they were seated, she asked questions.

'Are you sure you can trust the priest who helped us near Paris?'

'He is a good man.'

'Do you have all the necessary paperwork?'

Benjamin shrugged. 'What is missing, the priest will provide.'

'We have to leave everything behind.'

He shrugged again. 'So, what else is new? We left our shop and home in Berlin, and then the flat in Paris. What use are possessions if we are sent to a concentration camp?'

'Do you still have the gold and diamonds?'

He nodded. 'I will ask the priest for advice.'

'What sort of advice?'

'When to leave, which way to go, and who is the best guide.'

'Why don't you ask those families who are planning to leave? Ask Frau Weismann how the Schmidt family escaped?' He became distressed. 'What is wrong?' she asked.

'I don't know who I can trust. There are French people siding with the Vichy authorities who now do what their German masters want.'

They studied one another. Life bordered on the unbearable. Stay in Marseille and be arrested, or leave Marseille and run the risk of dying in the mountains.

He stared at her. 'Thank you, my good wife, I will ask tomorrow.'

Her face turned grim. 'Don't delay, Benjamin, make it soon.'

Thanks to the Nazi torturers, Louise sported a blister on her big right toe. Donald Caskie invited her to stay, but after chatting with her and remembering what Carstairs and his team told him about the old lady in the train, the Scot knew it was dangerous to hide this remarkable refugee at the Mission.

A kitchenhand came in. 'Two English airmen have arrived, Donald. They're in a bad way.'

'I'll be back, Miss Smythe,' said Caskie and for now, Louise was safe.

The Scot entered the adjoining room and exploded. The two RAF survivors were in full battledress. 'What are you doing in those clothes? If the police arrive, we're all dead. Strip gentlemen, now!'

The Englishmen were shocked but too tired and hungry to resist. They even needed a hand to get out of their muddy outfits. Caskie's helper provided them with food and street clothes while he stuffed their uniforms in a sack and left.

Down the dark alley at the rear of the Mission he went on the short walk to the quayside. He knew a dark and seldom used spot. He retrieved a couple of rocks from his secret stash, placed them in the sack, tied it tightly and dropped the sack in the Mediterranean. The collection of underwater Allied uniforms grew larger.

In their "new" ordinary clothes, the English pilot and rear gunner, ate ravenously. Louise, wanting to sort out her escape, went exploring. She knocked, entered and apologised speaking French.

'I beg your pardon gentlemen, I'm trying to locate Mr Caskie.'

The pilot spoke poor French with an English accent. 'He'll be back soon, Mademoiselle. Come and join us. There's plenty of tea.'

She joined them speaking French. 'Hello, I'm Helene Smythe.'

'Roger,' said the pilot, 'and this is Peregrine. We call him the Falcon.'

They shook hands and poured Louise a mug of tea.'

'You are English?' she asked.

'We are.'

'I speak a little English if it will help.'

They switched to English with Louise using her acting skills to add a French accent.

'I used to visit my great aunt in England,' she said.

'How nice,' said the pilot with the gunner sticking to grins and eating.

'She lived in 'ampshire, near the Old Forest.'

The men nodded. 'Lovely part of the world,' said the pilot.

'Lovely,' said the gunner.

Louise stopped speaking, bent a little and whispered. 'I am trying to find a party who will be crossing into Spain. If they can take a girl along, I will be so 'appy. I am a very good cook.'

'How jolly good,' said the pilot. 'We've only arrived so we're in the same ship, looking for comrades to help us escape.'

The conversation lapsed. The men ate and Louise sipped. Without warning, she pointed to the milk jug and spoke in fluent German.

'Milch bitte.'

The gunner's hand grabbed the jug before the truth dawned. He stared at Louise his face a picture. She went to stand when the pilot grabbed her left arm and twisted it. Pain exploded. Her unarmed fighting skills kicked in and she jabbed two fingers of her right hand in the man's eyes—hard. He let go of her wrist, and struggled with temporary blindness, his eyes throbbing with pain.

Louise grabbed a kitchen fork. The gunner jumped on the table and leapt at her. She swayed and as the man flew past, she stabbed the fleshy part of his thigh. He crash landed on the floor, and screamed adding to his comrade's yells. The new arrivals collapsed near one another. The finale involved Louise grabbing both chaps by their hair and giving their heads a right old bang.

The flying furniture and agony vocals drew a crowd. Donald Caskie returned and rushed to the eating area. Carstairs and his crew left their planning meeting and burst in from another door.

'She's done it again,' said Carstairs, both confused and impressed.

Caskie exploded. 'What have you done, woman?'

She replied in English. 'They attacked me, sir.'

'They attacked you? Why? What happened?'

'I discovered their little game.'

Caskie didn't understand. Nobody did. 'Well that's as may be, Miss Smythe, but it's no way to treat two of our brave boys.'

He bent to give assistance to the wounded. They needed it.

She spoke in Home Counties English. 'Alas, sir, they are neither brave nor our boys.' Everyone stared at her and the battered victims. 'They're Germans, Mister Caskie, who I suspect have stolen Allied officers' uniforms and arrived in your establishment planning to infiltrate your escape lines and destroy your brilliant work.'

Silence crash-landed. The onlookers were in shock. Not only did this slim and naturally beautiful woman best the two hefty males, she exposed a fraud which the others missed, and which might have caused their deaths.

Louise explained their schoolboy howler mistakes with English geography and idioms, and their response to a request in German. Her admiration club grew in number and intensity.

Carstairs extended his hand. 'I'm running out of award nominations for you, Miss Smythe.'

'Helene,' said Louise accepting his thanks.

But once the praise and thanks were over, a major problem arose. What to do with the two Krauts?

Carstairs and his crew were all for killing them. Caskie refused point blank.

'Okay, Padre,' said Carstairs, 'we'll drop them off at the gates of the nearest Allied-controlled POW camp. How far would that be then?'

Sarcasm filled the room. Caskie knew his life and work faced serious danger. But killing any unarmed person, military or civilian, to him would never be acceptable. He chose to stay in France to *help* people. To him, executing the enemy was verboten.

The Germans were regaining consciousness. Tied together, they squatted on the floor. Even if free, they were in no condition to escape. They moaned softly.

The others faced the question, what to do with them?

Louise made a suggestion. 'We could dress them in the clothes they wore when they arrived then dump them outside the Gestapo building where they tortured me.'

'Won't work,' said Carstairs. 'They'll protest long and loud in perfect German.'

Peters pointed out the obvious. 'If they speak, Padre, you're finished, and you'll have to escape with us.'

'Where are their uniforms?' asked Owen.

'Bottom of the Med,' replied Caskie who took control. 'Gag and tie them and put them in the room at the rear. I'll decide their fate after you lot are on your way.'

Carstairs and his crew didn't like that answer. They knew the Padre didn't have the will to kill. They agreed with his suggestion for now, and the trussed, gagged and terrified Germans were moved.

Louise approached Caskie. 'Sir, you know I'm English. It's not that I want to escape over the mountains, I *have* to. It's a matter of unmasking a traitor back in Britain, one who is already wreaking havoc like those Germans would have done to you and your colleagues here in Marseille. I beg you; help me join an escape party. I'm ready to go.'

'No, you're not.' She flared as this was not what she wanted to hear. 'Your foot injury will hold you back. You'll be in constant pain and hinder your fellow escapees.'

She fell silent. She went to argue, but he shut her down.

'I think you should go to a safe house, Miss Smythe,' he said. 'If the stories about your exploits on the train are true, and having seen your handiwork just now, I have no doubt they *are* true, then the Germans and Vichy officials will be hunting for you; even more so after your escape from the Gestapo HQ. I want to keep you safe.'

Louise gave half a smile. 'Thank you, sir. You're most kind. But staying safe doesn't appeal as much as escaping. I need to go home, no, I *have* to go home and the sooner the better.'

'That's our specialty. But we want our escapees to have the best possible chance of success.'

She came close to begging. 'But sir, I need to go.'

'Climbing mountains is tough but climbing mountains with an injured foot is courting a disaster. Let's move you to a safe house and give your body time to heal.'

She knew he was right. 'When will my rescuers be leaving?'

Her question threw him. 'Did I hear you correctly? How strange it is you should ask such a question when you've obviously been trained in how *not* to share information.' She realised her error.

'I apologise, sir.'

'Not required, Miss Smythe. May I suggest you think about escaping with civilians rather than military personnel.' She became both curious and disappointed. 'Fit serving soldiers will move a lot faster than ordinary folk who will struggle because of the terrain and their level of fitness. If your foot gives you trouble, with civilians the pace will be a lot easier.'

Her heart sank. Not for a moment had she considered waiting and then travelling with slow-moving refugees. Louise wanted to be back in Blighty tomorrow. The SOE mole could be causing mayhem even as they spoke.

'I'll take your advice, sir, and thank you for all you've done for me.'

'My pleasure,' he said, smiling. 'Collect your possessions and I'll take you to see the best doctor in Marseille, and then we'll find you somewhere safe to stay.'

Chapter 14

The Pyrenees

This mountain range between France and Spain has long been climbed by humans and animals alike. Smugglers have roamed here for millennia. Shepherds with goats, refugees from wars, tourists and hikers, and criminals and fortune seekers have all taken one or more of the hundreds of trails up and down these peaks.

A few years before the Nazis invaded European countries, the Spanish Civil War produced thousands of Spanish refugees who fled their homeland. Across the Pyrenees they hiked and settled in France. In WW2, the masses did an about turn and headed the other way.

The key for escapees, even fit men trained for war, was the guide. The best guides, known as passeurs, knew their onions. There were trails within trails and being able to find the correct one through the labyrinth was essential. Enemy patrols roamed the area and being arrested or shot remained a constant risk.

A few guides, curse them, took bribes. They were paid to lead the refugees into Spain, and paid more to deliver the unsuspecting travellers into the hands of the enemy. Bastards.

Then trekkers faced the weather. Climbing the Pyrenees tested even fit and able people. Crossing in the winter months pushed humans to breaking point. Frost bite happened often so even if you did make it, your reward might well include an amputation or two.

How the hell could elderly people and young children even start such a perilous journey, let alone survive and reach their destination? Desperation drives many to tackle unusual deeds.

The Pyrenees waited for people such as Benjamin Roth and his family, and a young Englishwoman known to some as Plum. Both had endured horrendous times of late, dodging death on a daily basis. Both wanted to escape Vichy France. Both needed to bide their time.

But those mighty mountains were patient and waited for refugees brave or mad enough to venture forth.

Marseille

Donald Caskie led Louise to a safe house in a Marseille suburb. Before setting off, he handed her a walking stick.

'Thank you, sir,' she said, 'but I'm fine to walk short distances on level surfaces.'

His slight smile belied his strong message. 'It's a prop, Miss, to ensure anyone watching thinks you are visiting for medical reasons.'

Louise took the stick. 'You mean the Germans are watching?'

'Possibly or it could be the Vichy police or more likely and more worrying, the concierge. He may well be in the pay of the authorities. Oh, and don't overdo the limp. I believe the best actors use subtlety. Does that make sense?'

She smiled inside. It did make sense, and she avoided over-acting.

They reached the large apartment at 21 Rue Roux de Brignoles, home to Doctor George Rodocanachi and his wife Fanny. Louise limped to the front door. The premises needed to be large because it often provided short-term accommodation for special visitors—escapees or evaders—Allied soldiers and airmen who were injured, captured or being hounded by the Vichy police, Germans and turncoat French. This was a safe house.

George led a checkered life; born in England to Greek parents, he studied medicine in Paris and, in his 60s, finished up working as a GP in Marseille. He and Donald Caskie were skilled in their respective trades and overflowing with courage.

'You'll like Doctor Rodocanachi,' said Donald. 'He and his good lady wife do a superb line in human kindness. He'll examine your foot and tell you how fit you need to be if you fancy a long walk.'

She glanced at her smiling companion. They knocked and a woman opened the door.

'Bonjour, Madame. This is Mademoiselle Helene Smythe.' The women greeted one another. 'Our friend needs to see Doctor Rodocanachi about a troublesome foot. Can I leave her with you?'

'Of course,' said Fanny offering a hand to Louise. 'Do come in.'

'I'll see you again, Mademoiselle,' said Donald and left.

Louise entered the waiting room. 'The doctor won't be long,' said Fanny, the doctor's wife, receptionist, and lifelong supporter.

Louise smiled at the other patients in the room. A couple, appearing stressed, sat with their two silent children staring at the new arrival. No-one spoke.

The children kept staring and Louise chose to break the ice.

'I like your doll,' she said to the smaller child. 'What's her name?'

The child turned bashful, looked at her mother who nodded. But even with Mum's approval, the doll owner stayed shtum.

Louise switched to her pantomime role-playing routine. 'I think I can guess her name,' said Louise teasing the now excited child. 'Is it Mathilde le Bon Bon Fiddlesticks?' The child smiled, shook her head and became hooked on the game. 'Is it ... Georgette Fifi Kiss-Kiss Butter Beans?' More head shaking from the girl with an ever expanding smile. 'Oh, now I know. It's Tiny Twinkle Toes Tina.'

The child could wait no longer. 'No!' she squealed, 'it's Heide.'

Huge mock disappointment burst from the actress. 'Oh, I knew that, I was going to say Heidi next.'

The happiness bubbled but ceased when the Doctor appeared. 'Bonjour. Who is next please?'

Louise indicated the family. 'This family is before me, Doctor.'

The medical man reckoned he knew his patients. 'I think they are for administrative documents whereas you, young lady, have a medical need.' Louise smiled at the parents who half smiled and the father nodded. 'This way please, Mademoiselle.'

'Thank you,' said Louise to the family, and then using her walking stick, followed the doctor to his consulting room.

He introduced himself and asked Louise for her details which he notated. 'So, Mademoiselle Smythe, what brings you to my surgery?'

'A minor injury to my foot, Doctor, and I'm ashamed to take up your valuable time on such a trivial matter.'

He moved from behind his desk. 'Let me be the judge.' He moved a footstool and indicated. 'Please place your foot here.'

Louise rested her heel on the stool, and the doctor removed her shoe and sock causing Louise to wince.

'Trivial you say?' he said examining the blister on her big toe. 'This is a burn and applied to the bare skin. Are you careless, Mademoiselle, accident prone perhaps?'

'Careless, Doctor, I wore sandals when cooking and spilt hot fat.'

He went to a cabinet and removed material. 'I can clean, bathe, and bandage the burn, Mademoiselle, but time will be your best medicine.' He worked on her toe. 'If I may say, Mademoiselle, despite being a good liar, you have totally failed to convince me.' He stopped work and studied her. 'This is a result of torture.' She said nothing and he resumed the treatment. 'The Gestapo is creeping ever further south.' Louise said nothing as he applied a soothing crème. 'Better?'

Finally she spoke. 'That's wonderful, thank you, Doctor.'

He applied a bandage. 'I'll give you some ointment and I suggest you change this dressing once a day. Let it breathe.'

'I will,' she replied then popped the question. 'I'm hoping to go walking soon, Doctor. How soon before I can go?'

'What sort of a walk?' She hesitated. 'Would it be over the Pyrenees into Spain?' She froze. He saw her discomfort. 'Relax, Mademoiselle Smythe, or whatever your name is. The Padre at the Mission and I are, as you English say, in cahoots, and even as we speak, there are three Allied airmen in my bedroom. They too are keen on long country walks.'

Louise tingled. 'I'm afraid I don't understand, Doctor.'

'I will be honest with you,' he said finishing dressing her toe. 'I am responsible for helping escaping airmen and soldiers go for a long walk over the Pyrenees to Spain. I tell you this because I have become aware of your exploits in recent days.'

Louise's nerves jumped. Was this a trap to make her reveal herself? 'Recently I helped five British airmen who told me of a brilliant young woman disguised as an old woman who single-handedly saved them from being shot. Apparently she speaks perfect English. They then rescued her from the Gestapo.'

'You seem remarkably well-informed, Doctor.'

He smiled. 'I understand you have your orders, but here are a few facts. You cannot stay here because I do not have quarters for females. You could stay with the Reverend Caskie at the Mission but they are often raided by the Vichy Police.'

Louise wanted to reveal all but remained silent.

'You cannot attempt a crossing until your toe recovers, at least a little, so that requires a new safe house. May I suggest you consider a stay in a monastery?' He stared at her. 'I believe you know a little about wearing a habit.'

That did it. Louise surrendered and spoke English. They both did.

'I am impressed, Doctor. What more can I say?'

'Are you the nun from Lyon who made a name for herself these past few days?'

'I am. But that is so far away. What have you heard?'

'Blowing up a railway, killing Gestapo officers, and being on the scene when a spy and a bishop were killed is the type of tale which spreads fast.'

'I see. But I'd rather not tell you my name, or have my identity revealed in case you or others would be punished by association.'

'Thank you,' he said. 'Sister Brigid is the Mother Superior of a fine group of Irish nuns nearby. They help Mr Caskie with donations of clothes. I can't think of a safer place for you to recuperate than with those friendly Sisters. I'll have my wife give you directions.'

'Again, thank you, Doctor, for medical help and wise advice.'

He showed her to the door. 'Come and see me in a week and we'll see how your foot is progressing.' They entered the waiting-room and he spoke to the adults. 'Monsieur and Madame, this way, please.'

'I will stay with my daughters, Doctor,' said the woman.

'No,' the doctor replied, 'I will have my wife sit with the children.'

Louise interrupted returning to her French persona. 'I would be happy to sit with the children.'

The parents hesitated. The doctor took control. 'Thank you, Mademoiselle. You are most kind. Come,' he said beckoning to the adults. They left with the mother giving her girls a warning stare.

Louise squeezed in between the two girls. She smiled and they warmed to her. 'Now, I know Heide's name but we haven't been introduced.' Despite the worry about revealing her real identity, having met Donald Caskie and George Rodocanachi, she chose to go back to her old self. 'My name is Plum. Who are you?'

The older girl spoke well. 'My name's Miriam and I'm nine.'

'Hello Miriam.' Louise then smiled at the younger child.

'My name is Sura and I'll be seven in ...' She turned to her sister seeking details of her forthcoming birthday.

'Miriam and Sura,' said Louise; 'two lovely names.'

'And we're sisters,' said Miriam. 'Have you got a sister, Plum?'

'No, only two brothers.'

'What are their names?' asked the younger girl.

'Henry and Edmund, and they're my big brothers.'

'Why do you have a walking stick?' asked Miriam.

'Oh, it helps me walk because I have a sore foot.'

'I have a sore finger,' said Sura showing the hand sans Heidi.

'Oh, dear,' replied Louise studying the invisible wound. 'Does Heidi know you have a sore finger?'

The child thought then replied. 'Yes because I tell her everything.'

'And so you should,' said Louise.

'Did you have a doll when you were a little girl?' asked Miriam.

'I'm still a little girl,' said Louise and sat straight showing a funny face. The sisters giggled enjoying her silly behaviour.

'No you're not,' argued little Sura who liked the lady who teased her, making her laugh.

The banter continued, and Louise worried her charges were making too loud a noise. To increase her worry, Fanny came into the waiting-room. The children fell silent.

'I do apologise, Madame,' said Louise. 'I have encouraged the children to be a little noisy.'

'And so you should. It is delightful to hear such happiness. There should be more of it.'

The door opened and the parents emerged. Their daughters wondered if they might be in trouble. Without being harsh, their Jewish parents in 1941 were automatically quiet, doing everything to avoid being noticed and making their daughters behave the same.

Louise smiled. 'Your daughters have been a delight, Madame, Monsieur. Congratulations on raising such wonderful children.'

Her statement said it all. The parents were relieved and proud, the daughters were bubbling, and the doctor and his wife were thrilled.

It was time to go. The parents wanted to thank Louise, but their smaller daughter couldn't help herself.

'The lady has a funny name, Mutti. She's called Plum.'

Chapter 15

Nunnery near Marseille

Louise wondered if nuns from different orders communicated with one another. Were her dynamic deeds in Lyon known to nuns in Marseille? She'd soon find out if her feats had travelled along the ecclesiastical grapevine. She knocked, and the convent door opened.

'Good afternoon, Sister,' said Louise to the woman wearing her habit. 'My name is Helene, and the Reverend Caskie and Doctor Rodocanachi suggested I seek shelter for a few days.'

The nun spoke with a lilt smothered in the greenest of Shamrocks. She didn't say, "To be sure, to be sure," but she did smile and say, 'Come away in, you're most welcome.'

Louise met Sister Brigid, the Mother Superior, equally as welcoming and who spoke with even more of an Irish lilt.

'You'll be safe here, my dear, and please stay as long as you like.'

What does safe mean? thought Louise, who thanked Sister Brigid and was led to a guest room. Her meagre possessions spoke of her refugee status. There was an absence of judgement in the convent.

'Meal time is in about an hour,' said her guiding nun. 'I'll come and fetch you when it's time.' She pointed. 'And the powder room is just across the hall.'

Louise smiled at the Sister's sparkling eyes, thanked the nun, settled in her room, and did feel safe. She'd escaped from Lyon when the world and its Mother were after her. She'd helped Allied soldiers escape. The Gestapo brutes who tortured her were dead. She heard the fake RAF airmen in the Seamen's Mission "joined" the Resistance.

But what will happen to me, and when can I leave for Spain?

She fell asleep and only a light tapping on her door woke her in time for a basic evening meal. The nuns made her welcome and although meals were normally consumed in silence, an exception was made for the visitor with Sisters chatting to the new arrival.

The polite discourse continued until Sister Brigid arrived and dropped a bombshell.

'Sisters, I have just heard some sad news. 'In Lyon, Bishop Vaine is dead.' The mood changed in an instant. Sisters made the sign of the cross, whispered prayers and became serious and worried.

'But I met him, Mother,' said a nun. 'He was relatively young.'

'That is true,' said Sister Brigid nodding, and Louise felt goose bumps all over.

'Tragically, he died in an accident. Apparently he fell to his death from a balcony in the cathedral.' A buzz raced around the dining room. The death of a church leader was big news and this method of dying ignited whispers.

'Did anyone else know or meet Bishop Vaine?' asked Sister Brigid.

Silence. Louise bit her tongue forcing herself to remain silent, to never mention the cleric she knew to be a tyrant, Nazi sympathiser, and murderer. She could have said, "I stood next to him when he fell as he tried to shove me to my death," but didn't.

'We will pray for Bishop Vaine's soul tonight in the chapel.'

The nuns murmured their understanding and the meal continued in silence.

It was about to finish when the nuns heard a loud noise as someone attacked the front door of the convent. A male voice shouted.

'This is the police. Open the door.' More door banging. 'Open now!'

The police were the cat and the nuns the pigeons although the sisters moved as if well-rehearsed. The nun, who took Louise to her room, took her arm. 'This way, Mademoiselle,' she said, and Louise found herself being led along a corridor at a fair clip, and into a small robing room. 'Put this on and say nothing,' said the nun handing Louise a habit. Louise hesitated. 'Hurry.'

Here we go again, thought Louise and placed the habit over her clothes. The large headpiece proved an excellent disguise. She was hurried to the chapel and shown to a place.

'Remember, say nothing,' whispered the nun. 'Kneel and pray.'

Louise did as ordered and sneaked a sideways glance. Each nun knelt with head bowed. Loud footsteps got louder.

Four Vichy policemen strode into the silent chapel followed by the nun who admitted the visitors and who scampered to her place. Sister Brigid performed what Louise considered to be a brilliant rendition of controlled rage. She spoke softly building a crescendo.

'This is sacrilege. I will report this outrageous intrusion to your superiors. How dare you enter the House of God like ... hooligans.'

'You said all that last time, Madame,' countered the senior officer. 'Again we will search the convent.'

'What for this time, guns and ammunition, or do you think we harbour escaping British airmen under our beds?'

The nuns watched in awe as their bold Mother Superior acted with dignified indignation. Fear enveloped Louise's entire body.

'We are searching for a woman,' said the senior policeman.

'A woman?' mocked Sister Brigid. 'You've come to a convent to find a woman? Now, whoever said the police are as thick as pig shit?'

Goodness; such language; and in a convent and to the police. The tension in the chapel grew thick enough to touch.

The police officer continued. 'This is no ordinary woman; she's special. Have you received any visitors in the last two days?'

Brigid evaded the question. 'And what do you mean by special?'

'I mean someone who would be right at home in this very room.' He gave another pause for effect. 'We're searching for a nun.'

Brigid gave them both barrels of sarcasm. 'Well, what a brilliant move. You seek a nun so you come to a convent. Magnificent!' She gave a sweeping gesture. 'Please, take your pick.'

Every kneeling nun, and one ring-in, watched like a hawk. The policeman moved around as he spoke. 'This woman, calling herself Sister Claudine, fled Lyon after she killed a senior Gestapo officer and one of your flock.' He paused again for effect. 'She murdered the Bishop of Lyon.'

Several faces copped a slap, Louise took an uppercut.

Sister Brigid remained strong and lied with conviction. 'We are too busy to be bothered with any pretend nun. We pray and collect goods to distribute to the poor. We even help the priest at the Seamen's Mission who, I point out, is a Protestant.'

The unimpressed officer sneered. 'We will search your convent from top to bottom. One of my men will remain to see no-one escapes. You will all stay here.'

One policeman stood guard; the others left. Soft murmurs were heard but stopped when Sister Brigid made a subtle shushing sound. The guard watched.

'Let us pray,' said Brigid. She began the Paternoster and the nuns joined in. Louise mimed at first but recalled her church-going days and spoke aloud but quietly.

When it came to, 'forgive us our trespasses, as we forgive those who trespass against us,' she fell silent. *That bit can't be true*, she thought. *Murderous, torturing bastards should be forgiven? Sorry, God, you'll need to re-think that part of the script.*

After the Lord's Prayer, Brigid began to sing a hymn with the nuns joining in. Louise mimed so as to be seen to be one of the Order.

After what seemed like an age, the Vichy police returned with the senior officer fuming. He checked with the guard who shook his head. The officer addressed the women.

'We have searched every room, cellar, attic, and cupboard, and found no trace of this dangerous nun. We are watching you. As with the Seamen's Mission, if you do anything to help the British or their allies, your convent will be closed and you, its inhabitants arrested.'

He glared around the chapel making eye-contact with anyone who returned his gaze. None did. Louise took up piety. He snorted and pointed an index finger at the massed gathering.

'Help the enemies of France and Germany and you will die!'

He stormed out followed by his colleagues. The sound of the disappearing footsteps lingered. A hubbub arose. Sister Brigid started to sing another hymn. The women joined in and as they sang, stepped into the centre aisle, genuflected, turned and walked out of the chapel.

Louise remained in no-man's land. *Do I stay or go?*

As the last nun made her exit, Louise glanced up to see Sister Brigid and a senior nun standing beside her.

'Congratulations, Sister. It has been a privilege to have you in our humble convent but now alas, you must go.'

Louise's eyes widened. *They're throwing me out.* 'I'm sorry, Sister, I don't understand. The police have gone.'

'And will be back as soon as someone betrays you.'

Louise gasped. 'Someone here will betray me? One of the nuns?'

Brigid gestured. 'Come, we have no time to lose.'

The other nun left. Brigid accompanied Louise, talking to her as they went to her room. 'I have learnt a lot during this war. Anyone is capable of betrayal, and treachery comes from the most surprising sources. Some French are as bad as the Nazis. Pack your belongings.'

Louise had nothing. The other nun arrived with male clothes.

'Put these on, especially the hat. You must appear to be a local.'

Louise removed her habit and added a coat, scarf and hat. 'But where am I going?'

'Relax,' said Brigid. 'I will have someone take you to a safe house. You'll be where anyone helping to free France is given shelter.'

Louise mixed gratitude with worry. 'I hope you will not condemn me, Sisters, for being present at the death of the Bishop?'

'Condemn you?' snorted the Mother Superior. 'Congratulate more like; the man was an utter bastard.'

They took her through the convent and out into a dark yard. A woodshed could barely be seen. When opened, the door creaked.

'Wait in here. Someone will collect you soon. The password is "The moon is round," to which you must reply, "No, it is not round, it is green." Goodbye and God bless.'

The nuns turned and went back inside. Louise closed the door and sat on a log. Her toe throbbed, and she thought about removing her shoe. Not being sure of anything she decided to remain and wait.

Being uncomfortable didn't help and depression came knocking. She needed to contact London but dared not for fear of warning the SOE traitor. Anyway, how on Earth could she contact anyone?

Her best chance of escape was blighted by the blister on her toe. Like millions caught up in the conflagration dominating Europe and beyond, she faced many unknowns.

She heard a whisper. Snap went her head. 'The moon is round.'

She whispered. 'No, it is not round, it is green.'

The door opened and a young woman, about 17, smiled in the dim light. 'Come, Mademoiselle, it's time to leave. My name is Antoinette.'

She left, and Louise followed. Climbing the convent wall with a blistered toe hurt like buggery. Once over, they headed into the forest. Antoinette put a finger to her lips, and Louise nodded. They walked for some time and never once on a road or even a track. At one stage they stepped into a stream and walked a fair way. The girl whispered.

'This is to distract any dogs, Mademoiselle.' The cold water produced a new sensation and felt good on her blistered toe.

Finally they went back into the forest and reached a property. A small light shone in a house. They crept through the yard and entered a barn. A cow complained and chickens flapped. A ladder rested against a mezzanine floor.

'Climb up there,' said the girl. 'If the Germans or Vichy police come, there is a tiny door at the back behind the hay. Squeeze through and use the rope to slide down. Then hide in the woods. I live in the farmhouse with my grandparents. Like me, they are your friends. We will come and find you when it is safe. I will return soon with food and drink.'

She left. Louise stared at the animals staring at her, then climbed the ladder. Acres of loose hay filled the mezzanine floor. She waded through and found the tiny door, opened it and checked the piece of rope, then made a spot in the hay and lay down.

The girl returned with food and drink. She climbed the ladder. They spoke quietly as Louise enjoyed her rural French supper.

'You can stay as long as you like,' said Antoinette. 'When you want to leave, I will take you to another safe house.'

'You're most kind. I would be dead without your help.'

The girl shrugged. 'We can't defeat the Germans on our own, so if we can help you and others drive out the Nazis, we are glad to do so.'

'A nun told me there are French people who betray neighbours.'

The girl nodded. 'Sadly it's true. And if the Germans catch us helping the British, the penalty is a bullet. They seem to enjoy killing loyal French civilians more than the British military. But amazingly, when one French helper is executed, another steps forward to take their place.'

They sat there in silence. 'I hope the authorities never come,' said Louise, 'and if they do, I hope I will not be asleep.'

'You won't be asleep. They don't know how to arrive quietly.'

Louise studied the girl. She made the Englishwoman, barely 21, feel old. 'Thank you again, Antoinette, you've saved my life.'

The women hugged and the girl slid off the hay and down the ladder. She left, leaving Louise alone and wondering what would happen next.

Chapter 16

Safe House near Marseille

Louise finally slept only to snap awake when a motorbike and police car roared up the drive of her safe house. The lights from the vehicles dominated the darkness. She grabbed her hat and coat and slid through the hay. Rather than do as instructed, she found a crack in the side wall with a bird's-eye view of the arriving police.

Her pumping heart seemed to be so loud the visitors must hear it. Did someone betray her? If so, why not come straight to the barn?

Police banged on the farmhouse back door, the one the family used. An old man, obviously the girl's grandfather, opened the door and was dragged outside. He stumbled and fell. One officer went into the house and Louise watched in horror as Antoinette got the same treatment.

The family dog ran around barking. His body might have been old but his loyal spirit helped him fight to defend those he loved.

One of the visitors wore a Gestapo uniform; the others were Vichy police officers. The senior policeman accused the family. His words floated clearly up to Louise in the still night air.

'You have been helping British airmen escape. This is a safe house for our enemies. Giving them help is a capital crime.'

The grandfather protested from his position on the ground. He knelt and clasped his hands begging for mercy. Louise wanted to vomit. *My kingdom for a weapon*, she thought.

Two of the police frog-marched Antoinette to their vehicle. She struggled, kicking and screaming, but had no hope against two powerful men. The old man could not believe the situation. He struggled to his feet and stumbled towards his granddaughter. The chief of the police removed his Ruby pistol and without hesitation, shot the old man in the back. He collapsed. In hysterics, Antoinette fought in vain as Louise bit her lip in frustration and rage. She wanted to race into the yard but without a weapon, froze.

The grandmother stumbled into the yard and knelt beside her prostrate husband. The dog kept barking and running to and fro. As the wife wept beside her partner of 56 years, the policeman stepped in behind the old woman and, using all his reserves of courage and daring, shot the frail, elderly French lady in the back of the head.

Louise screamed then died inside. Now she would be discovered. But the revving motorbike at the time covered her scream. The dog despaired and moved towards the man with the gun.

Louise held her breath. *Not the dog.* The police car turned around and the shooter ran to climb inside. She watched in horror as the police and Gestapo took off with the young woman. Her dead grandparents lay in their yard, one on top of the other, their faithful hound confused and incapable of helping his master and mistress.

Louise knew the risk any French person took in helping those fighting the Nazis. Here was proof. She witnessed the massacre and kidnap. *What will happen to Antoinette?*

Louise collapsed on the hay and wept. She wept for the family ruined for giving succour to strangers. She wept for the futility and helplessness she felt in returning their kindness. She wept for the dog now howling and alone.

I watched and did nothing. Would I have saved lives if I yelled and ran, distracting the killers?

Time meant nothing. The dog stopped barking. The cow made the occasional sound but otherwise the world on this farm in this corner of rural France remained at peace. There were two murder victims in the yard. If nothing else, they needed dignity.

Louise slid down the ladder, peered around the side of the barn, saw no movement and went to the dead grandparents. She knelt and recoiled in shock. The man, beneath his wife, made a sound. Louise panicked thinking he'd survived. *What can I do to help?* Whatever caused the sound, she discovered the man and his wife were dead.

From behind, she sensed movement and turned. The old dog growled at the stranger. Louise held out a hand and spoke softly. The dog sensed there was no threat. He walked closer and sniffed her hand. She patted him and saw his tail start to wag.

Using as much solemnity and respect as she could, Louise dragged the bodies into the corner of the barn with the dog following. She placed them side by side and arranged their arms so a hand of each touched the other. She found a piece of canvas draped over farm equipment, and gently placed it over the bodies. The dog followed and watched and whimpered.

Finding old fence posts and rocks on the property, she placed them on the canvas hoping to prevent domestic or wild animals interfering with the corpses.

Finally she ventured into the farmhouse taking the dog with her. The fire in the stove had faded but the warmth lingered. Washing hung on a string above the wood-burner. A newspaper lay open on an old armchair; the news might have been as old as the chair.

Louise wandered further into the house. Here cleanliness was next to Godliness. The beds were made and in the granddaughter's room, photos revealed family members, Louise assumed to be parents.

Where are these people? Who can I contact? Is there a friendly priest in the area? Are there neighbours? Are they friendly?

Louise ended up back in the kitchen and, despite the bloody and difficult experiences she'd endured since the start of the war, this latest episode burnt a hole in her heart and mind, even worse than the burn on her toe from the Gestapo.

She needed sleep and while the house seemed perfect, she thought it dangerous to sleep inside. She found food for the dog then locked it inside and returned to the barn. The old farmer and his wife were asleep forever.

She woke because the chickens and particularly the rooster were up and ready for the new day. She slid down the ladder, opened the back door, and the dog came out and cocked his leg. She needed to make one major decision—stay or go. She thought about the situation. Unless friends or relatives arrived, she'd be alone. The authorities will hardly come back—they think there's no-one here. If ever she wanted a place to hide, she knew she'd found it.

But where is the next safe house and who will take me there?

Okay, so having decided to stay, what now? A girl brought up in a rambling home on the edge of a Surrey village with no experience of milking cows, collecting eggs or cooking Coq au vin, struggled. She knew how to feed a dog and found food for the now friendly hound.

For her, breakfast tasted superb with a large supply of fresh eggs.

She wandered the property accompanied by the dog. A dirt road stood at the front with no sign of other houses or sound of any traffic. She reckoned she'd found the perfect safe house.

Milking the cow challenged her. Finding a pail and milking stool were the easy bits. The cow protested until, after trial and error, the milkmaid achieved success. Even the dog looked impressed. She led the cow into the backyard with grass aplenty, found food for the chickens then went inside to plan her future.

Marseille Adieu

Laron Roche made money smuggling. Born beneath the Pyrenees, he grew up climbing these mountains and copied his older brothers in carting goods from France to Spain and back again. No tax paid. His motto in life; *the government gets nothing.* During the Spanish Civil War he smuggled people. Refugees desperate to escape their homeland paid top peseta to flee. In WW2, refugees, particularly Jewish refugees, desperately needed to flee France, so Laron switched from Catholics to Jews and headed the other way.

At first he agreed to assist POW escapees and downed airmen busting to return home to Blighty.

But as the Germans pushed south and the Vichy government became more like the Nazis, Laron discovered his greatest profits were in guiding Jewish refugees.

He didn't advertise. Word of mouth within the Jewish community meant he could pick and choose his clients. He chose Jews with the biggest wallets. Gold and the right jewels were fine so if you were Jewish and wanted the best guide in Marseille, contact Laron Roche.

Benjamin Roth did just that. He obtained the necessary paperwork from the wonderful Gentiles, Caskie and Rodocanachi. But when he told the Padre he and his family were in a group being led by the passeur Laron Roche, Caskie nodded but said nothing.

'You are quiet, Padre,' said Benjamin. 'Is this man not reliable?'

'I've heard nothing bad other than his prices are high.'

Benjamin shrugged. 'You get what you pay for, Monsieur. It's a seller's market, and what price do you put on the life of your family?'

'True,' replied Caskie who held out his hand now grasped by Benjamin. 'I wish you and your family a safe and successful journey, Monsieur. I hope you will not be offended when I say "God bless".'

Benjamin produced a genuine smile, the first time in months, possibly years. 'We'll take all the blessings you can spare, Padre. Goodbye and thank you again for your wonderful support and advice. If I had any faith, I would gladly nominate you for sainthood.'

Caskie laughed, escorted Benjamin to the door and asked, 'If I hear of other refugees wanting to escape, are you able to take more?'

'Of course, but they would need to have deep pockets.'

'Do you prefer them to be Jewish?'

'No, we prefer them to be genuine refugees.'

Caskie understood. 'And you're leaving from the safe house in Rue Duverger tonight?'

'Yes, we leave at midnight on the dot. We were told it is vital to be clear of Marseille before first light.'

Caskie never lost his admiration for people who set out on such a long and perilous journey with little or no experience of climbing mountains. He raised a hand in salute. 'Goodbye and good luck.'

Safe House, near Marseille

Louise sat at the kitchen table planning her next move. The silence of the rural property was broken when she heard a voice. Someone called.

'Hello. Antoinette. Is anybody home?'

The dog barked and Louise shushed it, crept to a window to check the yard while hiding behind a curtain.

The visitor was male, about 20, wearing ordinary working clothes and certainly didn't appear a threat. Louise decided on the lie low approach hoping he would go away thinking the family was away.

He called again and, getting no response, turned and headed towards the barn. Louise moved. Anyone finding two bodies, shot from behind, would find it horrendous and ridiculously suspicious, let alone likely to bring the authorities or local Resistance in a hurry. Louise's safe house would no longer be safe.

She opened the backdoor and called. 'Hello? Can I help you?'

The young man turned, stared at Louise then approached.

'Who are you?' he asked in a polite but concerned way.

'I could ask the same question,' replied Louise trying to sound neutral.

'Where is Monsieur and Madame Lepage?'

'They are not here. They went to town on important business.'

'Has somebody died?' he asked.

'How did you know?' asked Louise hoping she sounded normal.

He shrugged. 'I heard that Madame's sister has been unwell.'

'She is.'

'And Antoinette, where is she?'

'She has gone too and they asked me to care for the animals until they return.'

The old dog walked to the young man and wagged its tail. 'Hello, Benjie,' said the man and the dog's tail wagged faster. He stared again at Louise. 'You still haven't told me your name.'

'Helene. I am a friend of a friend of Antoinette's. I was staying here when the family heard the news about Jeanne.'

'Who is Jeanne?'

'Madame's sister, the one who was ill.' Louise kicked herself for making such a stupid mistake. *Who the hell is Jeanne?*

Okay,' he said, seemingly convinced by the woman and believing her story. Louise moved further into the yard.

'Would you like coffee?' He nodded. She turned and went inside. He and Benjie followed. Louise fussed at the stove being ready for some sort of reaction. She turned and saw the man holding a knife.

'Hey!' exclaimed Louise. 'What are you doing?'

The knife waved and came close. 'Madame's sister is not Jeanne. Antoinette has no friends and you are a liar. Now, where are they?'

Louise held up her hands. 'Wait, wait! Please be careful. You might cut yourself.'

'I will cut you if you do not tell me the truth.'

'I will tell you if you put down the knife.'

The young man exploded. 'Tell me now!' She hesitated. He lunged. Louise stepped aside, grabbed his wrist, twisted it, and he screamed in pain, dropping the knife. She pushed his arm up his back. It hurt. He yelled. 'All right, all right.'

She pushed him into the old armchair, picked up the knife and threw it away, glaring at him. 'I will tell you but no more tricks; yes?'

He nodded. They settled. Louise didn't know him from Adam, and knew she needed a believable story, which didn't reveal her identity. Before she could say anything, Benjie wandered up with the knife in his mouth, grinning and with his tail wagging. He fetched anything.

The ice broke. Louise took the knife and explained. 'I am travelling to Marseille to help my sick mother. To avoid the Vichy police because my papers are forged, I asked the old folk for help. They took pity on me and I hid in the barn. The police arrived and killed them and took Antoinette away.'

The young man doubted her, hoping it wasn't true. 'I do not believe you.' When Louise gave more details, he became distraught and she realised he carried a torch for Antoinette.

'Where are the bodies?' he asked. She showed him. They went back inside. He broke down and explained how a young woman, a friend of his sister, had been taken by the Vichy last month, and kept in a brothel run by a Marseille businessman who bribed the police.

'Where is this brothel?' asked Louise.

'In Marseille.'

'Can you take me there?'

He stared at her. 'Why? What can you do?'

'A lot more than we can do here.'

'We?'

'Yes, both of us.' She studied him. 'I don't know your name.'

'Julien,' he said and continued to cry.

They discussed Louise's plan and Julien agreed with trepidation.

They waited till dusk, put the cow back in the barn, and left Benjie with food and water. Louise raided Antoinette's wardrobe making herself attractive in slacks and a pretty blouse and jacket. She carried her other clothes including her coat, hat and shoes in a bag. Julien smiled when she entered the kitchen.

'You look nice,' he said pleasing Louise.

Chapter 17

Marseille

They shared his bicycle and set off for Marseille. The back roads were good for avoiding patrols, but horrendous for sore posteriors as the fixed-wheel machine shook hands with holes and stones.

When Louise first explained the plan, Julien thought it insane but would do anything to save his girl. They reached the outskirts of the city. Louise didn't know this area. They dismounted.

'We're not far,' he said. They hid the bike in a dark backyard and walked until Julien stopped and pointed. 'There's the bar.'

'Okay,' said Louise. 'Do as we rehearsed, with the double and single blinks for the right and wrong man, and good luck.'

He glanced at her, forcing a smile, although that smile hid the fear ravaging his body. She leant in and kissed his cheek. 'Come on, be brave,' she said, and her hug forced him to put an arm around her as they walked towards the bar. 'Do this for Antoinette.'

Marseille boasted a seamy side before the war. Once hostilities began, drinking, gambling, and prostitution became even more popular.

The dim lighting suited the noisy bar, but voices stopped when the couple entered. They went to the bar and were given the once over by the barman. Without trying, Julien performed perfectly as a young man out of his depth with a woman of the world. He wasn't acting.

'What?' demanded the owner.

'Cognac,' said Julien without conviction. He, and the woman with him, were now the focus of attention. The owner mocked him.

'Does your mother know you're out tonight, sonny?'

The bar erupted. The drinkers fancied Louise and enjoyed the ridicule of her boyfriend. He maintained his little boy lost persona.

'I have money,' he said fumbling in his pockets.

Louise felt her arm being squeezed. 'Come on, darling, you need a drink with a real man.'

She glanced at the hoodlum then at Julien who blinked both eyes, the sign the stranger was the wrong man.

Louise treated her new beau with thinly veiled contempt. 'Pardon, Monsieur, but I prefer millionaires.'

Her punch below the belt helped her escape. She sat at a table. Julien stumbled towards her with drinks. He stopped when a snappily dressed middle-aged gent appeared.

'I'll take those,' he said. Julien surrendered, glanced at Louise, and winked with his left eye. He vanished, and as planned, went outside. The spiv eased himself into a chair beside Louise.

She sipped her drink, thinking about her character. She wanted money, and no man would ever get the better of her.

'I suppose you're the millionaire I'm after,' she said.

'I'm Enrico and the man who can help you make a lot of money.'

She'd heard such promises before when performing at the Folies Bergère in Paris. *My God, that was a lifetime ago.*'

'They all say that,' she said and sipped.

'Finish your drink, and I'll show you my establishment.' He searched for an answer in her eyes and liked what he saw.

She fondled the contents of her bag. The knife Julien produced in the farmhouse, now sat hidden inside the bag with her clothes.

He headed towards the rear of the bar. She followed. He pulled back a heavy curtain revealing a set of stairs.

'After you,' he said, and she climbed the stairs with him following, studying her bottom. At the top of the stairs, a lounge, offered sofas and dim lighting. It was the brothel reception area where three customers sat drinking, being softened up by company employees.

'This way,' said the owner with only one thing on his mind. They entered a room. 'My office,' he said. 'Take a seat.'

He sat opposite her. Louise wondered if she might be trying too hard. 'The best acting,' said her favourite thespian, Beauford "Nightie" Nightingale, 'is that which appears natural and effortless.'

'I can help you make serious money, darling. I run a tight ship. No drunks, morons, or spivs. You want a night off, you have it. Where are you living? I can find you a better apartment at a cheaper price.'

'Whoa, whoa, whoa,' said Louise holding up a hand. 'I need to see the colour of your money and hear from the girls.'

He liked her smarts. Pushovers were pushovers. She wasn't. Bedding an intelligent woman meant his self-opinion tingled.

'Understood,' he said. 'So, what's your name?'

She smiled at him, boasting. 'Plum,' she said staring back.

He leered. 'Nice; I like a juicy plum.' He stood. 'Right, let's meet the girls.' They walked past rooms from which came sounds never heard in a prayer meeting. At the end of the corridor, without bothering to knock, he opened the door. 'Ladies, we have a new girl; make her welcome.' He indicated with his head and Louise entered the Green Room. As she passed him, he whispered, 'I'll see you soon.'

There were half a dozen women either slumped on settees, applying make-up, or smoking. A couple showed a passing interest in Louise, the rest ignored her. She spied her target. Antoinette, her head slumped, sat at the end of the room. She saw her grandparents brutally executed while she was kidnapped and dumped in a brothel. Her life was over. Enrico the pimp and owner provided important Vichy cops with a free pass to his establishment in return for them turning a blind eye to his black market activities and brothel.

Louise worked her way through the room and sat near Antoinette who paid no attention to the new arrival until Louise whispered, 'Julien says hello'. Antoinette's head jerked up. She stared at Louise who put a finger to her lips. 'We have a plan. Behave normally.'

Someone knocked. Louise pretended to admire a painting.

The door opened and the women responded. Who was it and who would he choose? The middle-aged customer, a regular despised by all, grinned. Louise flinched and Antoinette froze. There stood the murderous Vichy policeman, assassin of Antoinette's grandparents.

He was so smug he attended in full uniform. 'Bonsoir, ladies,' he beamed. The women offered fake sincerity in their reply.

He wandered amongst the employees. He knew his target and reached Antoinette. 'Come along little girl. It's time you paid your dues to the Vichy government.' She hesitated. He snapped. 'Come here,' he spat grabbing her arm. Louise stepped forward blocking him.

'Experience, Monsieur, beats youth every time.' The sheer audacity of the young woman stopped the customer in his tracks. He examined her in detail as a farmer would a beast on market day.

'Next time, my dear,' he oozed, and led Antoinette away. Louise followed discreetly and watched the couple disappear into a room. She stepped outside the Green Room and waited. *When do I move?*

Time passed. Voices came from the reception area so Louise took off. She tapped gently on the right door and entered. Antoinette was partly undressed, but he was naked putting him at a disadvantage.

He went to protest then changed his mind. 'Okay, why not? Let's have a party.' He rubbed his hands and grinned. 'Who's first?'

'Get dressed,' snapped Louise to Antoinette who did so.

His expectation and sense of humour died in an instant.

'Hey! Who the hell are you?' barked the policeman. His authority lacked power due to his being naked. Juliet gave him both barrels.

'I am a witness to the two murders you committed tonight at the farm owned by this young girl's grandparents.' He became mute. 'You do know, Monsieur, even in Vichy France, murder is a crime punishable by death.'

He wanted to shout obscenities but struggled while searching for his underpants. Being naked put him at a disadvantage.

'It is my solemn duty to inform you, Monsieur, the Court has found you guilty and ordered your sentence be carried out forthwith.'

Now he fumed, and lost it. His mind exploded.

Who the hell does this woman think she's talking to? I'll have her head shaved, her body flogged then dragged through the streets as an example to anyone even thinking about criticism of the Vichy police.

Louise reached into her bag and produced the knife she borrowed from Julien. His anger evaporated and became fear. The officer's life flashed before him as Louise spoke to the still terrified, but now fully dressed young woman.

'This is for your grandparents, Mademoiselle,' she said and, remembering the advice of her SOE instructors in freezing Inverness-shire, fixated on the now terrified eyes of the victim and stabbed him once in his heart. His scream was stifled but not so Antoinette's. The stark savagery whacked the young woman. The flashback of what happened to her grandparents gave her lungs a massive boost.

Louise wiped her knife on the bed sheets and replaced it. 'Time to go,' said Louise and headed for the door. It opened and Enrico the owner arrived in a panic, the screams having brought him running.

'What the hell?' He saw the naked, bloody body of his most important, demonstrably dead client. Everything screamed disaster.

The owner glared at Louise knowing he'd been conned. 'You bitch,' he roared and lunged at her. She swerved, and he sprawled on the bed. She whipped his arm up his back. He cursed like the sailors down the road. Louise grabbed a chunk of his hair; dragged him up and, using his own momentum, herded him towards the window.

The cheap curtains offered no resistance as Louise launched the proprietor head first. The window shattered and he shattered on the footpath below. The fall from the second floor proved sufficient to make a broken neck fairly straightforward. And yes, it too was ugly.

Louise grabbed Antoinette and hustled her into the corridor. Two working girls stared at them in surprise. 'The boss said you can have the night off, ladies. Go and tell the others,' called Louise as she and Antoinette fled downstairs.

In the street, Louise looked for Julien. He ran from the shadows. He and Antoinette embraced with feeling, their tears running free.

'My apologies,' said Louise, 'but we need to move.' Julien broke free from his girlfriend and embraced Louise. Their praise and thanks flowed, and it took time for Louise to give orders.

'You need to return to the farm, bury your grandparents, and care for the animals, especially Benjie.' They nodded. 'The police and Gestapo will go mad but who will speak about tonight? The girls inside won't. You won't, and I'm leaving France. So, are we agreed?'

The young couple agreed and again hugged and thanked Louise.

'I borrowed some of your clothes,' said Louise removing the jacket.

'Keep them,' said Antoinette. Louise handed her the jacket.

'But I do need a favour,' said Louise.

'Anything,' replied Julien.

'I need to find Rue de Brignoles.'

'Follow me,' he said and, holding Antoinette's hand, led Louise through the back streets of Marseille, then stopped and pointed.

'Thank you,' said Louise, kissed them then ordered them to flee. They did and she knocked on Dr Rodocanachi's front door.

He opened it, asking, 'Who comes knocking at this hour?'

'Good evening, Doctor.'

'Ah, it is the lady who likes to go walking. Please, come in.'

Louise stepped inside as the doctor's wife appeared. 'Who is it, George?' She saw Louise. 'Oh, it's the young lady who makes little children laugh. Come in, Mademoiselle, come in.'

Roth apartment, Marseille

As Louise entered the doctor's apartment, Benjamin and Rachel Roth packed their bags with one crammed haversack each. Their pockets were full. Like many Jewish refugees, the best way to carry extra clothes was to wear them, which was not such a good idea in summer.

They were about to flee. Marseille became a city too small and too dangerous for Jews. It seemed the Germans would soon move south and worse, locals were turning on any Jew, French or foreign.

Other Jews in Marseille had escaped, over the hills and far away. Did they survive? No news was good news. Thanks to Dr. Rodocanachi, Benjamin obtained the papers he would need in Spain. They found a guide, and the Roth family was ready to leave.

The daughters slept while their parents wrote letters to family and friends. Would the letters arrive? Are the recipients alive? Is mail delivered to concentration camps? What a joke.

It was about 9pm. Raised voices were heard. Benjamin killed the dim lighting, straining to make out who was saying what.

'It's the police,' whispered Rachel. 'We must go now.'

'Stick to the plan,' said her husband going to fetch their daughters.

In the last few days they met with another Jewish family and formed a party of escapees. The guide was paid up front, and a rendezvous time and meeting place established. They were not due there until 11pm but this was an emergency. Each parent took a daughter. The rear door of the apartment opened to a walkway with stairs at either end. They closed the door, continually making gestures for the girls to be quiet. They tiptoed away from their flat to start an amazing journey. They headed to an apartment, a safe house.

Benjamin's gold and diamonds were buried deep inside his clothes. Please God, keep these people and their goods safe.

Chapter 18

It was late when Donald Caskie's phone rang. He dreaded the sound. It brought news of desperate arrivals or of people captured or killed. He knew the caller's voice.

'Oh, good evening, George; I hope this is not bad news.'

'Did you hear about the murders in the brothel?'

The clergyman gasped, almost joked. 'You are asking a man of God about activities within a bordello?'

'The chief of police and the owner met with unfortunate accidents.'

'That is terrible but my refugees have no interest in such places.'

The doctor said nothing, and the silence whacked the Padre. He knew it could be fatal to mention names on the telephone.

'So how are your patients, Doctor?' asked Caskie.

'All are improving, although your fellow cleric hopes to recover overnight.' Caskie took a moment to comprehend the term "fellow cleric." Then it whacked him—the doctor meant a certain former nun.

The minister struggled to comprehend Louise's achievements. Did the doctor mean Helene Smythe, the nun on the run, murdered two men? George continued.

'The Vichy policeman executed a young woman's grandparents, and kidnapped the granddaughter to work in the Marseille brothel. The murders and kidnap were witnessed by the religious.'

Caskie whistled. 'Vengeance is mine, I will repay saith the Lord.'

'Do you have any new social events on your calendar?'

'Yes, I do; happening very soon in fact and in the usual venue.'

'Good for you. I'll tell my friend,' said the medical man.

'Right you are, Doctor. Take care. Goodnight.'

'Goodnight,' said the medico and went to find his patient.

George found Louise drinking coffee being comforted by Fanny. Louise changed into the clothes and shoes she wore in the convent and had told the couple about the attack at the farm and the brothel.

'I will make up the back room, George,' said his wife.

'No,' he said, 'our visitor cannot stay here, it is too dangerous.'

Fanny protested. 'It is too dangerous to be out in the city and look at the time; it is late.'

'Please get ready, Mademoiselle. We have to leave now.' Louise felt her heart accelerate. She sensed this hair-raising night was not over.

Fanny went to stand up for Louise but George bossed their guest.

'Now, please, Mademoiselle.' He glanced at his wife and mimed the word *food*.

Louise followed him to the back door wearing the coat and hat from the Irish nuns. 'You need to look like a local,' they said. She did.

George kissed his wife. 'I'll be back soon, my dear.' She handed him a small parcel. He opened the door and peered out. The globe didn't exist and in the darkness he led Louise into the night.

She had questions but knew the value of silence. He knew Marseille and so kept to dark and narrow streets.

Turning a corner they walked along a road when a man appeared walking towards them. The darkness meant you couldn't see if he wore a uniform. George hustled Louise into the small garden of an apartment block. A dog in a ground-floor apartment barked and kept barking.

Stop that damn dog! An outside light came on. 'We must go,' whispered George and they went back into the street. The man was much closer and, when only a few metres away, turned into a block of apartments and disappeared. George stopped. He grasped Louise's hand, pressed something into it and handed her a parcel.

'Go where that man went. Knock on apartment 1a. Good luck.'

He squeezed her arm and left. She stood alone in an unknown street in Marseille. In the darkness she examined the material in her hand; cash, paper notes. The parcel contained food. She stored the items and thought she knew the score. *Where is apartment 1a?*

Sucking in a deep breath, she entered this next apartment block. As she drew closer to door 1a, someone stepped from the shadows.

'Good evening, Miss,' whispered a man.

She knew the voice and its accent. 'Reverend Caskie,' she said.

'Door 1a is over there.' He took her hand and pushed something soft into her palm and gave her a small package. 'God speed, Mademoiselle, and I hope you'll come to Scotland one day.'

He squeezed her arm and disappeared. In the darkness, Louise discovered even more money and food. She stuffed the cash in her trousers, the food in her coat, and walked to door 1a.

She paused although her heart didn't; it ran on the spot. She gently tapped on the door of 1a. Tension gripped her body. The apartment offered no light. From behind the door a woman's voice was heard.

'Yes?'

'Oh, good evening. I've been told to come to this address.'

The woman opened the door. 'Come in quickly and be quiet.'

Louise entered and waited in a hallway. The woman locked the door and stared at Louise. In the narrow darkened hallway, they were close enough to rub noses. 'This way,' said the woman.

She walked along the hallway, opened a door and Louise followed her into a room, dim but with enough light to make out a number of bodies, about 10, with most seated. The woman addressed the room.

'This woman was told to come here.'

Another voice sounded. 'Turn on the light.'

Louise involuntarily held her breath. A dim light shone and Louise saw a room full of people staring at her. Her mind raced and she wanted to say, 'Hello' or 'Good evening' or anything. Before she or anyone could speak, a voice rang out.

'It's Plum.'

The speaker, a young girl, nearly seven, clutched a doll named Heidi. Sura and her family met Louise at Dr Rodocanachi's surgery, and the children remembered the lady who teased and made them laugh. Sura lost all inhibition and ran to her new friend. They hugged.

The show of affection killed any objection anyone might have had towards the interloper. Benjamin, Rachel and daughter Miriam moved to Louise and welcomed her.

Louise felt the hairs on the back of her neck come alive. 'Is this a safe house?' she asked.

'It is,' replied Benjamin, 'and it's also the starting point for refugees escaping to Spain. You are welcome to join us, Mademoiselle Plum.' Now she understood. The doctor and the clergyman were in cahoots to save her life. There was a huge price on her head, and both men wanted her out of Marseille and out of France tonight.

The other escapees were introduced. She met a second family of four, to match the Roths, although Monsieur Otto Lunz looked much older than his wife, Carla, and didn't appear to be ready for a walk around the block let alone a jaunt over the 4,000 metre high Pyrenees. Their two sons, Ezra and Jacob, were late teens, early twenties and seemed fit and able. They were keen to have Louise join the party because she looked "interesting," her natural beauty shining through her male attire. Even a large battered hat couldn't disguise her curls.

A single, middle-aged woman, Mademoiselle Arnold, not related to anyone, was the 9th member of the party. Louise made ten and greeted all with her charming smile, thanking them for allowing her to join the team. Her smile disappeared when Benjamin said they were leaving at midnight.

'Tonight?' asked Louise with a mix of fear and excitement.

'We travel light with food and water a priority.'

Louise checked her possessions. 'I have both but not a great deal.'

'You need to pay the passeur when we meet him.' Louise nodded. 'Now, as a favour, Mademoiselle, to keep my children occupied before we leave, I wonder, could you please tell my daughters one of your stories?'

'Of course,' said Louise and took the girls into another room.

'She seems unprepared,' said Madame Lunz. 'How will she help us escape? We need all the provisions we can carry.'

'She is a kind woman,' said Rachel.

'And there will be plenty of water where we are going,' added Benjamin. 'I suggest we all sit and relax. We leave in half an hour.'

Chapter 19

The Freedom Trails

To travel from Marseille to Spain in WW2, thousands shunned trains, buses, bikes, or cars, and walked. They had no choice. As midnight approached, Benjamin announced their departure. His daughters were excited. They were told they were going on an adventure. With Mademoiselle Plum on board, life for the youngsters seemed perfect.

Benjamin addressed the group. 'We don't meet the passeur until we are clear of Marseille. This first part of the journey will be the easiest. We travel in style—in a milk cart.'

The group reacted. Benjamin went outside and returned in a minute. 'It's here. Please remember to remain silent at all times. It will be uncomfortable but think of the freedom once we reach Spain.'

'*If* we reach Spain,' murmured a worried Madame Lunz.

Louise worried as the others, even the young girls, had a bag or case of sorts. Her worldly possessions were on her back and in her pockets.

They moved quietly outside with Benjamin the unelected leader. He beckoned the others forward.

Their majestic mode of transport stood ready, willing and able; a milk cart complete with one horse and, most importantly, rubber tyres. Yes, the horse's clip clop was noisy but the wheels of the truck were silent. People were used to pre-dawn deliveries of milk and the escapees hoped the regular early shift would not attract attention.

With empty milk cans pushed to the sides of the cart, the humans climbed or were helped up into the middle, and made themselves as comfortable as possible. A couple wanted to complain about the cramped conditions. No-one did.

The horse last galloped in 1934. Off went the milk cart at its slow but steady pace. The refugees remained still—they couldn't move—

and wished the journey to end. It took almost two hours to reach the agreed spot in the countryside.

Laron Roche appeared and barked. 'Everybody out.'

'Should you be speaking so loudly, Monsieur?' asked a worried Benjamin. The passeur glared at him.

'You run the toilet breaks, compagnon, and I'll conquer the Pyrenees,' he replied counting heads. He wasn't happy. 'You have one extra. Someone hasn't paid.'

Louise stepped forward. 'That's me, Monsieur. I was offered a place at the last minute.'

Roche found it hard to be caustic to a beautiful young female. She offered possible fringe benefits although his love of money had always dominated his personality.

'You have to pay,' he said, sneering.

'Of course,' said Louise taking notes from her pocket. 'I hope this will be enough.'

He counted the notes. 'Not nearly enough.'

She'd divided her newly acquired cash into separate groups of notes and hidden them in different pockets. She removed one such amount, handed it over and lied. 'It's all I have, Monsieur. Once we are in Spain, I have contacts who will give me extra funds.'

He wanted to argue but stopped when Benjamin stepped in. 'I will guarantee any shortfall, Monsieur. Now, please, can we proceed?'

Roche snorted and addressed the group. 'We walk through the forest to a hut. This is an easy climb. Stay on the path and do not make a sound. If I say "Down", move into the forest and hide. Understood?'

The adults muttered their understanding and Roche set off. He didn't care how fit or frail they were. He'd been given his money, and they had damn well better keep up.

Being summer was a blessing. Cool, even cold nights were acceptable but wet could be a nightmare. The rain, with a crescendo in mind, fell softly. Everyone wore a coat and headgear to keep their clothes dry. The rain turned serious creating two problems—the walkers slipped and fell and, to prevent that, moved more slowly thus taking longer.

'Monsieur,' called Benjamin in the loudest whisper he dared. 'We cannot move at such a speed.'

Roche turned and saw his party spread out over about 40 metres. The Lunz sons were fit and able, and Louise made good time despite her nagging sore toe. But the others were a mess. Old Monsieur Lunz struggled being helped by his family, and the secretive and sullen Mademoiselle Arnold complained. Rachel helped her girls.

'Five minutes,' said Laron and walked into the trees to pee. When he returned the stragglers had caught up. 'The hut is another half an hour. It is easily seen off to the left of this path. Those who want to, come with me. The rest, travel at your own speed.'

He turned and headed along the path. The rain set in, and no-one went after Laron.

The sons moved to their father and Louise took the young Sura. Soaked and weary, they inched towards the hut.

'There it is,' said Louise and all spirits lifted even though the hike to the front door looked steep. Shepherds used the hut. Devoid of furniture, to the wet and weary travellers, it resembled a superb hotel.

They spread out collapsing on the floor, the perfectly dry floor. A few ate from their limited supplies, others slept.

'Mutti, I have to pee,' said Sura. Rachel sighed.

'I'll take her,' said Louise, and Rachel smiled her thanks.

'Me too,' said big sister Miriam, and Louise chuckled.

'Okay, ladies, form a queue and walk this way, please.'

Out into the rain they went with Louise trying to make it an adventure. They headed into the forest where Louise found a reasonably sheltered spot and with her knife made a small hole.

'What are you doing?' whispered Sura. Miriam knew.

'Plum is making a toilet for us.'

'Yes and the most important thing is that you don't fall in.'

The girls giggled. 'Shhhh,' whispered Louise and the children understood. It's not every day you squat over a hole in the ground in a forest in the Pyrenees as the rain splashes off leaves above as you make a splash in the ground; but needs must.

Louise guided the children back to the hut, their mother gave them a rationed amount of roll and cheese, and as the rain stopped and dawn broke, the refugees and passeur settled down to sleep.

Boredom became a problem but they knew their best hope of reaching Spain meant travel by night.

As dusk arrived, Laron ordered his charges to leave. Louise studied her fellow travellers. A few were decidedly shaky, the high climbing was still ahead, and the Spanish border days away. She worried.

Will this group fail and bring me down with them?

At least Laron slowed the pace. The reasonably flat path through the forest became a miniscule track on an incline. There were tracks everywhere. Only an experienced passeur knew which to take. Without Laron, they were lost. At least the fine weather helped but poor night vision slowed their progress.

Ordered to be quiet, Monsieur Lunz broke the rule when he yelled in pain. They all stopped. An enraged passeur hurried back to him.

'Are you insane? Do you wish to attract the whole world?'

'My father fell,' said older son, Ezra. 'He's twisted his ankle.'

'We can't stop,' argued Loran. 'We must be over the next ridge before sunrise.'

Louise joined the rear of the line. 'I'll help him,' she said. 'Ezra, let's each put an arm around your Dad. We'll walk him up the hill.'

'If you think this is a hill, wait till you reach a mountain,' said Loran. 'Keep up or else,' he sniffed then spat and left.

The others pressed on and the trio of Monsieur Lunz, his older son and the SOE agent limped along getting further behind. They pushed hard to reach two massive boulders when Louise stopped and ordered them to wait. They heard voices.

'We've caught up,' said Ezra with relief especially for his father. Ezra went to call when Louise slapped a hand over his mouth. His eyes screamed fear.

'Behind this boulder,' she whispered and steered the others back and to one side. They crouched under the rock.

The voices grew louder. They were male, speaking German. The trio froze and breathed silently. The two Germans came closer then stopped in the gap between the boulders where the trio stood moments ago. If the enemy kept going, the refugees were safe. But the men stopped. They lit cigarettes and smoked. The smell of burning tobacco drifted towards the refugees. If one of them coughed or sneezed or even stretched a stiff leg, death stood ready to swoop.

Louise held Monsieur Lunz with one hand and with the other felt the ground. She found a small stone. Throwing it across or behind the

Germans was risky. Throwing it away seemed better. She checked with her comrades, showed them the stone then took a deep breath.

Heave. It flew and landed. It made a sound then settled. It didn't start a rock slide. It could have been made by someone climbing the mountain en route to Spain.

The Germans came alive. They spoke in low voices. One pointed in the direction of the sound. They dropped their cigarettes and crept away. The trio waited until the enemy left. The refugees felt fantastic.

'Let's go,' whispered Louise and through the boulders and up to the ridge they went. Even Mr Lunz senior found a new lease of life. They were over the moon when they spied a fellow refugee.

Benjamin beckoned and they scrambled into a cave. It was hardly luxurious but fantastic with the group re-united. A second night on the "road" and most thought so far, so good. Or was it?

They had two hours before sunrise but no-one wanted to continue; other than the passeur. Safe in the cave, the refugees settled. The young girls asked when they would arrive in Spain, and their mother worked hard to take their mind off the long distance still to go.

Louise remembered her SOE training about living off the land. Anyone would struggle here unless you could hit a bird with a stone, or fancied a main course of moss washed down with rainwater. She made her rations even smaller. Rachel offered to share their meagre supplies but Louise kindly refused. Her water intake never faltered.

As the others slept, she went for a walk. Hearing voices she moved towards them. From behind a rocky outcrop, Benjamin and Loran argued quietly. She struggled to hear but got the gist.

The passeur reckoned the journey time kept getting longer, which it did, and so wanted more money. Benjamin gave his word that once in Spain he would raise the funds to pay an agreed extra amount.

Loran snarled. He accused Benjamin of lying, and how he, Benjamin, had no incentive to pay extra once they reached Spain.

'I give you my word,' said the now worried Jew. 'I do not swear on my children's lives but this is the equivalent. I will pay you the extra once we arrive in Spain. Name your price.'

Louise sensed disaster. If the passeur demanded more money and it didn't appear now, he could betray the group or walk away. They were struggling, and losing their guide would be catastrophic.

She called in a quiet voice. 'Hello?' The two men fell silent and watched her appear out of the gloom. 'Good evening, Messieurs.'

Benjamin breathed easier when she arrived, Laron turned curious.

'I am having trouble with my foot and wondered if either of you have any medical training.'

When blindfolded, Benjamin could strip a clock and put it back together, but troublesome toes were not his forte. Laron offered.

'I'll check it,' he said wanting to put his hands on the woman.

'I'll see to the others,' said Benjamin and left.

Louise sat and removed her right shoe. 'I hurt my toe last week and the doctor said I need to go slowly.' She gingerly removed her sock revealing the bandaged toe. 'What do you think?'

He knelt beside her and stared at the bandaged toe. He touched her ankle. 'Where does it hurt?'

'Obviously not there.'

He gently squeezed her foot, massaging it. 'Is that better?'

In the gloom, their eyes shone like lights.

'Yes,' she whispered. He kept massaging but moved his hand above her ankle to her calf.

'I'm sure I can help you on this trip. I could massage your foot at night after we reach each destination.'

She massaged his mind. 'I don't like being outdoors.'

'There's no problem. I know huts and caves.'

She gently removed his hand. 'Okay, Doctor, till tomorrow night.'

He liked what he heard. He liked her, well, like isn't the right word. He helped replace her shoe and her toe gave a shout of pain. She winced.

'Sorry,' he said and helped her to stand. He wanted to kiss her. She found that idea revolting.

A whole day in the shelter ramped up the boredom issue. No-one complained when they heard a plane. 'Go further back inside,' said Laron, and the refugees obeyed. He peered out as the plane headed away. Benjamin and Louise crept forward.

'German,' said Laron. 'That's why we travel at night.

As dusk arrived, Laron spoke to Herr Lunz about the terrain ahead. The description made the old man even more miserable.

Off they went with the same formation; Laron leading, Louise and older son Ezra helping Herr Lunz, with the others in-between. Above the tree line gave them no cover thus making night travel essential.

The ground cover of hardy moss-like grass included a path, if you could call it that, with uneven rocks as stepping stones. The path followed a zig-zag route heading ever upwards. In the darkness, you took one step at a time. Louise despaired. On their third night of travel, at this rate, the war would be over before they even reached the summit of their trail.

The trio at the rear stopped whenever the patriarch said, 'Rest'. By the time they caught up, the others were settled in a shelter of sorts beneath an overhanging rock face. Laron fumed.

'This is not our destination for tonight.'

'We need to rest,' said Louise.

Laron stormed off. At just after midnight, they could and should be walking for another four hours. Louise checked the others. They were acting brave despite their misery. Disaster encircled the group.

Benjamin took Louise aside. 'I'll have a word with Laron,' he said and went after the passeur.

Louise sat with the girls and teased them in-between asking serious questions about their health. Their mother loved the way her daughters were distracted. Mademoiselle Arnold quietly scoffed.

As Benjamin hadn't returned, Louise went to find him. As she approached a huge boulder, she heard the men before she saw them. Their voices, though soft, were full of anger and frustration.

'This is not what we agreed,' argued Laron. 'Five days, six at most. This is our third night and we are nowhere. Back in Marseille, I have other people ready to go. I am losing money.'

Benjamin begged. 'I promise I will pay you extra in Spain.'

'You're a liar,' hissed Laron and pushed Benjamin.

Louise decided to intervene and stepped carefully forward.

Loran flew into a rage, grabbed Benjamin's coat lapels and pushed him against the rock face. 'You have gold hidden in your pockets, Jew, you all do, and you will pay me extra now!'

Louise appeared, scaring them. 'Stop it,' she hissed frightening both men. 'Do you want to tell the Germans we're here?'

Then she gasped. They were on a narrow path with a moonlit drop into the void only a few metres away.

'Keep out of it,' snapped Loran, his interest in sex nowhere near as strong as his lust for cash. 'Unless you pay me now, I'm gone.'

'No,' gasped Benjamin, in desperation grabbing Loran. 'Please, I beg of you.' Loran slapped Benjamin who fell on his knees. Louise stepped in and punched the passeur's chest. He staggered, enraged.

The Jew has gold and the woman's a tease.

Loran seethed wanting his pound of flesh. Louise pleaded.

'Stop Monsieur, I have money. Here, take it.' She rummaged in her pockets and produced her last collection of cash. He went to snatch it but she pulled it away at the last second. He raged.

'On condition you continue until we are safely in Spain.'

Now they were controlling him, setting conditions, for him the last straw. He would break bones first. He shaped to kick the prone Benjamin, slipped and fell on his face. He slid down the moss but lying flat he grasped the vegetation and rocks and stopped his descent. The others watched in horror. Louise crept forward offering her hand. He swore at her refusing any help.

He wanted out and his pride restored. He stood too quickly. His centre of gravity moved. He teetered in slow motion.

The expression on Laron's face reminded Louise of the face of Bishop Vaine just before he fell from the Cathedral balcony in Lyon.

Terror grabbed Laron as his arms whirled, faster and faster. He grasped at air, already thin at this altitude, with nothing to grasp.

Benjamin and Louise froze as the experienced guide who knew the Pyrenees backwards, fell backwards and gave voice to his emotions. The scream endured and echoed around the mountains.

Any Vichy or German patrol would not believe it to be a shepherd yodeling for his flock, not at that time of night, or at any time. Death lingered in every echo. In the nearby shelter, those awake glanced at one another in alarm. Rachel found a new depth to her misery.

Laron's skull smashed against a rock. He lost consciousness, and the rolling passeur kept rolling until he disappeared. The refugees watched the darkness swallow their guide.

The two survivors stared at one another as the scream and rock fall sounds faded. 'What do we tell the others?' whispered Benjamin.

Louise's face grew worry lines. 'Surely, Monsieur, the more important question is how the hell do we get to Spain?'

Chapter 20

64 Baker Street, London

As the driving force behind the creation of the SOE, Prime Minister Churchill urged its agents to set Europe ablaze. But he worked on the big picture and left his trusted lieutenants to run the day-to-day operation.

If Mr Churchill dropped in on the SOE in Baker Street as Louise and Benjamin watched their passeur drop into eternity, he would not have been best pleased. The F or French Section had become a bit hit and miss of late with the misses ahead on points.

In Vichy controlled France, Louise discovered two SOE agents were captured by the Gestapo, and only her daring raid with a local priest saved the life of one agent. The other died in his Gestapo cell.

But were the agents careless or betrayed? Louise discovered the truth. They were betrayed. In Lyon, she found an Englishman working for the Germans with a contact in London, in the heart of the SOE. As the Englishman tried to kill her, she shot the traitor with a pen gun, and as he lay dying about to reveal the name of the SOE mole in London, a cleric, of high standing no less, murdered the spy.

But then this killer, the bishop, in trying to kill Louise, found himself on a rapid trip to Paradise, or perhaps elsewhere.

So, Louise knew about the mole in London but not his or her identity. If she told the SOE in London a viper lurked within its bosom, the traitor could flee, do more damage, or cover their tracks.

No, Louise must have London believe she's dead, reach England undetected and, without revealing herself, find the rat wrecking the SOE. With Louise believed to be dead, the most likely outcome would see the mole continue.

Her plan was simple. Flee France to Spain and from Gibraltar, reach home. And all that looked good and was on track until her guide fell off the Pyrenees.

Back in London, Buckmaster addressed his colleagues. 'I'm worried about Lyon. We have agents betrayed, dead or missing. Why? What's happening there?'

'The radio operator, Alfie, is alive and in touch,' said Frenchman, Jermain Attard. 'But his latest report confirms 'is partner is dead and our fake nun, Sister Claudine, is missing.'

'But why?' pleaded Buckmaster. 'Why are we failing our agents?'

Vera Atkins seemed reluctant to speak. 'We have slipped up on occasions, sir.' Buckmaster looked displeased.

'Meaning?'

'If we give agents an instruction and then don't follow through at our end, we could be, probably *are* doing them harm.' She paused and Buckmaster worried.

'Explain,' he said.

'Our agents begin a message with a simple code word. It means nothing to the enemy but to us it means they're free to transmit. Recently, sir, you reprimanded an agent for omitting the code word.' Buckmaster went quiet. 'It could have been omitted because the agent was under duress. He followed orders and yet you reprimanded him.'

Buckmaster shook his head. 'It never happened,' he said and changed the subject. Alas it *did* happen and the boss made a schoolboy howler, which may have placed an agent in harm's way.

The current problem in the SOE was not only the mole in their ranks, which was catastrophic for agents abroad, but the fact nobody in Baker Street knew the mole even existed; nobody, that is other than Louise Wellesley.

The Pyrenees

Benjamin and Louise made their way back to the others. Both volunteered to break the news. Louise insisted on being the one. As they approached, they heard groans, and hurried.

'It can't be true,' said Rachel, and Benjamin's fears multiplied.

'What?' he asked. 'What's not true?'

Rachel explained. 'Mademoiselle Arnold said she heard a story about our guide, how on one trip a baby cried and went on crying. The mother tried everything to hush the little one. The sound carried and everyone feared it would bring a Vichy patrol. Apparently our wonderful guide suggested the child be silenced—permanently.'

'Nonsense,' said Louise, 'and anyway it will never happen to us.'

Well, did that statement stop the conversation?

'What do you mean?' asked Madame Lunz, her anxiety catching.

Benjamin took over. 'There's been an accident. Monsieur Roche has suffered a nasty fall.' Benjamin tried to break it gradually. His audience clung to his every word. 'I'm afraid he's passed away.'

Groans and gasps buzzed around the cave.

'He's dead?' croaked the already shaken Monsieur Lunz in disbelief. Benjamin nodded.

'What kind of an accident?' asked Ezra.

Louise replied. 'He slipped and fell and hit his head.'

'Are you sure he's dead? Can we try and help him?' asked Mademoiselle Arnold.

'We can't help him,' said Benjamin. 'He fell off the mountain.'

There were more reactions of despair and fear. 'It's the end,' said Monsieur Lunz. 'We are lost and will finish up like him.'

Misery flooded the group. The two young Roth girls didn't fully understand but knew something bad had happened. They cried and clung to their mother. Her tears mixed with their tears.

Louise spoke in a soft and calm voice. 'I know this is awful. But what is important is staying positive. We are alive. We have one another. Let us rest, try to sleep and in the morning, make a plan.'

No-one argued. What was the point? They were as good as dead. No-one thought they could survive. No-one spoke.

Near dawn, Louise went for a walk. She returned as the light improved. The mood in the cave didn't, it reeked of despair. They were alone, lost and would starve.

'Listen,' said Louise with a plan she created over her walk. 'I have a suggestion.' She called on her acting skills to speak a certain way and to convince people of her sincerity and self-belief.

The group became eerily silent. Louise began.

'I have studied maps of the Pyrenees. I believe I can find a way to the Spanish border. I have been trained to travel through the countryside and survive. If you will agree to me going out to scout the land, I will return with a route to follow. At least, please let me try.'

She paused and no-one spoke. Then Benjamin moved to Louise and embraced and thanked her. His two daughters ran to her and joined the group hug. The others were grateful although Mademoiselle Arnold and Otto Lunz were skeptical and quiet. What alternatives were there? None. Either they would trust this young woman or stay here and die.

Now, hope appeared, slim, yes, but it existed. The group settled and Louise moved around talking to her fellow refugees. The Lunz parents were a worry. His frail body seemed physically unable to make the journey without help. His wife seemed psychologically troubled, her spirit crushed. Louise spoke quietly to her.

'We have come so far, Madame. Rest and gather your strength for our final journey.'

She wanted to cry. 'I have lost everything; my beautiful apartment, my clothes, my shoes. If I survive, I will have nothing.'

Louise studied the woman's shoes. They were expensive and perfect for a hotel lobby, a wedding reception or cathedral but totally wrong for mountaineering. *Why choose them in the first place?*

'We have all lost belongings, Madame. I have lost friends, and my brother has been horribly disfigured at sea escaping from France, but unlike so many of our friends and family, we are alive.'

Carla Lunz was struck dumb, forced to confront her self-pity. She imagined the beautiful young woman to be worry free. Louise continued.

'I have seen people tortured and die with my own eyes. They cannot fight for freedom ever again but *we* can, Madame, *we* can.'

She studied Louise, admiring the young woman's strength and depth of character, but said nothing. Louise squeezed Carla's arm, smiled at her sons and husband, and moved to the Roths. The parents supported her and the girls worshipped her.

She spoke in a soft voice to the whole group. 'I'll go as far as I can to find a way forward. I'll go in the daylight because I need to be able to see where we can go. Please stay here and do not go outside. I'll be back as soon as I can.'

'Be careful,' said Madame Lunz.

Louise gave a restrained smile then blew a kiss, and every member of the party, especially the two little girls, waved and wished her well.

'Be careful, Plum,' were the last words she heard from the lips of Miriam Roth.

To travel in daylight carried an obvious risk, but Louise needed to see into the distance, to find the route they would take, and travelling at night meant travelling blind. Her compass-reading skills were solid and she rejoiced knowing she carried a magical invention created by the boffins back home. She held a simple magnet which, when placed in water, always turned to point north.

She spotted pools so scampered down the rocks and moss, and placed her magnet in the water. She waited and watched. Slowly the magnet wavered then settled. Now she knew her directions.

Keeping close to overhanging rocks to avoid being seen, she climbed seeking the best vantage point, relatively easy for a fit SOE agent, even one with a blister on a big toe. The frail Monsieur Lunz would consider this an impossible climb. This became Louise's major problem. Find the right way of course, but unless she avoided tricky climbs, the right way would be impossible.

How can I get an old man and young children over the Pyrenees?

She couldn't go too far; just enough to explore further along the road to freedom. Satisfied she knew their next leg, she headed back.

To say they welcomed her return would be an understatement. Without this young woman taking over their expedition, they were dead. Their food supplies were low, their bodies bruised, their spirits shattered, and their knowledge of the area, zero. They craved news.

'I've found the route for our next stage. It does include a small climb but once we reach the top, we have a fairly even path to follow.'

'Where will we stay when we arrive?' asked Rachel who worried her children could not survive sleeping in the open.

There are shelters along the way and pools of water. I even saw a small lake.'

She did but far away in the distance and not close to the route she planned. She herself needed a rest, and everyone tried to sleep before the expedition, now sans passeur, resumed.

Darkness fell in the Pyrenees and it was time to leave. Above scattered clouds, the sky became a sea of ink. 'I'll lead,' announced

Louise, 'and Ezra and Jacob, you can help your father, and Benjamin you can bring up the rear and help anyone in trouble.'

'Of course,' he said admiring Louise more by the hour.

'I'll maintain a steady but slow pace so take your time. We should easily make our destination before dawn. Okay?' Heads nodded. They were afraid, even terrified, but took heart from the woman with natural leadership skills. She oozed confidence even if inside she felt as sick as a dog. Their new journey began.

The night air nipped their faces. Talking was forbidden but occasionally Louise could hear voices. She chose not to reprimand anyone. Better to keep moving and hope they kept up. She worried because the climb she mentioned before they started was about to begin. This would be a major test.

She wondered if Otto Lunz's sons reprimanded their father as he kept up with only the odd complaint. The Team Tortoise plodded forward. The climb used a track of sorts. Rocks and grass were either side with the slope always heading up.

Louise climbed. In the dark, she searched for a rock or foothold. She stepped where she thought the safest place to put your feet existed. The slope increased.

Now, the complaining kicked in. 'Help me' and 'I can't go any further,' were two comments floating up to Louise.

She turned and encouraged them with short sentences such as, 'Take your time.' 'We'll soon be there.' 'We can do this.'

The labourious trekking dragged on. Even Louise doubted they would make it. When she heard a scream, she feared they were doomed.

Otto Lunz slipped and fell. His sons in front and behind managed to catch him. The screams were from his wife and Mademoiselle Arnold. Louise hurried as carefully as she could back to the accident. The old man groaned and lay still. Louise knelt, desperate to make the best of a bad situation.

'Where are you hurt, Monsieur?' He groaned.

'I think it's his leg,' said Ezra, supporting his father's head.

Louise squeezed his shin. 'Tell me when it hurts.' He continued to groan softly. She assumed it to be a bone problem and not muscular, but what would she know? She squeezed his knee producing more soft groaning. She pressed his hip and the old man howled; the sound perfect for attracting enemies on the hunt for escapees, and for telling the world the refugees now included a cripple. Wild animals took notes.

If Otto Lunz had cracked a bone in his hip, he was no longer able to walk. For him, the climb was over.

'Let's all sit and rest,' said Louise, and walked on a bit to think. Benjamin joined her. She stared at him in the fleeting moonlight.

'What are our options, Mademoiselle?' She didn't answer so he answered for her. 'We can leave him here and send help when we reach Spain.' Both knew he would certainly die. 'Or we could carry him to Spain.' That sounded even more far-fetched.

'Or we could kill him and carry on,' said Louise thinking aloud.

Benjamin's face turned white. 'I cannot believe you mean that.'

'Of course I don't but I have been trained to consider all options before deciding on a course of action.'

'What is this training you talk about, and who are you, really?'

'If I told you, Monsieur, you would not believe me.' She grasped his arm. 'Come, we have the solution.'

She moved back to the injured man, disrobing as she moved. She knelt beside Otto Lunz. 'I regret we do not have any drugs to ease your pain, Monsieur, but we do have a stretcher to carry you the rest of the way.' The others gasped.

She spread her coat on the sloping ground and tucked it in beneath him. They lifted his shoulders and guided his upper body onto the coat. He screamed when they lifted his lower body. She ordered his sons and Benjamin to take a position. 'When I say lift, we lift.' Each of the four took a corner of the coat. 'Ready,' said Louise, 'and lift.'

The patient yelped in pain but settled when lying on the coat.

'We should be thankful my coat is made from the finest wool, and we are more than halfway through our journey.' The wool bit was true, the halfway claim a wild and hopeful guess.

They all seemed better, stronger because of the courage and determination of their new leader. She found solutions to problems. She alone became the reason they would carry on. Under Louise's instruction, the three males and Mademoiselle Smythe stepped off holding the homemade stretcher. Otto Lunz appreciated the effort others took on his behalf and kept his complaints to a minimum. Up the mountain went this odd collection of Jewish refugees and the actress doubling as an SOE agent.

Louise urged her fellow carriers on. The women and children were behind but always the group moved forward.

The males found being a stretcher-bearer tiring. Their muscles yelled but none dared complain. If a woman can carry her share of the load, then so can they.

Finally they reached the summit. Louise bubbled with pride. She knew they were past the toughest part of her planned leg.

'Let's rest,' she said as they lowered the patient to the ground.

They waited a good fifteen minutes. Before them was a path of sorts on mainly flat land. In winter it would be covered with snow. Louise rallied the troops. She wisely asked the four carriers to swap sides giving their other hand and arm some respite. With the land relatively flat, they made reasonable time.

She knew of no cabin or cave to aim for. She faced a quandary. With broken bodies and dwindling supplies, she needed to move as fast and as far as possible. Finding the border wouldn't be her biggest challenge; rather it would be getting there before they died.

They needed to stop every twenty minutes or so to prevent one or more collapsing. Even a fairly fit Louise suffered cramp.

As soon as she found a place of shelter, she would take it. Even with hours of darkness left, finding a safe camping spot was essential. They didn't have a choice when the moon disappeared and the clouds decided to send down precipitation.

'Over here,' called Louise as she headed towards the face of the mountain. Huge boulders rested against one another. By crawling between the giant rocks, they were out of the rain; yes it was cramped and uncomfortable but beggars can't be choosers.

She crawled towards Otto. 'How are you, Monsieur?'

'I'm alive, thanks to you.'

'Well done,' she said then, 'may I borrow your stretcher for a while, please?' He didn't hesitate. His family helped him roll on his good side and Louise claimed her coat. She addressed the group.

'I'll go forward and find a better place to shelter and see if I can locate our final path to the border. Please stay here and I'll be back as soon as I can.'

Their faces showed their admiration for the woman they knew to be the difference between life and death. If she entertained doubts, they were never on show. As Louise crawled out towards the rain, she passed little Sura with tears streaming down her cheeks.

'Oh, Sura,' said Louise, 'what's all this crying for? Soon we'll be in Spain and you will be free to play.'

The child stared at her favourite lady and sobbed. 'I've lost Heide.'

'Oh no,' cried Louise.

Rachel explained. 'She lost her when we were climbing the last slope. I explained how Heide will find her own little cave and stay dry.'

'But she'll have no-one to talk to,' cried the inconsolable child.

'I have to go now, Sura. You try and get some sleep.' Louise kissed the child's head, gave her mother a weak smile then stepped out into the rain. She dropped to the path they were on and then, she didn't know why, turned left heading back the way they came.

This is insane, she thought as the nasty rain pricked and stung her face. Her coat and hat were a Godsend. She reached the top of the ridge and headed back down where they first carried Otto Lunz. She slipped and landed hard on her bottom.

Now she attacked herself. Searching for a lost doll was madness; getting injured when they were so far along the climb was insane.

She carefully traced her steps down the mountain. The weather gods became bored and threw in some variety. A flash of lightning was followed by thunder which bounced around the mountains.

'Great,' said Louise and decided enough was enough. As she turned, another flash of lightning lit the desolate place but shone on the limp body of Heide. Louise wept for joy, her tears swamped in the rain. Heide was found. Louise kissed the doll, buried it inside her clothes and headed back up the mountain.

Reaching the summit, and about to take the path to return to their current hiding-place, she saw a path of sorts on the ridge. She could never ask the others to take this steep and bumpy route. Besides, a sheer drop on one side made any sort of slip or fall a disaster. In the dark and wet, she took this course, parallel with the track below.

She could go no higher. Could she see the best path to the border from up here? No, and it meant she would have to go out alone in the morning to find their new route meaning another 24 hours with little food. No, she must find the direction now and have the others push on in the daylight.

She trod carefully peering through the rain at the landscape beyond. The storm continued to rage and as she moved further along the ridge, a massive bolt of lightning flashed lighting the Pyrenees and she saw it; a ribbon reflected in nature's lamp—a river.

'Yes,' shouted Louise. A river can tumble down a mountainside but also meander through plains. She'd studied a map of the Pyrenees and believed she knew this river. It might be the waterway her famous ancestor and namesake, Arthur Wellesley, crossed in one of his many battles, and it could well be their ticket to freedom.

She searched for a way down the ridge, found one and slithered to the track the refugees trod about an hour ago. She saw the two boulders, their makeshift shelter, and headed towards them.

'Hello,' she called when close by, and voices and sighs full of relief and happiness bounced back. Soaked, she crawled into the space. Rachel helped her out of the wet coat and hat. They all stared at Louise. The terrifying storm meant each adult wondered if they would ever see the young woman again.

'I have two bits of good news,' she said, and expectations soared. 'There is a river away to our right. I'm pretty sure it's part of the border between France and Spain.' Hearts beat faster. 'If we can reach that river, and cross it, we will be in Spain and free.'

There were smiles in the dark. Hope sprang eternal. Feelings of joy fought to surface. From wondering if their leader had been struck by lightning and lay dead in an abyss, they had news to shout about. She not only returned safe but spoke of the possibility they might yet triumph. Fit military men struggled at times crossing these mountains. Here were untrained civilians, including an injured elderly man and young children, who now dared to believe.

Rachel spoke first. 'You mentioned two bits of good news.'

'Oh and so I do,' said Louise and pulled a rabbit out a hat in the form of a doll called Heide. Hearts lit up and the squeal of a little girl brought joy.

'Heide,' she exclaimed and hugged the doll to her chest.

Louise thought, *Might that be an omen?*

Chapter 21

The Pyrenees, France

Food became a luxury. The adults could bear the hunger but not so the children. 'I'm hungry, Mutti,' said little Sura, 'and so is Heidi.' The little girl's joy at being reunited with her beloved toy was overpowered by a rumbling tummy. Her parents cringed not being able to feed their daughters. They kept promising they would soon be safe and could have lots of food.

The rain passed and the new day turned sunny. Good weather for pushing to freedom. Louise made a decision and addressed the group.

'I know travel by day is unwise but with our supplies low and the river near, I say we go now. We can see the path. What do you say?'

The others agreed—what was the point in disagreeing?—and they prepared to start again. Louise's wet coat meant having Monsieur Lunz being carried on a damp garment. Would that make him ill? But the sun shone and the promise of freedom encouraged everyone.

The big question lingered; how would they reach the river? Should they go back to the ridge where Louise first saw the waterway? Should they push on along the mostly flat track, and hope to find another way to get off the mountain?

Louise didn't want to make the decision alone so spoke quietly with Benjamin. She described the options. He gave his opinion.

'I know we have to climb down at some stage but if we try and do so now, it might be too much for Monsieur Lunz.'

'And for those of us carrying him,' added Louise.

'Yes, but if we can see the river below us, it will be an incentive to climb down.' Louise nodded. 'It's your decision, Mademoiselle. You are an inspiring and magnificent leader, and I bless the day we met.'

Louise forced a miniature smile being grateful for his kind words but knew danger waited whichever route they chose. Getting this final decision wrong could wreck their chances right at the death.

'We'll keep going along this ridge and look for a way down as we travel,' she said. They lifted Otto Lunz, and the ragtag, struggling band of Jewish refugees led by an English actress limped forward.

Stoppages for rest and water became more frequent. The sun climbed higher and shone with a fierce glow. The children took it in turns to constantly complain. Louise watched Otto who seemed to become delirious at times. They had placed a handkerchief on his face to shield it from the sun. At least Louise's coat dried.

The path gradually edged higher and soon everyone could see a space of only about ten metres between their path and a steep drop off the ridge. The adults stopped speaking. Rachel helped her daughters with the two other females, Madame Lunz and Mademoiselle Arnold clinging to one another out of fear of stumbling and falling. Louise knew how delicate things were and ordered another rest. They searched for shade.

Then they heard it. A plane sounded somewhere in the distance. It grew louder. Panic kicked in albeit in a quiet manner.

Ezra announced the fact. 'It's a plane. We have to hide.'

'Over there,' said Louise indicating with a nodding head.

They moved towards a rock face with haste; great haste for so weary a group. Little shade was available with the sun ever climbing.

'Drop,' said Louise and after settling the patient on moss, she joined the others crouching against the rock wall.

Now they saw the plane. It circled. Louise watched. A few refused to do so. Ezra whispered.

'Will they shoot us?'

Louise shook her head. She spoke half the truth. 'We are not important.' She could have said, 'They will report us to the nearest patrol and they will soon be heading our way.'

The plane flew away and most of the party sighed with relief. Louise made a decision.

'I'll go on ahead and find a way for us to climb down. Stay here and rest. I won't be long.' As she left, the words of encouragement and thanks from the others were muted. They were oh so close to giving up. She disappeared along the track.

It became steeper and narrower. *This will never work*, she thought. Carrying Otto along this track is impossible. She turned back wondering where to go, and how she could convince them to go on.

Moving closer to the group, she heard strange sounds. A female voice wailed. Louise hurried. The others heard her approaching and turned to her. She sensed their news but moved closer to be sure. She studied faces. The Lunz brothers had tears streaming down their cheeks. Louise glanced at Benjamin who shook his head.

'Monsieur Lunz has passed away,' he whispered as Rachel tried to distract the girls.

Bent double in pain, Carla knelt beside her dead husband. Louise knelt next to her. 'I am so sorry for your loss, Madame.' She wanted to say more but reckoned silence and respect were best. Louise gave each of the sons a hug. No words were needed.

The saying that every cloud has a silver lining flashed inside Louise's head. The business of carrying Monsieur Lunz had become a massive handicap. Now, being free of such a burden meant the others could push ahead with relative speed. His death might mean saving the lives of the others. But what would happen to the body?

She moved aside and nodded to Benjamin who joined her.

'We can't bury him,' said Benjamin. 'Even with tools and soft earth, we haven't the strength to dig any sort of a grave.'

Louise put her point of view. 'But we can't carry him. The path ahead is far too steep.'

Benjamin studied Louise and gave his thoughts. 'We must involve his family.' Louise agreed. 'Not his wife; ask Ezra the older son.'

'Ezra,' said Louise in a soft voice. He joined them. 'We're so sorry for your loss, but as cruel as it seems, unless we press on, we'll all suffer the fate of your dear father.' Ezra understood but couldn't face the fact about leaving his father behind, alone in the mountains. Louise spoke bluntly. 'Would he want you to stay here and die?'

Silly question.

'My brother and I are fine but our mother will not want to leave.'

Louise gave an order in the most sympathetic way. 'Then you must persuade her to come with us to Spain and to freedom.'

Ezra understood. 'But what do we do with my father's body?'

'We can bury your father beneath many rocks,' said Louise.

'Many, many rocks,' said Benjamin. 'It will be done with great respect and his body will return to the earth.'

Louise drew strength from having a sympathetic Jewish soul on hand to explain the situation, and comfort the bereaved family.

But Ezra's distress continued to grow. 'He cannot be buried above ground. It is forbidden by Jewish law.'

'Was your father religious?' she asked.

Benjamin answered for the man he did not know. 'Mademoiselle, in these crazy anti-Semitic times, every Jew is religious.'

Louise's stomach churned at her ignorance. She didn't know how but made a promise. 'We will dig a grave to ensure your father is below ground.' She and Benjamin stared at the young man. He grimaced and spoke from the heart. There and then he came of age.

'Thank you, both of you; my family is deeply grateful for your kindness.' He kissed Louise's hand. 'I will have my brother take my mother back along the path while we prepare the grave.'

Ezra behaved like the head of the family. His father would have been proud. Ezra and his younger brother whispered to their mother, and Jacob led her and Mademoiselle Arnold away. Benjamin asked his wife to do the same with their girls, and Rachel and her daughters followed the grieving widow.

Louise and Benjamin studied the area then she spoke. 'See if there is any place suitable for a grave.' She pointed. 'Try over there.'

They both searched. Ezra joined them and Louise experienced joy when the son chose the grave site; a mossy area between low boulders. He used his hands to tear at the moss. The others joined him. Ezra and Benjamin found stones with an edge of sorts and Louise produced the knife she used to kill the Vichy policeman in Marseille. The three of them worked at removing the moss and attacking the soil. She stabbed and broke up the earth and the men placed it to one side.

It wasn't deep or even but was made with love and respect. 'You collect some stones, Ezra,' said Louise, 'and we'll fetch your father.'

They laid the old man in his final resting place. It was not a deep grave but certainly well below ground. Louise and Benjamin placed the removed soil and then the moss respectfully on the body. This took time. Ezra fetched stones. These were added with Benjamin making a sort of headstone. When they finished, using his left hand, Ezra placed a pebble at the top of the grave.

Louise whispered to Benjamin. 'I think you should wait with your family. Ezra can bring his to pay their last respects.'

Benjamin left and Louise stood beside Ezra before suggesting he collect his family. He did. He and his brother led their mother to the burial place and Louise stepped back.

So now, alone in the Pyrenees on a glorious day as the world went about its business of killing, a family said goodbye to a beloved husband and father.

Madame Lunz took strength from her sons. The close family grew closer. Their grief grew stronger but never stronger than their determination to escape.

Louise led them to the Roth family and Mademoiselle Arnold.

'Thank you everyone for the way you helped Monsieur Lunz. I believe he would be grateful. And I know the best way to honour him would be for all of us to complete our journey over the Pyrenees.'

She studied their faces. The Lunz family members were in tears. The Roth girls were weepy because of their rumbling tummies, and their parents were being crushed not being able to feed their children. They'd run out of their last food supply; sugar lumps washed down with rainwater. Mademoiselle Arnold remained inscrutable. But all were touched by Louise's words. She pushed the positive.

'I will go first and Monsieur Roth will bring up the rear. This is our final part of the journey. Soon we will climb down to the river and cross into Spain.' Another pause as she produced a winning smile of hope. It caught on. It was unusual to see sad, desperate people with tears in their eyes all trying to smile.

Let's go,' said Louise, checking her pockets to see if she had any spare reserves of hope.

Chapter 22

The Pyrenees, France

Walking along the relatively flat ridge made their progress okay. But life became scary when the path grew narrow with the drop on one side only two or three metres away. When the wind became a stiff breeze, Louise heard little Sura complaining. The massive drop to the right scared everyone.

'I'm scared, Mummy,' she cried. Louise stopped and turned around. Rachel was doing it tough. Her husband brought up the rear in case anyone stumbled or struggled but handling the two girls, and keeping herself upright and moving, made Rachel's life hell.

Louise addressed the small child. 'Let me carry, Heide,' she said. Sura thought less of the tricky geography. 'Remember I found her and I promise I will care for her until we are off the mountain.'

The child sought guidance from her mother and received a nod of approval. Louise accepted the doll and carefully stored it inside her jumper. Then she turned her back and knelt.

'Now you can ride on *my* back.' This shocked the group. Louise regretted saying it the moment she bent to receive her passenger. The child again hesitated but with her mother's nod, stepped forward and placed her arms around Louise's throat. Ouch.

Memories of climbing obstacles and carrying packs in the wilds of Inverness-shire flooded back. Straining her legs, Louise adjusted her new backpack and set off. Full points for bravery but all the adults had one idea bubbling in their minds—this was a disaster in waiting.

They struggled along in silence. The death of one of their group brought not only sadness but the reality of grief. If Monsieur Lunz can die, why not me? Louise carried a child, kept up everyone's spirits, and searched for a route to get off the mountain. But now, for the first time, even she doubted her ability to survive.

No food, little water, inexperienced companions including young children, and, since the appearance of a buzzing aeroplane, the definite prospect of patrols out searching for them. Stopping because of the daylight wasn't an option. Time became their enemy. Stay high in the sky and die of starvation or exposure. Hide and die anyway. No, reaching Spain was essential and the sooner the better.

Then Louise struck gold. Away below her she saw a sheet of pebble-like shale. Beyond this mass of stones lay a mass of grass or moss with even a few stubby trees and, away in the distance, the far away distance, a river. If correct, they were looking at the border between France and Spain. She stopped, knelt and Sura hopped off.

'Thank you, Plum,' smiled the adoring girl.

Louise addressed her "team". 'Let's have a brief rest and then we'll climb down.' They sat in a group. 'The loose stones will be slippery. I mean they will move so we'll have to travel sitting down. Then there is grass and hopefully a path. And if you cast your eyes away in the distance you can see a river. On the other side is Spain.'

The sighs and quiet words of happiness stopped when Madame Lunz spoke.

'But how do we cross the river? I cannot swim.'

Murmurs of concern replaced the previous murmurs of delight.

'Is there a boat, Plum, or a bridge?' asked Miriam.

'We'll find a way,' said Louise. 'We've conquered the mountains and I'm sure we can conquer the river.'

The positive words brought silence. The girls ceased complaining about hunger pains. Benjamin moved to Louise with his back to the others. He spoke quietly.

'If we travel down in daylight, patrols will see us from miles away.'

Louise knew that but argued. 'And if we stay here without food, how long before your daughters collapse and have to be carried?'

They were literally between a rock and a hard place.

'What about a compromise?' asked Benjamin. 'We stay here for a few hours then move when the sun is setting?'

Louise pondered the idea. Whichever move they made, danger reared its ugly head. 'Okay,' she said. 'I'll go on and find shelter. Please tell the others.'

He did. Louise returned with good news. 'There is shade further along. Follow me.'

Talk about a slow-moving group. They were dead on their feet. Louise stepped in, placed Sura over a shoulder like a fireman. Such a simple action inspired or shamed the others into moving.

They reached an outcrop of rock and collapsed in the shade. They passed around their remaining water.

'Rest,' said Louise, 'conserve your strength for the final push.'

'What strength?' asked Mademoiselle Arnold and silence returned. Louise wanted to slap the woman for her constant complaining.

The sun departed and dusk arrived. Louise surveyed her fellow travellers. The males were awake and keen. The sons helped the older women and Benjamin helped his wife. The girls whined.

'Follow me,' said Louise. 'Let's go to Spain.'

She led them back to the spot where a descent seemed possible. She went first. After about fifty metres, she reached the large area of ancient granite and slate broken into small rocks like shale. She stopped and beckoned the others to move towards her one at a time.

'Lean backwards,' she called. Ezra helped his mother and Jacob guided Mademoiselle Arnold. Benjamin took Sura and Rachel held Miriam's hand. All eight made it to the shale.

'Sit,' said Louise and demonstrated. 'Move using your hands like this.' She demonstrated, lifting her bottom and moving it further down the slope. 'As you can see the stones move. Don't worry. So long as you remain low, you will be fine. Don't stand up and don't hurry. Take a rest if you need to. We're heading for the grass down there. Okay, let's go.'

She set off giving her bottom a hard time. The others copied her with mixed results. The children found it fun but the two middle-aged women reckoned it was torture.

Louise refused to go back and help anyone. They couldn't fall; they were already on the ground, and if she gave help, they would never make it to the river. Everyone must help themselves.

Eventually they reached the grass and declared it the nicest vegetation in the world. They rested; their posteriors in need of a massage.

Louise sensed pride. 'Congratulations everyone, you all did a brilliant job. Now, this next part is tricky. It's dark so watch your step.

Travel in pairs as before. We stand but move slowly. Check each footstep. Be extra careful.' She turned around. 'Where's Jacob?'

'Call of nature, Mademoiselle,' said his brother.

'I've run out of pee,' grumbled Madame Lunz.

'Hey,' called a voice and panic struck the group.

Louise made a shushing sound as Jacob returned, stepping carefully through the grass and between the scrubby bushes. 'There's a path over there,' he said.

Louise explored and couldn't believe her luck. They'd found a small path, ideal for sheep and goats and, right now, for a group of refugees. 'Over here,' she called in a whisper. The others moved.

The discovery gave all the adults a surge of happiness.

'Well done, Jacob,' said Benjamin.

Louise continued being positive. 'This is a huge stroke of luck. We must always take care but this time we can see where to put our feet. Stay in pairs and please, no talking, not a sound.'

She set off wanting to go faster than the others but mindful of their condition, settled for a steady pace.

In the darkness, they made good progress when Louise nearly died. She turned and held up a hand. She whispered with fear in her voice. 'Stop!' The party stopped. 'Not a sound.' The others wanted to know why. The adults reckoned they knew and knots grew in their stomachs.

Louise waved. 'Move over there and drop when I say.' They moved. Sura scratched her leg and went to complain but tasted her mother's hand as it wrapped around her mouth. Rachel's face turned the little girl to stone.

Louise whispered. 'Drop! Do not move or make a sound.'

All nine refugees buried themselves in the grass and low bushes. They knew why as distant voices could be heard in the still night air. A torch beam flashed. The words were French and the men were Vichy police hunting refugees having been tipped off by a spotter plane.

Knowing the escapees were women and children, the searchers with guns held little fear of their quarry. They were not on the same path as the hunted, but still headed in their general direction.

Louise decided. If the group remained here, the odds were they'd be discovered. She must do something; lead the police away, attack them, even surrender, and thus leave the others to escape.

Benjamin crouched beside her. She whispered. 'I will lead them away.'

'No,' he whispered in fear as much for her safety as for him and his family. She ignored his protest.

'If I'm captured, wait till they're gone then take the others to the river. Cross where you can.'

'Let me come with you.'

'The others need you, Monsieur. You can lead them to freedom. I know you'll be great. Good luck.' She squeezed his arm and moved. Benjamin's heart wanted to scream.

Louise's body craved a rest but her mind drove her forward. The heavy cloud cover helped and she knew about positioning for a surprise attack using the wind to her advantage. She removed the knife from her belt and gave the enemy as wide a berth as possible.

The police were talking about where the refugees were last seen. They kept talking as they came closer. A short, scrubby bush stood near the path. Louise crouched behind it, ready to strike. She knew she could kill the first policeman but the second would easily shoot her. She made a plan.

The men drew closer. She could hear them and then see their shapes in the gloom. In single file they came up the mountain. Louise crouched above them. She waited until the first man passed then she sprang at the second. He was flattened. The first officer spun around and struggled to grab his rifle slung over his shoulder.

Louise grabbed her man in a headlock with her knife at his throat. His eyes grew wide. The other man pointed his rifle but straight at his partner.

'One false move and I cut his throat,' hissed Louise.

'Don't shoot,' begged the man being held.

Dragging her prisoner closer, Louise strengthened her position, and spoke to the first man. 'Come forward where I can see you,' she ordered. 'Drop the rifle and raise your hands.'

After a tense moment, the first man started to walk forward. He came closer but continued to point his rifle at his colleague and Louise. Her plan seemed hazy. She had no idea if it would work. Then the first man stopped. Tension ran wild. The man with the rifle changed direction and walked backwards. Louise lost control.

This first man kept backpedaling. Without a gun, what could Louise do? If the man disappeared into the night, she was stuck.

In desperation she tried to gain control. 'This is what is going to happen,' she said.

'No, *this* is what is going to happen,' said a third policeman who lagged behind his two fellow officers, heard the incident and crept forward to press his rifle against the back of Louise's skull. She recognised the circle of a gun barrel. 'Put down the knife.' Louise hesitated. 'Do it now or I shoot.'

Louise dropped the knife. Her prisoner grabbed it and all three men trained their rifles on Louise. The late arrival stepped forward and smashed his rifle butt against Louise's head.

She fell, clutching her head, trying to absorb the pain while thinking of any possible move. Her well-used routine of keeping her enemies talking swung into operation.

'I surrender, Messieurs. I am trying to cross to Spain to join my husband who is a wine merchant. His business has been confiscated by the Nazis.'

'You are a liar, Mademoiselle,' said the third officer. 'You are a nun on the run with the code name of Plum.' Louise froze. 'We have been tracking you since you murdered two of our colleagues back in Lyon.'

Louise died inside but admitted nothing. Her head throbbed with pain. 'A nun?' she scoffed. 'Me? Are you serious?'

'There are many people who would like to meet you, Mademoiselle. Someone in London wants you dead but many in Lyon and Marseille want you alive. But first we will need to soften you up a little.' He turned to his colleagues. 'Do we toss to see who goes first?'

They laughed.

'You have the wrong person. I have never been to Lyon.'

'Undress you evil English bitch,' said the gun waving officer. 'Oh, and feel free to scream as loud as you like. The only people who might hear you are those bloody Jews you tried to save, and they're useless. Where are they? All dead?' He barked. 'Now strip.'

On the side of a mountain in the Pyrenees close to the border between France and Spain, Louise would have preferred a bullet here and now to what they planned. She faced an intolerable choice. The

Gestapo in Marseille or the Vichy police in the Pyrenees was a choice between evil and evil.

Her captors smirked and sneered, goading her as she removed her coat. They were spread out so if she tried to rush at one, the others were free to shoot her.

Standing there sans coat, she stopped.

'Undress,' snapped the third officer.

Louise defied him. 'No, I won't. You'll have to shoot me.' All three raised their rifles. 'But then what will you say to your Gestapo pals?'

She taunted them, picked up her coat and dressed. The Vichy police were confused. She spoke the truth, her worth being a million times more alive than dead.

'If you kill me, when the Gestapo find out, you are all dead.'

She was right. They muttered and agreed not to kill her but to rape her. They moved in. Each came from a different direction. The first raised his rifle to strike her. She ducked and smashed his face with her fist.

That's it, she thought, *now I'm dead*. But her captors didn't yell their rage but rather their pain. With a rock apiece, Benjamin, Ezra and Jacob leapt from the darkness and attacked the two still standing police from behind. Killing would never be a part of the nature of these refugees, but here they found a special motivation.

Louise broke the neck of the officer with the bloody nose, picked up his rifle and shot the one being attacked by Benjamin. She turned to help the brothers who between them bashed the skull of the third officer. All three Vichy policemen lay dead.

Standing in the darkness, Louise stared at her three heroes. 'Messieurs, what can I say?' she asked. 'You have saved my life.'

'We were returning the favour, Mademoiselle,' said Benjamin.

'Or Sister,' said Ezra.

'Or Codename Plum,' said Jacob.

Louise dragged one of the bodies, talking as she did. 'Forget what you heard. We need to cover the bodies and weapons. Help me.' They did. 'In the morning a plane will be searching for them.'

'And us,' said Ezra.

She replied. 'They'll be too late. We'll be in Spain.'

Chapter 23

A river in the Pyrenees

In the darkness, they dumped the bodies and weapons close together, and used grass and stones to cover them. Talk about a crude job. They headed back to the females. 'Not a word to the others,' said Louise. 'The police fired, probably at an animal, and went away so now we must reach the river before they come back.'

'What if they ask questions?' asked Ezra.

'Please do as I ask,' said Louise. 'Now come on, Spain awaits.'

After the violent incident, life was no picnic with the two younger males and even Benjamin never having behaved as they did. Killing someone was unreal but Louise's status meant they did as requested.

Ten minutes later all nine resumed their journey not discussing the latest bloodbath. As Benjamin and the brothers Lunz picked their way down the mountain towards the river, they each pondered the claims they overheard about their leader and her seemingly fantastic history. Is she a nun on the run? She killed with ease tonight. Who wants her dead in London? Is she a liar? She can't be just a nurse.

Descending a mountain can be dangerous but less tiring than ascending. The thought of their journey's end gave all the adults a lift. The closer they came to the border, the more their hearts sang with their expectations continuing to rise.

Louise heard the sound first. She would have preferred no sound.

A sleepy, meandering river is whisper quiet. A busy, angry river snarls. She heard the anger long before they reached the river.

Benjamin caught up with her. 'I don't like that sound,' he said glancing at Louise, 'the river I mean.'

She ignored his comment feeling wretched. 'How are the others?'

He ignored her comment. 'If the river is as it sounds, we can't cross into Spain; not here anyway.'

She kept going. 'Let's get there first.'

They did and collapsed. Exhaustion followed by devastation. They found no shallow, slow-flowing stream but a swiftly flowing deep and angry beast. Crack troops couldn't cross this monster. Exhausted civilian refugees stood no chance. Sweet dreams became nightmares.

'Let's rest,' said Louise to the prostrate party. Here they were, in the open, exposed and dawn an hour or two away.

'We can't stay here, Mademoiselle,' said Benjamin knowing he stated the bleeding obvious. Their hunger pains turned nasty. The younger men were survivors but the older women and girls were out on their feet.

Louise could not believe that despite losing their guide, suffering a tragedy, and being attacked by Vichy forces, they would reach the border only to be halted by Mother Nature. Benjamin spoke the truth. They couldn't stay here.

In the pre-dawn darkness, trees could be seen upstream; a forest on the French side. She pointed. 'Those trees will give us cover.' The older women complained. Louise addressed the brothers. 'One last trip, gentlemen, please. It's not far.'

They helped their mother and Mademoiselle Arnold, while Benjamin and Rachel helped their girls. They reached the thick and overgrown forest. Louise took them a short way in then declared this to be the spot. Nobody argued. They were running on empty.

She moved about finding branches and returned placing them between forks in adjacent trees. The men saw her plan.

'Branches, undergrowth, anything you can find,' said Louise, and soon they built a crude shelter. It was good timing as the heavens opened. Occasional drips broke through but without the shelter, it would have been misery heaped upon misery.

The children fell asleep. The adults clung to the belief they would not die. The rain eased and Louise whispered to Benjamin. 'I'll take a walk upstream. Make sure nobody moves.'

He whispered back. 'You catch a fish and I'll dig for potatoes.'

She forced a grim smile and set off upstream.

There must be a way to cross; there just has to be.

As she trudged along, her heart grew heavy. She thought she was travelling the wrong way. The banks became steeper, the water more angry. She couldn't keep walking and leave the others to fend for themselves. She approached a rise and decided to climb and see what the river did beyond. If nothing, she would turn back, and say what?

Then she saw it; a bridge. Well, it looked like an obstacle course to test would-be SOE agents. She hurried to investigate.

The steep bank frightened her with the river out of control. But attached to each bank, high above the torrent, she made out a narrow wooden bridge with ropes. It danced in the wind. She crept forward then climbed onto the first planks. Holding the rope on each side, she moved forward. To welcome her, the bridge swayed, she swayed and the river, ten metres below laughed and called her a coward.

It must have been a hundred feet across with the bridge dropping at its mid-point. Then, through the gloom, she saw a light.

Surely not a customs office at such an out-of-the-way bridge?

Back she went, hurrying. It looked dangerous, terrifying even but represented their best, their only chance of freedom. She chose to lead the others to the bridge without describing it in detail.

If I describe it, they'll never go there.

Back at the camp site, the others were quiet and miserable or asleep and it seemed, waiting to die. Louise played it low-key.

'I have news,' she said in a calm voice. 'There's a bridge upstream.'

The girls didn't stir but the others were awake and talking.

'A bridge?' asked Madame Lunz. 'Is it a bridge to Spain?'

'It's not far and there may be Spanish officials on the other side.'

'Can they help us?' asked Rachel desperate to feed her daughters.

Louise hesitated and they sensed danger. 'They might but they could stop and even arrest us.' A solid groan escaped from the refugees. 'But if we cross now, they may be asleep.' She almost begged them. 'I know this is our best chance.'

The brothers helped their mother and Mademoiselle Arnold to stand. Both women looked exhausted.

Benjamin encouraged Rachel, picked up Sura and walked. Miriam struggled along with her mother.

What a sight. Eight Jewish refugees and one young female SOE officer from Surrey staggering beside a raging river towards the world's most flimsy bridge they knew nothing about. Louise kept thinking about her pitch once they saw the ramshackle structure.

Carrying his younger daughter, Benjamin arrived first. He refrained from reacting not wanting to frighten the child. He knew she would never cross this bridge. The others arrived and, in the gloom, stared at the waving ropes and wooden slats.

This to these good people represented literally a bridge too far. As they gasped, and stated unequivocally they would not even attempt to cross the bridge, Louise took action. She spoke to Benjamin who shook his head. Rachel was keen to be a part of the conversation. She too shook her head. Louise argued. The parents discussed the offer and then decided.

Standing well back from the bridge, they lifted Sura onto Louise's back. Using string which held the refugees' few belongings together, Sura's hands were tied under Louise's chin. Then Sura's ankles were pulled around in front of Louise and those too were tied together. The child became attached to her carrier. Louise needed her hands free.

Sura's parents kissed their daughter, several times. Louise didn't have time for speeches and fond farewells. She worked out a simple plan. Hold on to the ropes at all times. Put your feet close together on the slats. Take small steps. Do it. Go. She shuffled towards Spain.

If the child cried, it made no impact. The river's roar dominated. Step by step, Louise moved forward. From the bank, you couldn't see much in the pre-dawn gloom. A collective gasp erupted when Louise stepped too close to the edge and the bridge tilted. She froze and gripped the rope either side as if for dear life. No, it *was* for dear life.

She paused, re-positioned her feet and set off again. Closer and closer she came to Spain. She reached the end of the bridge, steadied herself then fell forward. When she stood, she stood on Spanish soil.

The hut for the customs' officers seemed deserted. A weak lamp burnt above the door. Louise hurried into the trees, undid Sura's wrists and ankles. The child hugged the lady she loved. Louise gave instructions with the child told to sit, to not move or make a sound and soon her Mummy and Daddy would join her.

'And Miriam?' whispered the frightened child.

Louise smiled. 'And of course your lovely sister. Now wait here, and be quiet.' She kissed Sura and slipped away back to the bridge.

One down and seven to go.

She reached the other side and made a decision. 'Ezra, you take your mother. Clara's hands were placed around her son's waist and tied together. Then Louise gathered everyone in close and gave a lesson on crossing the bridge.

'You saw how I did it. You only have to cross once. The person in front never lets go of the ropes. What did I say?'

They spoke. 'The person in front never lets go of the ropes.'

'And we only take very small steps. What do we do?'

The chorus sang as one. 'We only take very small steps.'

'Good, now when you're across, go to Sura, stay together, lie low and don't make a sound. Yes?'

Nodding heads made Louise feel marginally better although her heart still battered her ribs. She walked with the mother and son.

His bravery shone, her bravery ran away. Louise leant in and whispered to the widow. 'Your dear husband wants you to do this, Madame. You can do it. Do it for him.'

Carla couldn't speak as she and her son stepped onto the bridge. He did well, taking tiny steps in a set rhythm. His mother closed her eyes and when she opened them they were safe.

Louise spoke to Benjamin. 'It's time to take your daughter, Monsieur. Can you carry her on your back as I did with Sura?'

What a stupid question. Louise helped lift the older sister and her hands and feet were tied. They were running out of string.

Up to the bridge stepped the German Jew, the man who once ran a jewellery business in Berlin, who fled to Paris and then through France, and who recently walked across the Pyrenees, was now charged with carrying his daughter across a rickety bridge in the dark with a whipping wind causing the river below to froth at the mouth. After all this man had endured in recent years, his latest task was nothing, easy, it was child's play.

'Rope and feet, Monsieur,' said Louise. 'I'll take care of your wife.'

He stared at Louise. He hoped they survived this crossing and the war itself. He wanted to tell the world about this young woman, and to do all he could to repay the massive debt he knew he owed her.

Louise watched the father and daughter inch across the bridge. A lump formed in her throat. Could this be their moment of freedom? Could this group of refugees finally escape tyranny?

She watched as Benjamin crossed to the other side then she turned back to see the three remaining people.

'Mademoiselle Arnold, I will take you,' said Louise.

'I can't,' replied the older woman, shaking with fear. Her tear ducts were empty, her hunger pains gnawed away inside her brain. Louise made a decision and spoke to Rachel and Jacob.

'I'll take her before she gives up. You two cross after me. Okay?'

Rachel and Jacob nodded. 'I will lead Madame Roth,' said the teenager who, like his older brother, had become a man during this perilous trek over the Pyrenees.

Louise squeezed their arms. 'You're both wonderful people.' She handed Jacob her last piece of string. 'I need you to tie Mademoiselle Arnold's hands. He understood. Louise worried and spoke to Rachel and Jacob. 'We have no more string.'

They put on a brave front. 'We will be fine,' said Rachel and Jacob.

Louise gave them a grim smile then led Mademoiselle Arnold to the bridge. Louise hugged her. 'Hug me, Mademoiselle, hug me.' The woman did as instructed with fear and trembling. Jacob moved behind Louise and tied the older woman's hands. She groaned. Louise persisted and they stepped onto the swaying structure.

'Now we will dance, Mademoiselle. We start with your left.' She patted the woman's left thigh. 'Small steps, and when I say, we start. Yes?' The woman's eyes filled with fear. Louise gripped the rope either side of the bridge facing backwards. 'Ready, dance.'

Louise took a small backward step with her right foot and surprisingly, Mademoiselle Arnold stepped forward with her left. Louise repeated the routine with her left foot. Her partner obliged and small step by small step they crossed the bridge. The fact their bodies were pressed tight helped. Mademoiselle Arnold could feel another beating heart and when they reached the Spanish side, Louise fell backwards causing her dance partner to land on top of her.

Benjamin and Ezra were on hand to help the new arrivals. Louise waved to the final pair. They could only just see her in the gloom.

As the penultimate couple danced their way across the bridge, Rachel and Jacob discussed their routine. Jacob would go first with Rachel behind him, her arms around his waist, clasping her hands together. They knew the routine. Take small steps in a steady rhythm with Jacob clinging to the ropes. Their crossing became their destiny.

The wind grew stronger and the bridge swayed more than it did for any of the others. Their progress became snail-like. They reached the middle of the bridge where the slope now pointed upwards.

'Are you okay?' shouted Jacob, his voice almost lost in the wind.

'Yes,' shouted Rachel, petrified and thinking only of her girls. As Jacob took a step, a slat on the bridge in front of him broke free and took off in the wind. Staring forward, he stepped into the gap, stumbled and fell to his knees. Rachel screamed, her cry lost in the roar of the water below. Jacob's arms howled with pain. His grasp on both ropes weakened. The bridge swayed and bucked. It flipped from side to side. Louise and Benjamin watched in horror.

Rachel saw the problem and released her hug. This meant her link to Ezra vanished. She stood, her body wavering. Ezra sensed her missing, and froze still gripping the ropes. He turned his head and saw naked fear on Rachel's face.

'Grab me,' he yelled and thrust his backside towards her. She grabbed his coat and pulled herself in and wrapped her arms around him. He rose. With her grip so tight, he struggled to breathe. He rubbed his right heel against her right shin and, as if a conductor, they struck the same note moving forward, stepping over the space.

Slowly, slowly they crept towards Spain. Closer, closer they came to freedom with the wind deciding to have one last throw of the dice. Louise and Benjamin were side by side with a hand extended towards Jacob. He could see their faces and kept going, his steps now even shorter. He faced a momentous, life-and-death decision; when to let go of the ropes and grab the outstretched hands?

Jacob needed to tell his partner he was about to dive forward. How? What if she didn't hear him? He prayed, hoped, assumed she would be dragged with him. He let go of the ropes and lunged at the waiting helpers. They grabbed him and pulled.

Stunned by this sudden move after so many slow and tiny steps, Rachel panicked. She clung to Jacob but her hands slid down his body. She clung to his ankles. The wind demanded a consolation goal. It blew like hell and the bridge danced a jig. Rachel lost her grip, fell on her face and slid sideways, towards the edge. What could she grasp? Fresh air. The rope, too far above, and the slats rocking like crazy, could not stop her momentum as she slid towards her death.

Benjamin dragged Jacob to Spain. Louise dived towards Rachel and with her right hand, grabbed the top of Rachel's coat. Still the mother edged closer to the edge. Louise strained every muscle to stop Rachel's movement. The swaying bridge ramped up Rachel's momentum making Louise's task close to impossible. In slow motion, Rachel started to slide off the bridge.

Now lying flat on her belly and partly on the bridge itself, Louise used her left hand to snatch at Rachel as she prepared to drop. A handful of Rachel's hair stuck in Louise's hand.

Rachel screamed in fear. Louise screamed louder. 'Pull my legs!'

Benjamin, and now Ezra and Jacob, seized Louise's ankles and pulled. Hanging by her hair and coat, Rachel grabbed the swaying slats. As the males dragged Louise back, Rachel clung to the bridge becoming a brake on Louise's backward movement.

Louise screamed again only this time at Rachel. 'Let go! Let go!'

Now, that request would never be obeyed by someone in Rachel's situation. She wanted to live so clung to the bridge. When she started to slip out of her coat, her hair became the only connection to Louise. Forget about the pain that caused.

Rachel, brave woman indeed, did what her brain told her not to do. She let go of the slats allowing Louise to drag her forward, hanging on to Rachel's hair and her disappearing coat.

Benjamin left the brothers pulling Louise, and flattened himself on the bank holding out his hand to his wife. Louise kept inching backwards. Rachel witnessed the lot. She flung out her right hand and, tried to secure a foothold on the bank using a flailing foot. Benjamin took the risk and leant dangerously close to the edge. If his wife would fall, he would too, helping her survive the thrashing river.

Rachel stretched her hand, cupping her fingers. Benjamin ignored her linking method and lunged for his wife's wrist. He grabbed it in a vice-like grip. He pulled, Louise lifted and Rachel rose, level with the slats, and threw her left leg on to the bridge. The raging river lost.

The refugees collapsed gasping for air. Their feelings of elation were never voiced. Celebrations would come later. Or would they? The party looked up to see two uniformed men. One spoke.

'Bienvenido a España.'

Chapter 24

Spain 1941

Stress grabbed Louise and began to strangle her. Since parachuting into France, her life plunged from crisis to crisis, and these last few days, the closer she came to freedom, the bigger the hurdles she faced. Now, as dawn broke in Spain, had she finally failed?

Despite massive odds, she and the refugees made it only to be met by two officers from Spanish customs. But why were they here? The bridge hardly offered an easy passage to smugglers or refugees. The officials worked in a basic building. How busy were they?

Louise heard of refugees who crossed the border only to be detained and handed to Vichy officials or the SiPo (Gestapo). Spain might be neutral but Franco remembered the help Germany gave in his recent civil war. Spain listened sympathetically to Nazi requests.

But why capture and return elderly Jewish citizens or children? Who benefits? It was illogical and counter-productive to Germany's chances of winning the war. Ah, but of course, such a move became understandable once you added pure evil to the mix.

The brothers Ezra and Jacob helped Louise to stand. Dawn crept above the horizon and, in daylight, she saw two Spanish faces. Louise spoke not even elementary Spanish although could add *por favor* at the end of a sentence.

She observed. In the thick forest her fellow refugees were like her, out on their feet. But where were the children and older women? Surely they were not arrested or worse?

Both officers were armed but their hand guns were holstered. One officer addressed Louise speaking in Spanish. 'This way,' he said, pointing.

How he knew Louise held the position of leader she didn't know. He indicated the building set back from the bridge. The only door faced the forest away from the river. Louise followed the two men, scanning the surrounds for any sign of the children. She saw no-one and her heart sank. For Benjamin and Rachel to survive the Nazis, the Vichy and the Pyrenees only to then lose their precious daughters would be beyond belief.

Louise turned her head. Back on the river bank, Benjamin knelt beside his exhausted wife. How could he find the words to tell her their children were dead?

One officer opened the door to their HQ and beckoned. Louise stepped up and inside. She saw only one room. A desk and chairs were close to the front. Two single beds were on either side. A closed door presumably opened to a bathroom. The sight at the far end lit her heart, as seated at the only table, were the widow Lunz, the spinster Mademoiselle Arnold and between them, two little girls with what appeared to be doorstop slices of bread and cheese covering most of their faces.

'Plum,' cried Sura and waved delighted to see the lady who found her doll, and carried her over the Pyrenees, and then over the bridge from hell in the darkness and rain.

Louise explored under her jumper, produced Heide, and walked to the child. She squealed with joy, Louise lost control of her tear ducts, and the two gentlemen with Spanish blood smiled.

When the brothers and the Roth parents made their way inside, the touching reunion would have melted the coldest heart.

Both Spanish officials were fathers, the older with grandchildren. Whatever their politics or orders, they did what their heart told them to do.

Coffee and bread and cheese became manna from heaven.

Whilst finding her body and mind take up dancing and singing, Louise tried to focus. Her mighty achievement in escaping from France was but one part, one step in her long, long journey.

No-one in London knew if Louise Wellesley was alive. She wanted to keep it that way. She must travel through Spain and reach Gibraltar and from there fly home. But only then would the real test begin. She must uncover the SOE mole.

The unexpected reception from the Spanish officials brought joy to all. It could not have been a more remote location, and the refugees spread out, feasting on a basic but beautiful breakfast. Louise sat outside in the forest, against a tree, with coffee and a piece of sausage. She imagined she was dining in The Ivy restaurant in London with Noel Coward at the next table. She refused to swallow keeping each morsel in her mouth for as long as possible. Bliss. Heaven.

But then she crash-landed back on Earth. Two questions pummeled her brain. *What next and do I travel alone?*

For the last few days, she became the leader of this group of refugees. *Does that make me responsible for these people?*

She could hear the girls in the building chatting away. 'There's even a proper toilet, Mutti,' said Miriam.

Louise's conscience clapped its hands. She couldn't imagine embracing each of her refugee comrades, wishing them well, then heading off on her journey leaving them, God knows where, on the Spanish French border. *I can't leave them. I must help them escape.*

But first she needed to know their current location, and that of the nearest town with a railway station. Her SOE training told her to make for the British consulate in Barcelona. She knew she couldn't hold the hands of her companions forever. But once she discovered the local geography, and chatted with Benjamin, decisions could be made. She went back to the hut.

A lifetime ago she attended a finishing school in France and made friends with another student, the rambunctious Matilda Gonzales-Jones. They hit it off and became best friends. Matilda's parents were Spanish and Welsh and thanks to Matilda, Louise learnt a few Welsh sentences, but only one in Spanish.

The uniformed men, armed, fit and well fed, assumed the new arrivals who arrived from France as bedraggled, unarmed, exhausted and starving refugees spoke French and as they, the officials didn't, settled for pointing and nodding.

The refugees long deferred to Louise as their leader. They agreed without question to have Mademoiselle Plum act on their behalf. She took a punt, and remembering the sentence taught by Matilda, Louise spoke to the officers. '*Usted es la nalga de caballo.*'

The others were flattened; the refugees were in awe as their charismatic leader could not only do so much, but now something new—she could speak Spanish. Was there no end to her talents? Well, actually in this case her specific language skills were non-existent.

The officials broke their silence by laughing, and not a mere chuckle or smirk but belly laughs which were so out of place in this remote hideaway. Louise worried.

The officials recovered. The first tried his fractured English. 'Oh, Senorita, you are very funny.'

Louise took the plunge and replied in English. 'Sorry, gentlemen?'

'Ah, Inglés,' said the second man. 'Someone is playing you a trick, Señorita. You have spoken, how you say, the insult.' Louise now knew Matilda had set her up. 'In Spanish you have called me a horse's ...' He turned and patted his posterior.

'Arse,' said Louise, and the Spaniards laughed again. 'Si, a horse's arse.' But at least now the language barrier collapsed.

She asked questions and with their broken English and a map on the wall, she discovered their current location, that of Barcelona, and details of the train services. There were few trains in this area with bus services their best option. The refugees listened, hooked on the details.

Everything flowed swimmingly with only their mode of transport to be resolved. Being safe from Vichy or Nazi officials brought joy. Knowing how far they were from Barcelona put a real dampener on their excitement. They were exhausted but even fit and well, how on Earth were they going to cover the hundreds of kilometres to reach Barcelona? Walk?

Louise decided to do nothing for now. Obviously they couldn't stay here. They were extraordinarily lucky to have found two Spanish officials, who not only didn't arrest or report them but went out of their way to help. Their hut though offered only temporary respite, and if Louise wanted to stay with the group and continue as their leader, she needed a plan.

She wandered in the forest and studied the bridge they crossed, and wondered if they would have attempted the task in daylight. Apart from the never-ceasing roar of the river, the only sounds she heard were the birds singing beautifully in Spanish.

But everything changed when she heard shouting from the Spanish officials. They sounded angry, even scared. She raced back.

'What's happened?' gasped Louise, panicking.

'Our supervisor is coming, Señorita. We saw his car. He will be here any minute. If he finds you, he will arrest and deport you. Tell your friends to go from here away.'

The others already understood. Rachel had a daughter's hand in each of hers and wanted guidance. 'Where do we go?' Her face showed pain, the old pain she suffered in their trip over the Pyrenees.

Louise pointed. 'Go into the forest and hide.'

Ezra and Jacob were helping their mother and Mademoiselle Arnold. 'Follow Rachel,' called Louise, 'and hide.'

Benjamin arrived. 'I've made a quick check to see we haven't left anything.'

'Great,' said Louise and pointed in the direction taken by the others. 'Go.' He took off and she ran back to the building. Coming out, one of the officials bumped into her.

'No, Señorita, you must leave.'

'I left my toiletries in the bathroom. I will be only a moment.'

She raced to the bathroom as the sound of the supervisor's car grew louder. The two officials went outside to meet their boss.

Louise had left nothing in the bathroom. What toiletries? She pretended to go there but stopped by the desk and cut the telephone wire close to the floorboard. She peered around the door, and saw the boss getting out of his car with the subordinates lining up preparing to salute. She ducked and ran bent double. Crashing into the forest, she dropped and froze. No cries, nothing. She made it.

Once she knew the Spaniards missed seeing her, she scrambled into the forest and found the others. She spoke to Jacob and pointed. 'Take the ladies and girls, and walk that way until you see the road. Hide in the trees and wait for me.' Jacob hesitated. 'Go, go!'

So used to Louise's leadership, the females and Jacob left. Louise gestured to Benjamin and Ezra, and set off. 'Follow me.'

They did and when close to the hut, she whispered her plan. The men stared at her and then one another. Is she joking?

The supervisor's car faced the way it came. The meticulous official could well have been German. He even obliged by leaving the key in the ignition.

Louise quietly opened the driver's door and hopped in. She released the handbrake. 'Okay,' she whispered and Benjamin and

Ezra put their backs into it. The vehicle rocked but wouldn't move. 'Push!' whispered Louise.

'We are,' they hissed between grunting.

She hopped out and joined the shoving team. The car moved slowly but then picked up speed. Louise jumped from the running board into the car. 'Jump on,' she whispered. They did although pushed with one leg as if on a scooter. The road began to slope downwards and soon the free-wheeling vehicle got moving.

Louise steered and after a minute, looked to her right, spotted her would-be passengers, and slammed on the brakes.

'Jump in,' she cried. 'Hurry!'

The fearful but excited refugees scrambled aboard, the car now full of human beings with the driver the only person not sharing a seat. She checked to see everyone had boarded, turned the ignition key, and fought to find first gear as the car kangaroo-hopped away to where she didn't know. Car thief was added to her CV.

Each bump sent passengers on small journeys within the car. Bumping and knocking one another brought pain but the fact they were driving, yes driving through Spain, gave them all a solid serve of excitement and satisfaction.

It sure beat the pants off walking.

Louise tried to think. She'd cut the phone in the building so it could be a while before Spanish authorities were searching for them. The fuel gauge showed half full.

Should she take roads and follow signposts to Barcelona and risk being seen by someone in authority? Should she take back roads and run the risk of becoming lost? Should she stop and ask directions?

When she saw a signpost for Berga she knew where to go. The map shown to her by the officials listed this town and its location. Buses ran between Berga and Barcelona. If she could help her fellow refugees onto a bus, she could honestly feel her responsibility for their wellbeing had ended. They would have to make their own way from Barcelona.

She took the road to Berga. Conversation lagged within the car until Rachel spoke up.

'Mademoiselle Plum, I do not have the words to explain what you have done for all of us.' Everyone listened, hanging on Rachel's unprepared speech. 'We all owe our lives to you. We will never forget every single act of bravery and kindness you have done, and I only wish we could repay you.'

The others gave strong and instant support. Little Miriam summed up the mood. 'I love you, Plum.'

'So do I,' added Sura, 'and so does Heide.'

Louise wanted to cry. 'Thank you, everyone, you are most kind; all of you. But soon I think we will need to go our own ways.' The mood flattened. 'We're heading towards Berga where I'm hoping buses run to Barcelona. I will catch a bus and from there catch a train to Madrid and then to Gibraltar.

Smiling for the first time in ages, Benjamin responded. 'But that is what we plan to do,' he said. 'From Gibraltar we will find a ship to America.'

'My husband wanted us to do the same,' added Carla Lunz, hidden with so many adults and children sitting on and around her.

'You can come with us to America, Plum,' said Miriam.

The driver smiled and the car ran beautifully.

Chapter 25

Travelling in Spain

The car entered the outskirts of Berga around lunchtime. Running low on fuel, the fear of being spotted, and wanting to be out of Spain in the shortest possible time, pushed Louise as she drove around looking for the bus station.

She saw a sign, turned into a quiet narrow street with high rise apartments on either side. Residents on floors above ground level hung their washing in public view.

'Can we all please hop out sensibly and quietly?' she asked. They did and gathered in their two groups. Louise drove the car up on the footpath so as not to block the road, and then left the ignition key and joined the others.

'If questioned, remember to use your documents from Marseille. Keep your story simple. You are refugees fleeing Nazi persecution and wish to settle *outside* Europe.' Heads nodded. 'Any questions?'

No-one spoke. As Louise delivered her final instructions, Benjamin interrupted. 'Pardon, Mademoiselle, I would like to make a speech on behalf of everyone.'

Not meaning to be rude, Louise cut him short. 'Thank you, Monsieur Roth, but save it for when we meet again in New York or London.' He was hurt, understood her reasons, yet remained determined to do something for the young woman who saved his life and those of his wife and daughters. Louise kept leading.

'Let's walk to the bus in separate groups. Let's stay apart and if we think it's safe, we can meet up in Barcelona. Now, money; are we able to pay for tickets and hotels?'

She kept cash for such an occasion, as did the others, and ever since their passeur left the group by disappearing down the side of a French mountain at a rapid speed, their reserves were intact.

They set off walking on different sides of the roads. Louise joined the Roths. She discussed tactics with Benjamin as they reached then waited under a bus shelter.

'I am buying a ticket only for Barcelona, Monsieur,' she said.

Benjamin misunderstood thinking she could not afford to pay for the added journey to Madrid, and then on to Gibraltar.

'Allow me to pay for your extra tickets, Mademoiselle. It would be an honour.'

Louise felt awkward. She knew the British Consulate in Barcelona would be her first port of call when fleeing through Spain. Her training taught her never to reveal unnecessary information.

'You are most kind, Monsieur, but the truth is I have friends in the city who will help me.'

Benjamin copped a whack. This sounded like a definite goodbye. He and his family, particularly his young daughters, were in love with the woman who saved their lives time and time again. Besides, they knew they were safe with Plum by their side. In Spain, despite there being far less pressure from Nazi and Vichy officers hounding Jews, the refugees were always on edge.

'I understand,' he replied, 'but will you allow me to purchase your ticket to Barcelona?' His eyes broadcast his feelings. How could she refuse?

'Thank you,' she said and watched as he went to the ticket-office.

She sat with Rachel and the girls as the bus would not depart for an hour or more. They chatted about anything other than the war. The girls seemed normal, which Louise struggled to understand.

How do young children experience such trauma and retain their innocence?

Benjamin returned, handed Louise her ticket, and then remained standing in front of her. Rachel sat on one side of Louise and Miriam and Sura the other.

'You can sit next to Mutti, Papa,' said Sura pointing to the empty space on the bus stop bench.

'Thank you, darling,' said Benjamin who remained standing. He studied Louise who sensed something was about to happen. 'I wish to remain standing to make the speech you asked me not to deliver before, Mademoiselle. We have a little time, n'est-ce pas?'

'Oui,' said Louise touched by his kindness.

Rachel knew her husband's resolve and even the girls understood the occasion was special and remained quiet. What could Louise do? Being surrounded by people with whom she shared near-death experiences made it easy for her to relax.

Benjamin spoke and as he did, Madame Lunz, her sons and Mademoiselle Arnold walked towards him. They stood behind the bench. Surrounded, Louise waited. Benjamin knew his thoughts.

'These last few years have been disastrous for all of us, and these last few days, catastrophic. Sadly for Jews, fleeing persecution is normal, and has been for thousands of years. In this war, many Jews have suffered and died, although some have been lucky to survive. We are a few of the lucky ones; we have survived thanks to luck, but also thanks to many miracles made from courage, all of which came freely from one person. I am ashamed to say I do not even know her real name, but like my daughters, I am happy and proud to call her Plum.'

Louise found it hard to swallow, and her eyes grew moist as Benjamin continued.

'I am not a religious Jew but I know the Talmud teaches that, he who saves a single life saves the whole world. We have been blessed to meet a woman who not only helped us but saved us. We are the blessed Jews saved by a Gentile.

'She does not see our culture or religion. To her, we are equals. You, dear lady, treated us as fellow humans, and to a Jew that makes your kindness and sacrifice a thousand times more important.'

A tear trickled down Louise's cheek followed soon by two more.

'We will never forget you, Mademoiselle. My young children will never forget you, and God willing, they will tell their children about the woman with the funny name and the heart of a saint. Your bravery, skill and sacrifice will be remembered for generations.'

Now, Benjamin found a lump building in his throat. Louise didn't try to stop her tears. Other adults dabbed their eyes. This first safe opportunity to express their heartfelt feelings became supercharged with emotion as it seemed they would most likely be saying goodbye. Leaving aside a miracle, they would never see this young woman again.

Benjamin built his speech towards the denouement. Louise, amidst her swirling emotions, thought his script and delivery would have graced any stage with class and power.

Benjamin reached into his pocket. 'I wish to make a presentation, Mademoiselle. I am a jeweller by trade, and have carried something with me from Berlin to Paris to Marseille, across the Pyrenees and even across the most terrifying bridge in the world.' The adults smiled although not Mademoiselle Arnold who was never happy unless she was miserable.

'I have a diamond which I believe is the most perfect I have ever owned. I have been keeping it for the day when the first of my daughters chooses to be wed. But its great value, its worth could never equal or repay the value of my life, and of my family and of our friends.'

Louise sensed feelings of love from all around.

'I wish to give you this precious stone, Mademoiselle, and I am proud to do so. I hope it will forever remind you of your time with the Jews in the Pyrenees.' He opened a piece of black velvet to reveal the sparkling and seriously expensive diamond. Gasps were heard. Louise's mouth opened and stayed open.

She struggled to speak. 'Thank you,' she almost said, her throat blocked with a giant lump of emotion.

'And when the day comes for you to become engaged to be married, I will be delighted to have the stone set in the most beautiful golden ring. Find me, Mademoiselle, and I'll come to you no matter where my address might be.'

He too started to lose control as his voice quavered. He handed Louise the stone in its piece of velvet.

'Free of charge,' said Rachel, reprimanding her husband.

'But of course,' said Benjamin and they all applauded.

Silence settled on the near empty bus station as the entire refugee party waited for their leader to speak. Before she could, the youngest member of the group popped the question.

'Are you getting married, Plum?'

Infectious laughter erupted from all except the surly Mademoiselle Arnold who managed to scowl.

Before Louise could respond, Benjamin returned for one final sentence. 'I think you should call it a Plum jewel.'

Louise wanted to smile but struggled with emotion. 'I will,' she said, 'and thank you for your kindness. The gift is wonderful but your words, their meaning and your friendship mean as much if not more.

I hope you will all reach freedom and live long and healthy lives. Shalom,' she said turning to look at all of them.

'Shalom,' said every Jew with feeling.

That's all Louise managed to say as her tears took over. The others patted or hugged her and drifted away. They remembered their leader's advice to travel in separate groups. Do not be seen together.

Rachel took the girls for a walk and Benjamin sat beside Louise. 'If I may offer advice to one so wise, you must find somewhere clever to hide your jewel, Mademoiselle. It is worth a small fortune.'

Louise gazed at him. 'Thank you, I have the perfect place.'

She planned to remove the cyanide pill hidden in the special button on her shirt and replace it with the Plum jewel. She would carry it with her back to Blighty.

She stood and he did likewise. 'I will go now to secure your gift.' She kissed the jeweller from Berlin on both cheeks, then slipped away to the Ladies to secure her present. Despite concerns, she dropped the cyanide tablet in the lavatory and flushed it.

Pray God I never have cause to regret that move.

Waiting for the bus and being away from the others gave Louise the opportunity to plan her next move. It had to be reaching the British Consulate in Barcelona. She even remembered the address.

But what would she do before then? Travel alone? Under what name, and should she reveal her true identity in the British Consulate? Would being an SOE agent grant her preferential treatment? Probably but then she worried that revealing her real identity would weaken her chances of exposing the SOE mole.

If she told anyone she was Louise Beatrice Wellesley, and worked for the SOE in Lyon, London would be informed immediately.

Wrong. She must remain anonymous. She must return to London unannounced and find a way to uncover the traitor in Baker Street. But how? How could she do that?

Then the idea whacked her. *Of course, why didn't I think of it before?* She returned to the bus stop and found Benjamin. 'A word if you please, Monsieur,' she said, smiling at Rachel and the girls.

She took him aside and told him her plan. 'The friends I have in Barcelona are working with the British government. My real name is Helene Smythe. I worked as a nurse for the Allies and fled when the war turned against the British Expeditionary Force. I am not French but British.'

Benjamin absorbed her details. 'I know you have received special training; no-one could have done what you did in the Pyrenees without it. But forgive me, Mademoiselle, I do not understand why you are telling me all this.'

She explained. 'I will have a better chance of getting help if I am travelling with your family and your daughters are in my charge.'

Benjamin still didn't understand. 'Pardon but I'm still confused.'

'With your permission, I will become the nurse and governess of your daughters, and travel with your family as we return to England.'

Benjamin smiled with joy. His creased face developed new creases. 'But that means we can travel together to England.'

Louise knew the Roths harboured plans to flee Europe. 'But are you not going to America?'

'America, England, it doesn't matter. We need a country where Jews are not persecuted.'

Louise smiled. 'Then we agree. I will be in charge of your children and there is only one rule.' She paused. He longed to know. 'No-one, and especially your daughters, must ever call me Plum.'

She knew if any government official heard the woman claiming to be a British nurse answered to the name of Plum, the SOE would discover she was alive before she even reached Madrid, let alone Gibraltar or Blighty.

Benjamin understood the command but never the reason. 'I will tell my family the wonderful news,' he said and went to leave but stopped. 'And your new name is Mademoiselle Helene Smythe, and everyone must call you Helene.'

Chapter 26

Barcelona, Spain

On the bus, the Roths and Louise sat in the front, the others towards the rear. Benjamin and Rachel knew about the new governess but getting young girls to follow the rules seemed fraught with risk. It would be so easy for little Sura to call Louise, now Helene, Plum.

'It's a game, girls,' said Rachel. 'We pretend Helene is your teacher.'

The bus arrived in Barcelona and they all alighted. The two groups waited apart, and Louise asked the Roths to remain where they were as she approached the others.

'I am taking the Roth family to the British Consulate. If we do not see one another again, I hope you continue to travel with safety and find your land of freedom. I would like to hug you all but who knows, we may be being watched.' She smiled at them. 'Good luck.'

The brothers and their mother wanted to hug Louise but understood the situation. They nodded and Louise slipped away. Mademoiselle Arnold's face remained set in stone.

Louise hailed a taxi and all five headed to the British Consulate.

'Because I'm British, I will go first.' The parents understood. Louise turned to the girls. 'Now girls, I am your nurse and teacher and my name is ...?

'Helene,' the children chorused.

Louise smiled and led them into the building. They waited in a reception room until a middle-aged man entered wearing a three-piece suit with a badly tied bow-tie and a matching pocket handkerchief. His moustache came alive when he spoke perfect English.

'Good afternoon, may I be of assistance?'

Louise surprised the Roths with her reply in flawless English. Since they first met Mademoiselle Plum in a doctor's waiting-room in Marseille, she almost always spoke excellent French.

'Good afternoon, sir. My name is Helene Smythe, once a nurse with the British Expeditionary Force, and I'm hoping to arrange passage back to England for myself, and the family for whom I now work as nurse and nanny to these delightful girls. I'm hoping the British Consul is able to assist us.'

She did this well setting out every detail. Does the Consul assist British citizens? Indeed, so all that remained was to check the bona fides of those involved and send them on the next leg of their journey.

'Will you step into the Consul's office please, Miss Smythe?' He indicated and she left. At the door she turned to smile at the Roth family. She wanted to wink but thought better of it.

She took the offered chair. 'My name is Nicholson, Miss Smythe, assistant to the Consul. I regret his absence but I'm sure I can help. Do you have your papers, please?'

She provided the papers created in Marseille. He perused them in detail then smiled and handed them back.

'All in order but I must say, you've made an extraordinary journey from Northern France to Spain. However did you make it?'

'I enjoyed good fortune, sir, plus help from courageous friends.'

'Jolly good show and well done you. We hear all sorts of tales from chaps who were shot down over France and Belgium. There were RAF men here the other day who told us about a young woman disguised as an old woman who disarmed a Vichy thug and, can you believe it, broke his neck and threw him off a moving train.'

'That sounds remarkable,' replied Louise, trying to think of her acting classes which covered how to display believable shock.

'Now, about your family; I assume they're non-British refugees?'

'Yes sir, but all with official papers.'

'No doubt, but while your clearance to Madrid and beyond is straightforward, alas I cannot say the same for them.'

'Oh, I understood we Brits welcomed people driven from their homes and forced to flee Nazi persecution.'

He wasn't expecting such a reply and disliked being held to account. 'We do but in war time, resources are stretched, enemy agents are everywhere and procedures must be followed.'

Louise pondered her next move. She sensed an obligation to the Roth family. If she played her hand now, would it be too soon? Would it work? Would she be revealing her true identity?

'Mister Nicholson, we have a train to catch to Madrid in two hours. I hope you can provide *all* of us with the necessary paperwork to proceed through Spain and on to Gibraltar.'

He saw her staring at him. Something troubled him. This woman knew something or someone important. She performed her routine in a calm manner, her face emotion free. She uttered no threat or dropped any important name but still he became uneasy. She did know VIPs—The King, Queen and PM for starters—but let her superb acting skills portray a sense of danger unless he granted her request. Apparently it's one test of great acting; achieve your goal with what appears to be an absence of effort. Nicholson yielded.

'Please have your employer and his family bring me their papers.'

The five of them left the Consulate with official permission to proceed. Louise showed with her face they were not to speak. They stepped into the street and were shocked to see the other half of their refugee team, the Lunzs and Mademoiselle Arnold, walking towards them. Neither group knew what to say.

The second group reached the door. Benjamin opened it for his friends. Nobody spoke. It was eerie. Jacob helped his mother enter and Ezra indicated the door for Mademoiselle Arnold. She gave a tiny shake of her head and indicated he should go first. He did. Just as she was about to enter the building, she paused, stared at Louise and spoke in flawless English.

'I hope you enjoyed a successful visit, Miss Plum.'

Stunned best described the reaction of all the others, and especially of Louise Wellesley who felt her blood run cold. Before Louise could reply, the woman, who sounded like she hailed from Chelsea, SW1, moved inside and Benjamin closed the door.

'Station,' said Louise and the family departed.

Nicholson welcomed this second group of callers, and Mademoiselle Arnold performed the Louise routine by entering the office alone for an interview. The assistant to the Consul met his match for the second time that day and with a woman on both occasions.

She introduced herself. 'I am Lady Miranda Bonneville-Clegg. My husband is Sir Crispin Bonneville-Clegg, secretary to the Secretary of State for War. I was betrayed by your former fellow diplomats in Paris in 1940 when the Germans arrived. I have lived under appalling conditions for almost two years until finally escaping a month ago. I have been travelling under an assumed identity for weeks and am barely alive.'

'I'm terribly sorry, my Lady,' said the obsequious Nicholson. 'How can I remedy the situation?'

'Find me a seat on the next available plane to England. Can I fly from here?'

'I regret not, my Lady. Gibraltar is your nearest exit point.'

She sighed. 'Oh well, needs must. Kindly arrange for my journey to Gibraltar at your earliest opportunity.'

'Of course; and does the same apply to your travelling companions?'

She scowled. 'Good God, man, are you insane? They're German Jews. I put up with them in order to survive. I need to lose them.'

'I see,' said Nicholson trying to play the diplomat.

'Do you?' she barked. 'Mosley understood. Jews are a blot on the English landscape, and the sooner I'm shot of them the better.'

Nicholson mumbled, 'I understand.' He paused. 'So may I ask how you managed to escape from France, my Lady?'

'I walked, and no thanks to you or any British consulate.'

'Good God, you've achieved something outstanding, my Lady. Crossing the Pyrenees on foot with German Jews is truly remarkable.'

She downplayed her reply. 'They weren't all German Jews. We had an Englishwoman in our party. She seemed to know what to do.'

'Did you say an Englishwoman?'

'Yes, she came out of here as I arrived. The others called her Plum, although why I have no idea. Now, are my papers ready?'

Nicholson fussed. 'I can have them ready in two minutes.'

'Good, and is there another way out of here? I can't bear facing those Jews ever again. And whatever you do, don't give them any papers.'

He prepared and handed over her documents, showed her out via a side entrance, gave the Lunz family a pathetic excuse, and asked them to return tomorrow. Defeated, they left not daring to ask about the so-called French spinster who betrayed them in a heartbeat. They headed to the station hoping to find their real friend and saviour.

Inside the Barcelona station, Louise asked the Roths to wait while she went to find provisions, and to check on the others. As she went food and refugee hunting, she passed a park and saw the three Lunz family members. She hurried to them and heard their news.

'Stay here,' she said. 'I'll be back soon.'

She walked briskly to the British Consulate and sent the pulse of one Jeffrey Nicholson racing.

'Miss Smythe,' he said, 'was there something you forgot?'

'The three people travelling with the Englishwoman who arrived after we left have not been given clearance to travel to Madrid.'

Nicholson made a terrible liar. 'Yes, there was a minor problem with their paperwork.'

'Bollocks,' snapped Louise shocking the diplomat. Matilda Gonzales-Jones, who used the word often, would have been proud.

'I beg your pardon, Miss Smythe,' replied Nicholson, giving a good impression of a person in a huff with bells on.

'I'm guessing the other Englishwoman pressured you into delaying their approval by dropping names to impress and intimidate.'

'How dare you? Lady Miranda Bonneville-Clegg's husband is ...'

'I'll make this easy for you, sir. Either you give me the papers for all three of those people here and now, or I'll contact Number 10 and the Palace informing them how you've been bribed.'

Number 10 proved more than enough to deflate his faux rage and pomposity. By throwing in the Palace, the man's legs turned to jelly. He blustered and flustered trying to defend the indefensible.

'The papers, sir, now,' she threatened and watched as he produced appropriate documents. '*I'll* fill in the names.'

He stamped the documents before handing them to Louise. She studied them. He persisted with his pathetic posturing.

'I have never been so insulted.'

She smiled. Her acting skills enabled her to switch effortlessly to a friendly, satisfied customer. 'Thank you,' she said before switching personalities again. 'And if you ever mention my name or the word Plum to anyone, I'll send your name to MI5, 6 and 9 questioning your loyalty to the Crown. Are we clear?'

'Yes, of course.' What else could he say? My God, she was utterly believable and ferociously intimidating. Mind you it helped because her threats were real and possible.

He escorted her from the Consulate and wiped the sweat from his brow with brandy his immediate port of call.

Louise hurried to the park to give the widow and her sons the passes. They struggled to express their thanks using tears as words.

'These will take you to Madrid. From there, you need to choose. Portugal or Gibraltar are two options. Choose wisely and travel well.'

She hugged all three or rather they all hugged her. There seemed no end to their gratitude. Time and again these last few days she helped them when they were desperate. Even now, seeing them alone and forlorn in the park, she saved their bacon.

'Take care of your mother, gentlemen,' she said to Ezra and Jacob. 'Make your father proud.'

She left them and went searching. Finding food, she returned to the station and the family Roth. As always, their gratitude knew no bounds. Once settled, she took Benjamin aside and explained the possibility of an enemy within their ranks. He could not believe it.

'But she claimed to be a French spinster from Paris,' he gasped.

'Forget her and concentrate on your family.'

As a safety precaution, Louise suggested they take a taxi to a nearby station and catch the Madrid train from there. What could Benjamin say? Her faultless leadership saved them time and again. He explained to Rachel and they set off to find a taxi.

The next station was several kilometres down the line. There they finished their meal and waited for the train to Madrid. It arrived. Louise searched for the Lunz family but didn't spot them in the crowded carriages. The Roths and their governess boarded and settled down for the long trip.

When the local officials asked for their tickets and passes, Louise held her breath. She and the Roths were okay. Phew.

Next stop, Madrid.

Chapter 27

Madrid, Spain

They arrived in the city at dusk. The Pyrenees-crossing refugee party became three groups; the Roths and Louise, the Lunzs, and, travelling alone, the English anti-Semite, Lady Miranda Bonneville-Clegg. None knew the others were on the same train.

Louise gathered her family as she perused the crowded platform searching for any threats. She didn't see Lady Bonneville-Clegg who alighted and saw her. She in turn didn't see the Lunz family who alighted and saw her. They watched the woman who deserted them as she moved to an official. They saw her speaking to the official and pointing in the direction of Louise Wellesley.

Before Ezra and Jacob could do anything, the official summoned two colleagues and headed along the platform toward the Roths. They were upon the family and their target in a few seconds.

Other passengers stepped aside as the posse of officials went for their prey. Their Spanish meant little to Louise but their manner and actions left her in no doubt.

They arrested her. She was worried, with the Roths distraught. The daughters cried, clinging to their parents. Louise contemplated using her unarmed combat skills, whacking the officious officials and sprinting for freedom to anywhere in Madrid. She wisely decided against it and allowed herself to be frog marched away. Benjamin and Rachel wanted to help Louise so much it hurt. They fumed, dumbfounded as she disappeared through a doorway on the platform.

There were other interested witnesses. Lady Bonneville-Clegg smiled to herself seeing her plan to prevent those Jews from ever getting within a bull's roar of her beloved green and pleasant land starting to work. But then other witnesses were the two young men she left to rot in Barcelona. They watched the developing drama, discussed the matter and made a decision.

Louise landed in an office where an official heard the details of her arrest. He spoke a smattering of English. 'So, Señorita, you claim to be French and English and have entered Spain under false pretences.'

'No, Señor, it is not true.' She went to retrieve her papers but two men grabbed her hands. They twisted her arms and it hurt. She winced. The men were ordered to search her. She let them.

They searched and Louise dreaded their clammy hands touching her body, as much for lust as loot, but her fear exploded when they found the knife under her clothing. She silently cursed herself.

Her bad situation became seriously worse. Louise saw her chances of escaping Spain disappear.

Elsewhere on the platform, Lady Bonneville-Clegg headed towards the exit. She would seek any British presence to confirm her journey to Gibraltar. Her wretched experience of traipsing through Europe with Jews would soon be over. She moved with other passengers towards the exit.

Crash. A yob stepped in front of her, blocking her path. She fumed, prepared to remonstrate and found herself staring at Ezra Lunz. His face oozed intent.

'Out of my way,' snapped Miranda.

Ezra didn't move, and saw the woman's face show fear when something sharp pushed against her spine. It was a pencil.

'Move and you're dead, Mademoiselle,' hissed Jacob from behind.

Her first response in a public space was to scream. The hooligans would panic and run. Or would they? She sensed their resolve.

'Go on, Madame,' whispered Ezra. 'We want you to scream, to make a fuss, and then we can use the distraction to rescue the woman who saved your life, and who you have just betrayed.'

'What type of evil person are you?' added Jacob.

Twenty metres away, a woman clutching two small girls, screamed and kept on screaming in French. 'My baby, my baby, someone's taken my baby.' Her daughters joined the distress.

Miranda saw this distraction as her chance to escape. 'Help!' she screamed in English. 'Help, I'm being kidnapped!'

The Lunz brothers wanted this reaction. They threatened her, causing her cries to grow more frantic. People reacted to the two separate scenes of distress. When a third broke out, the station's passengers got the message. This was not a safe place.

A man, a doppelganger for a certain Jewish Berliner, shouted loud and long, 'Fuego! Fuego!', and now the masses moved with speed.

Inside the office where the officials were about to throw the book at Louise, the sounds of panic upset all three men. The senior official ordered the other two to investigate. They left and the sole official ordered Louise to turn around. She did.

'Hands behind back,' he ordered and Louise complied. As he went to place handcuffs on her wrists, a sudden and throbbing pain shot up his leg. Louise stomped on the man's foot in the right place for maximum impact. He lost interest in his work and pretty much anything else as she turned, grabbed his ears and jerked his face downwards to meet her rising knee. The agony from his foot collided with the agony in his nose.

Footsteps were heard and Louise panicked. She prepared to fight the returning officials as two males burst in. Ezra and Jacob were reversing the favour and arrived to rescue their heroine. She grinned.

'Are you okay, Mademoiselle?' asked Ezra.

'I'm fine and delighted to see you both. Let's go.'

They headed out once she had searched for and found a set of keys. Clutching them, she pulled the door closed, locked it and ran after the young men. The keys landed in a bin.

The platform turned into a heaving mass or mess of humanity, and the perfect scenario to make an escape. Only the arrival of Louise settled the nerves of young Miriam and Sura. Rachel assured her daughters.

'See, I told you Plum would come back.'

'But Mutti, her name is Helene,' protested the well-trained Sura.

Louise hugged the girls and bent to kiss their heads. 'You can always call me Plum, girls. But come on, it's time to go.'

Benjamin joined them and Louise saw him smile, something rare yet wonderful. 'Welcome back, Mademoiselle,' he said. 'It's nice to have your team do something for you for once.'

Ticket collecting vanished, and so the Roths and Louise were soon out in the streets of Madrid. She kept studying the surrounds.

'Across the road,' said Benjamin nodding, and Louise saw Madame Lunz and her sons waiting, all smiles with a smattering of laughter. They were getting ever closer to their destination scrambling over the many obstacles in their path.

But even with the finishing line seemingly in sight, they knew the whole thing could come crashing down at any moment. Everyone, even the children, stared at Louise. Their thoughts were as one.

Where to now, Mademoiselle?

She sensed their question. 'We need to find a hotel, somewhere small and quiet where we can rest before our journey tomorrow. I think we should travel together now. It has risks but as you just proved, it does have benefits. Yes?'

There followed instant and forceful unanimous agreement. Even the children voted in favour. 'Let's spread out but keep within sight of each other. We need to find a hotel.'

They set off and after a short distance, Ezra whistled. He and his brother waved. Louise and the Roths walked to them, and saw two hotels in a side street.

The SOE agent went into both and made enquiries. She came out of the second and signaled. Two rooms, six beds, two children and six adults. It could best be described as cramped, embarrassing and an awful predicament, but after what this group endured in recent times, they were in paradise.

Creeping downstairs early next morning, Louise made enquiries. Flashing her charming smile, the middle-aged hotelier happily assisted the attractive young tourist. She could have sought directions to the station or British anything, but instead sought somewhere unusual.

After unsuccessfully searching for even a basic breakfast, Louise rounded up her sheep and took them across town. No-one asked where they were going, how long it would take, but simply put their total trust in the woman who now meant the world to them.

After a good half hour traipsing across Madrid, heads drooped and children complained. Louise urged them on, studying the notes she made in the hotel and observing signs and places.

She spotted what she wanted. 'Over there,' she said, and led them to a mixture of buildings with many raised voices and people carrying boxes, bags and baskets. She told the others to rest and took Benjamin aside.

'I think the trains are too risky. I've assaulted a railway official, and the lovely Mademoiselle Arnold has certainly branded you and the others as criminals or worse, Jews.'

He understood. 'But Gibraltar, Mademoiselle, we cannot walk.'

'True but there is an alternative. Come with me, s'il vous plaît. A young woman accompanied by a senior male carries more power.'

She led him into the busy market. There were stalls selling fruit, vegetables, cheese, bread, sausages and other local produce. She searched for trucks, vans, any type of vehicle which might offer transportation. If a farmer came to Madrid to sell their wares but left with an empty vehicle, any chance to make money on the return journey must appeal.

Many men didn't understand, several were heading north but one man pointed to another shouting his wares. Louise approached.

'Pardon, Señor. Habla inglés?'

This stopped his "Buy my oranges" routine dead in its tracks. He'd never been stopped by such a beautiful young woman before and with so unusual a question. He spoke a little English. She explained her need. He would be returning with some goods but had plenty of room in the back of his truck. The haggling proved interesting. Louise negotiated well and when the driver pushed for more, she turned and went to walk away. They did the deal.

The group needed to kill time and the young troops were becoming restless when the time to board the "coach" drew nigh. There were pros and cons in accepting this form of transport.

Forget seating, enjoy the free fresh air, and any unsold oranges were there for the taking. Springs above the axles didn't exist or work and the whiff of manure from sundry animals tiptoed around seeking clothes to decorate.

Despite all this, the move proved a lifesaver. An all-points bulletin flew down the railway line with Louise and her tribe wanted for sundry offences. A battered fruit truck sailed along uninterrupted. They were free, dripping with orange juice, and drawing ever closer to Gibraltar. The trip proved tough; six hours is a bloody long time.

With a little extra cash and a double smile from Louise, Juan, the now friendly fruiterer, pushed on to the border. Louise and the others couldn't believe it when they saw the sign *Gibraltar*. In the back of the truck, the refugees cried and kissed one another. In the cab of the truck, Louise leant across and gave the driver a powerful kiss on his cheek. He would dream about it for ages. They left Spain.

In Gibraltar, finding the right office and officer for lost Brits wanting to go home took little time. Louise asked her friends to wait in the street while she went inside. Now, a new hurdle appeared. Now, she needed to persuade whoever she met they were dealing with the nurse Helene Smythe from London, England who wanted desperately to return home to continue her nursing career as part of the war effort.

She wondered. Did the servile Nicholson in Barcelona give her away? Did the appalling Lady Miranda Bonneville-Clegg get here first and report Louise, the Jew-loving Brit? Did a plane have a seat for her, and were there berths on a ship for her friends? Were they home and dry, or was there a new disaster just around the corner?

Chapter 28

Gibraltar

'You're in luck, Miss Smythe,' said the official. 'There's a plane leaving this evening. I'm not sure if there are any seats left. You'll need to ask at the airport.'

'That's wonderful,' said Louise, finding it hard to believe she could be in England before midnight. 'I'm travelling with refugees who are not British. Is there any chance they could find a ship?'

'What papers do they have?' Louise explained. She was handed a note. 'Tell your refugees to see this man at this address. He knows every ship coming in and going out of Gibraltar.'

Her heart sang as she went to meet the others. They suffered mixed feelings. Finding a contact for a ship was magnificent news, but having to say goodbye to their friend and saviour brought a torrent of tears and sadness. Would they ever see her again?

There was much hugging and no shortage of tears as they all said goodbye to Louise. She couldn't stop crying. The children were inconsolable. 'I don't want you to leave, Plum,' they howled through their tears. But she did.

Or rather they left for the docks and Louise waved until they were no longer in sight. Now she needed to concentrate on *her* next move. She must get back to England, find the SOE traitor in London and do so incognito. She must survive, and expose and remove the mole. Easy. Ha. She headed for the airport.

'It's the last seat, Miss,' said the man arranging the passenger lists. 'Takeoff is 2045 hours. Be here well beforehand and trust me, latecomers miss the flight.'

He wrote her name on the list. She went for a walk along the sea front as the sun slid beneath the waves. Her recent life flashed before her. Ever since she parachuted into farmland near Lyon, she faced dangers and strangers aplenty. It was kill or be killed. And to escape all the chaos and bloodshed, she walked out of France into Spain.

All the adventures and near-death experiences she and the others endured in recent times came alive in her mind. It became a magic lantern show with scene after scene of pain, threats and death. She looked out to sea. The waves were miniscule. She stared at a scene of peace. No wind and little sound. Is the world really at war?

She checked her watch. Better to be early. She headed to the airport. Thoughts filled her head. *Will the key to my flat in Maida Vale be in its hiding-place? Is my mother alive? Where are my brothers? How are my brothers especially Edmund with his badly damaged body? Does the SOE mole know I'm alive and coming for him or her?*

She walked inside the terminal, more of a large shed, and went to the reception desk. As she waited, a voice sounded behind her, one she immediately recognised.

'So you made it after all, Miss Plum.'

Louise didn't want to turn but couldn't stop herself, and so faced Lady Miranda Bonneville-Clegg.

'Good evening, madam,' said Louise in a civil voice thanks to an upbringing by parents who stressed the importance of good manners regardless of the situation.

'Travelling alone are we? Lost your Jewish hangers-on I see.'

'Madam, I'll thank you to call me by my proper name, Miss Helene Smythe, and to keep your contemptible and racist remarks to yourself.'

Louise turned in time to address the booking officer, who gawped at the exchange between the two women. Louise sensed hatred from the woman, whose life she recently saved, burn into her back.

'That way, Miss Smythe,' said the officer pointing and, staring straight ahead, Louise walked to the aeroplane.

She didn't see three gentlemen who recently arrived with the purpose of watching Louise leave. They knew her real name and wanted to be sure she flew away safely. The males were Benjamin Roth, and Ezra and Jacob Lunz, three of her biggest fans.

They climbed the ground beside the airport to obtain a good view. Louise walked across the runway. The men remained silent but in their hearts wished her bon voyage.

She reached the portable steps ready to board the aircraft.

To obtain a better view, the three men decided to climb higher on a path beneath the famous Gibraltar rock. The moon appeared as if to honour the woman they freely described as wonderful; she who did so much for a small group of Jews and now, apparently, one solitary Gentile.

The sea sparkled. The runway jutted out over the water. It might easily have been a scene befitting a movie with themes of romance, intrigue and destiny. Lights, camera, action!

From high above, the three men watched as the propellers moved. Even from such a distance, the roar of the engines carried in the still night air. Taxiing, gradually the aircraft turned to face the water then prepared to depart.

It hummed, racing along building speed until, as if responding to a conductor's baton, lifted then climbed heading towards the moon.

Those three men standing on the path beside the famous Rock of Gibraltar wanted to wave or salute or cry out, "Good luck, Plum." They knew they were blessed to have even met, let alone lived with and survived thanks to this brilliant and courageous young woman.

The pilot took the aeroplane on a sweeping arc preparing to head to England. It kept climbing then, without warning, fell silent. The night air took on an eerie atmosphere, terrifying even. The spectators shivered in the mild conditions. Surely the engine noise wouldn't fade in an instant. The men on the Rock froze. The engines misfired. What's happening? On board, the crew and passengers panicked.

The engine roar became a whine as the aircraft literally fell out of the sky. The pilot and co-pilot fought to right the helpless machine. They failed and a huge plume of water erupted as the sea swallowed the giant bird.

The men on the Rock saw their silence turn to disbelief. It took them an age to speak or move. They'd made the trip from their hotel near the docks to witness the escape of the one person who made their freedom possible. Instead they witnessed her death. Tragic didn't come anywhere close enough to capture their feelings. And how in God's name could they explain this event to their families?

The panic at the airport remained controlled. Aircraft casualties were common in war. But where were the enemy planes and anti-aircraft batteries? Such guns here were Allied guns and silent. Nobody shot at this plane or any plane, it simply crashed. No-one on board could possibly have survived. The passenger list contained such names as Lady Miranda Bonneville-Clegg and a Miss Helene Smythe. It would not be long before a list of passengers and crew would be sent to London, and from there a dreaded telegram would arrive at military and private addresses.

Ten minutes before take-off, Louise took her window seat in the Dakota. Her mind raced and her heart struggled to keep pace. She stared at nothing and no-one. The handful of passengers arrived with departure only minutes away. Louise sensed someone about to sit next to her then glanced up when they spoke.

'Oh dear, fancy meeting you again,' said Miranda of title fame.

Louise turned away then spoke without thinking. 'Would you like the window seat?'

Miranda shrugged. 'Scared of flying are we?'

Louise stood and moved to the door. 'You'll need to take your seat, Miss,' said the cabin officer. 'We're about to go.' She paused then brushed past him. 'Miss!' he called causing other passengers to turn.

She jumped down the steps as the ground crew started to pull them away. They were shocked at her sudden arrival, and more so when she helped them push the steps across the tarmac.

High up on the Rock, the three observers saw the ground crew doing their thing. The door on the Dakota closed and Louise disappeared into the night.

She shocked herself. Something came over her. Something pushed her to move as far away as possible from the woman she now despised. She set off on foot heading towards a hotel, anywhere to find a bed for the night. As she trudged along in the moonlight, she stopped to watch the Dakota make a turn then, without reason, fall from the sky.

Shock gripped her soul. She wanted to pinch herself. *Did what I saw really happen?* She cheated death and knew not why. It took minutes to start breathing normally. When she did recover, she saw the light. She knew her future path.

Helene Smythe died. If anyone knew she survived Lyon and then the Pyrenees and said so, they didn't have all the facts. She took off in the Dakota which plunged into the sea with the loss of all on board.

And the crash gave her an advantage, a super lucky break. She could attack the SOE mole anonymously. She could invent a new ID, return to London and work undercover. Tingles of excitement teased her body, first from getting off a doomed flight, and second because she now enjoyed a free hand. But to flatten her excitement and nerves, a new problem arose. *How the hell do I get home?*

She knocked on the door of a cottage with a B&B sign. An elderly woman wearing a dressing-gown over her nightdress opened the door. Seeing a young woman put the landlady at ease. Using perfect manners and a range of apologies plus a wonderful English Home Counties accent, Louise found herself in a single room at the back of the house. She couldn't sleep. Breakfast was a cracker. She headed into town.

If she returned to the RAF station and asked for another ride home, who would she be? If Helene Smythe or Louise Wellesley, her cover would be blown. Waiting for and travelling by ship would take forever. The SOE traitor could be betraying agents right now.

I need a new identity and a plane ticket today.

Her cash supply hovered above empty and having paid for her bed and breakfast, "Skint" became her new nom de plume. The eye-watering diamond secreted in a button on her shirt didn't help.

Louise headed into town. Shops were opening. She wanted to remain anonymous but needed a free flight back to Blighty as soon as possible. She peered through shop windows looking for a discounted fairy godmother.

It wasn't a matter of choosing the best option; the cupboard lay bare. She sat on a bench. The one idea which kept coming back involved the word *stowaway*. If she could sneak aboard a flight and then sneak off at the other end, all would be well.

But is there a flight? What type of aeroplane?

How can I become a stowaway? Think logically, girl. Go where potentially helpful people congregate.

She headed for the RAF Mess. The deserted venue, due to the early hour and last night's tragedy, killed any wish to drink. She heard sounds and went around the back. Someone made crate-stacking noises below ground in the cellar. Louise devised a plan. She practised sniffing and moved her home address to Bethnal Green in London's East End. She messed her hair and spoke like a Cockney.

She yelled. 'Oi oi, is ya down there Guv'na?'

Work sounds stopped. After a pause and silence, a head appeared. The publican, Dickie "Tricky" Carter blinked in amazement.

'Blimey girlie, youse is a long way from Spitalfields.'

'Beffnil Green if youse mus' know.'

Dickie climbed out displaying his liking for the goods he sold. His trousers fought a long-running war with the Battle of the Bulge.

'Wotcha want, girlie?'

'A bacon sarney anna free ride 'ome to Blighty, please kind sir.'

Dickie laughed. 'You'll be lucky.'

Louise laid it on with style. 'I 'ave it on good orfority dat youse is t'geezer what can fix anyfink in Gibraltar.'

Dickie bathed in her flattery. She intrigued him. Not for a split second did he think she was anything other than a girl from London's East End. He took pride in being the black market boss in Gibraltar and, for a price, could obtain anyfink for any geezer.

'So wot's y'story, darlin'.

'I promised t'King an' Queen I would do a turn for 'em at t'Palace only I missed me boat didn't I? I 'ave t'be back in London by tomorra or else I is brown bread.'

'Well we can't have that now, can we? You bein' a pretty young fing an' all. So you're performin' for their Majesties at the Palace?'

He studied her and she smiled. 'Nah, it ain't true, Guv'na. I never performed for the King and Queen at Buck House.'

'I fought you was havin' a giraffe. So wot's the true story?'

She laid it on with a trowel. Any audience would be teary listening to Louise's tale. 'Back 'ome I met wot I fought was this diamond geezer an' he told me he loved me.'

'Okay, I know what's comin' next.'

'I stowed away on 'is ship. 'E promised me a beautiful gaff 'n all 'ere in Spain, only after 'e's 'ad 'is wicked way wiv me, 'e tells me 'e's got a missus an' four dustbin lids. Dat got me real Tom 'n Dick, and so 'ere I is, on the floor bein' all coals 'n coke, wiv no passport an' no nuthin'. Wot am I gunna do, Guv'na?' Out came the tears.

Dickie bought her tale of woe. He moved to her and she let him embrace her. 'There, there, m'lovely. Dickie won't let you down.'

Having recently climbed a major mountain range while living on meagre rations, Louise weighed in as a skinny flyweight dripping wet. Dickie was an overweight heavyweight complete with beery breath and a veranda over his toolshed. She wondered about her next move. Could he provide the necessary and if so, what would he charge?

She broke free. 'I'm Fanny and I reckon you're a Stan.'

'Dickie,' he said.'

'Yep, Stan or Dickie I fought. Now Dickie, if y'don't mind me sayin', y'gaff's a bit on t'fireman's hose. 'ow about I gives it a bit ov spit 'n polish?'

She didn't wait for his answer, removed her coat, pushed up her sleeves and started collecting glasses, plates and cutlery. He beamed.

'Kitchen frew 'ere?' she asked carrying a tray of empties out of the mess. Dickie needed to pinch himself; this must be a dream. Hungover, feeling poorly, and shattered at the loss of all passengers and crew in last night's inexplicable crash, out of nowhere comes a gorgeous young female who sets about cleaning his mess, the mess of the Mess. He wanted to help this girl more than anything else.

She spent the next two hours washing the items needed in the Mess and then the Mess itself. She scrubbed the floors, washed the windows and scraped years of grime from the oven. She washed the curtains in the sink then took them into the yard to dry in the new day's sunshine.

Dickie kept thanking her and then ordered her to stop.

'Fanny, enough. Come an' sit down.'

'I ain't finished, Dickie.'

He feigned anger. 'I said, come an' sit down.'

She did. He pushed a steaming mug of tea and a plate of biscuits to her. The tea tasted sweet but the biscuits were an obstacle course.

'Fanks,' she said and whacked him with one of her smiles. His toes came alive.

'Now we need to talk, girlie.' He sounded serious. 'There's a geezer in charge of cargo; everythin' comin' and goin' between 'ere and 'ome'. 'e owes me big time. 'is tab's a mile long. Poor bastard's a bitter and twisted wreck. But if I knock off his bar bill, I reckon 'e can pop you aboard an' get you safely tucked away on the next Dakota.'

Louise knew the hairs on the back of her neck were dancing. 'You'd do that for me, Dickie?'

'But you'll need to watch 'im cos 'e treats women like dirt.'

She hopped up and gave Dickie a hug, planting a sloppy smacker on his unshaven cheek. He thought he was Christmas.

She took over. 'Now after I finish me tea, I'll start on tidyin' y'gaff.'

What could be say? 'Blimey, girlie, you sure you don't wanna stay?'

She laughed, finished her tea and sauntered off to explore Dickie's hovel. Sorting and cleaning, she made the job drag. Dickie's Mess became the perfect hiding place because wandering around Gibraltar, she might be seen. Of course she didn't know her fellow refugee travellers were still weeping after her untimely death last night.

The Mess filled up for lunch and Dickie found Louise. 'You there, Fanny?' She was on all fours giving the bathroom a thorough clean, its first in ages. 'That geezer's 'ere. Come in the snug for a chat.'

He left, she made herself half decent and entered the snug.

'There you are,' said Dickie. 'Fanny, this is Ronnie Culpepper. 'E's the chap what can sneak you aboard the Dakota.'

Louise moved forward extending her hand. 'Pleased t'meet ya, sir,' she said, trying for the humble but standoffish approach.

He grasped her hand complete with excess sweat. 'Call me Ronnie,' he leered. 'There's a plane leavin' t'night at 8. You'll need to be at the hangar by 7. Can you be there?'

'Yes sir, I mean, Ronnie.'

'Wrap up cos it'll be cold in wiv the cargo.' He stared at her and Louise knew he was mentally undressing her. 'Okay, be there at 7.'

'Fanks,' she said forcing a fake smile and left.

'She's a nice girl,' said Dickie.

'There's no such thing as a nice girl,' added Ronnie swigging beer.

The Mess manager threatened his customer. 'If I 'ear she doesn't get home in one piece, your tab'll be back on.'

Louise prepared, being dressed ready for an English adventure. Dickie's Mess had customers aplenty keeping him busy pulling pints and serving sandwiches. At half six from the back of the bar, she coughed. Dickie came out to the kitchen.

'You all set?' he asked.

'I am, an' it's all 'fanks to you, Dickie.'

'Nah, my pleasure.' He kissed her cheek. 'Now you take care, girl.' She headed for the door. He called. 'An' say 'ello to their Majesties.'

She flashed a dazzling smile, one which would stay with him throughout the night; actually it stayed with him throughout the war.

SOE HQ, Baker Street, London

Maurice Buckmaster once worked for the Ford Motor Company. The old Etonian worked hard for years in France. When the balloon went up, he served in different capacities until he joined the SOE in Baker Street where he went on to become a high-flyer.

Often at his desk for 16, even 18 hours a day/night, when events were dangerous and missions failed, Maurice endured pain when his agents in France struck trouble. If they were captured or killed, he became a mess. Dog tired, he answered his phone.

'Rusty, long time no see. How are you old chap?'

A Wing Commander in the RAF, Rusty Reynolds also worked on another dangerous job, overseeing bomber crews flying missions over Europe; their survival rate being as bad if not worse than SOE agents.

'The same as you; trying to keep our chaps out of harm's way.'

'This isn't a social call, Rusty, so what can I do for you?'

'Did you hear about the Dakota that crashed after takeoff from Gibraltar the other night?'

'I did; bloody disaster, and not a Jerry in sight.'

'I think one of your agents might have been on board.'

Buckmaster sat up as if shot. 'What? Who?'

'A Miss Helene Smythe.'

Buckmaster struggled to remember the name. He knew the real and code names of all his agents but Helene Smythe didn't ring a bell.

'What have you heard?'

'A while back, five of my men were shot down and escaped through France. On a train from Lyon to Marseille, they met an old woman who turned out to be a young woman in disguise. As some Vichy thug tried to shoot one or more of my chaps, this beautiful young woman snaps his neck and throws him off the train.'

Buckmaster knew the stunning Sister Claudine from Lyon was missing presumed dead. Was this unarmed combat expert Louise Wellesley aka Sister Claudine?

'That could have been one of my agents,' he said.

Reynolds reacted. '*Could* have been? How many beautiful young women have you got in Lyon with those combat skills?'

'Not many; only one actually.'

'My chaps made it safely to Marseille where they heard this woman had been captured by the Gestapo.' Buckmaster's chest pain kicked in. 'Keen to return the rescue favour, the five RAF boys did the right thing by the damsel in distress and got her out.'

Buckmaster cringed. 'Did the Gestapo torture her?'

'Not badly. And while still in Marseille, and in the digs run by that Caskie chap, she discovered two German bastards dressed in RAF uniforms and knocked them out. That's when my boys discovered she was called Miss Helene Smythe. Soon after, my chaps got themselves over the Pyrenees but sadly never heard of her again.'

'Right,' said Buckmaster now waiting for the denouement.

'I looked through the list of passengers and crew on that Dakota and I'm sorry to say, Maurice, it includes the name Helene Smythe.'

Buckmaster fell silent. The news hit hard. He really liked Louise Wellesley, code name Sister Claudine. And she was so young.

'Thanks, Rusty. I'll arrange to tell her family. Talk soon.'

Buckmaster put down the receiver as Vera Atkins entered, saw his face, and knew it meant bad news.

'Louise Wellesley is dead,' he whispered.

It took Vera a few seconds to compute. 'Do you mean Sister Claudine from Lyon?' He nodded. 'What happened?'

'She was on the Dakota that crashed into the sea at Gibraltar.'

'Oh, no. But how did she get from Lyon to Gibraltar?'

'Must have been on one of those Freedom Trails.'

'Well, she wouldn't have crossed the Pyrenees alone.'

Buckmaster shrugged. 'She was using the name Helene Smythe.'

'Why? And how do we know Helene is Louise?'

He explained the heroics. 'I'll need confirmation. But can you chase up her next of kin?'

'Sure,' said Atkins as Jermain Attard and Royston Black entered.

Atkins looked at them. 'Sister Claudine is dead.'

Chapter 29

Gibraltar

With her hat and coat pulled tight, Louise made her way to the airport. Head down, she didn't see the person coming towards her until they collided. She bumped him, he stumbled dropping bags of shopping spilling the contents.

'Sorry,' she said bending to pick up items.

'Mademoiselle,' gasped the person and Louise looked up and at the face of Ezra Lunz. He stifled a scream. 'You're alive.'

He hugged her and wouldn't let go. Eventually each explained their whereabouts on that night and Ezra's tears flowed.

'Wait till I tell the others,' he said and hugged her again.

Feeling fantastic, she broke free, but this time had a flight to catch.

A Douglas C47 Dakota rested in front of the hangar. Louise waited in the shadows. Ground crew came and went. She heard their chatter.

'On board there's a mix of POW escapees and blokes who were shot down and escaped through France.'

'Bloody amazing,' said his mate as they shoved a trolley to the rear of the aircraft. 'They deserve *two* medals for what they've done.'

Their chat stopped when Flight Sergeant Ronald Culpepper appeared. 'Get that gear on board then report to the terminal. There are VIP cases and other bits of baggage to load.'

The men did as ordered and left. Ronnie checked the area. Shadows made hiding easy. 'You there?' he called softly.

'I'm 'ere, Flight Sergeant,' said Louise, walking from the darkness towards him. He waited for her to arrive.

'In here,' he said indicating the open plane door. He helped her up and she felt a hand on her back, presumably as a form of support. When she pushed off into the aircraft, Ronnie's support transferred from Louise's back to her buttocks. She moved to the tail and he followed. Cramped best described her position amongst the cargo.

She squeezed in and observed. 'Lucky I'm thin.'

'You're lucky full stop. Just squat in there, and put a sock in it.'

She did and made herself uncomfortable. No padding, no peeing, good for hiding, and a wing and a prayer seemed appropriate.

'If you make a noise and are sprung before take-off, you'll be thrown off. If you make a noise after take-off, you'll be arrested when you land. So shut it. I'll be back before you go.'

He left and Louise tried moving one leg one way and then the other. Cramp prepared to get busy but who cares because, within hours, legs and fingers crossed, she'd be back in England. She knew not where but somewhere, and right now, anywhere in Blighty beat the pants of anywhere in Continental Europe.

The boxes around her were an odd mix of foodstuffs. She tried to relax and wondered if pinching something to eat would be seen as treason.

She heard passengers. They sounded exhausted. The hubbub and activity continued. Then she heard him and his hoarse whisper sounded close.

'Oi, are you still there?' Ronnie "The Creep" Culpepper returned.

'Yes,' said Louise desperate to remain undiscovered.

'I wanna give you a chance to thank me for getting you on board.'

'Fanks and I mean it.'

'Yeah, well, I need you to prove it.'

Louise knew what he wanted but not the method of delivery. In the semi-darkness she again studied the material around her.

'You know I ain't got no dosh,' she whispered, carefully breaking into the packages.

'Forget the money, darlin', let's have a bit of fun, only you'll need to be quick.'

'I'm stuck. I can hardly move.'

'Yeah, but I can come to you, if you take my meaning.'

What a prat, thought Louise.

'Can you see me?' he whispered.

'Only your belt and trousers.'

'That'll do. I'll shove me best friend through the gap and you can work your magic, but hurry.'

'Okay,' she replied and prepared to do the business.

It didn't take long. The sex-starved Flight Sergeant pressed his body hard against the boxes with his trying-to-be erect penis poking through the small gap. He waited in gleeful anticipation. The first sensation he enjoyed sent adrenalin coursing through his body. It hit a brick wall though when the second sensation took over.

Louise started with a couple of drops of a honey entrée, but soon provided the main course of red hot chilli paste, generously sloshing the cooking ingredient on the eagerly waiting Private John Thomas.

Ronnie withdrew in fear and trembling, not knee trembling, and grabbed his now burning member making a bad situation worse by rubbing the added substance to his once pink joystick. The hot chilli paste packed a kick like a mule and Ronnie prepared to scream.

His brain screamed back. Make a fuss and the word will be round the Mess, not to mention the Rock, about Ronnie and his painted plonker. He spat a string of rude words at the stowaway then lurched to the plane door and tumbled onto the runway. Ouch! Double ouch!

Louise froze wondering when she would be discovered. Her heart beat would surely give her away. But the roar of the engines and the cries of the ground crew told her the escape had begun. The nearby plane door slammed shut and the aircraft taxied into position.

Okay green and pleasant land, let's be havin' ya.

For a wartime journey, the flight went well and with no refreshments, adverse weather or stray Messerschmitts, Louise even caught herself snoozing. She dreaded the prospect of having to stand up with cramp well and truly at home in both legs.

Many questions hammered her brain. *Where will we land? How will I disembark without being arrested? Where will I go when we do land? With my new name, will my Helene ID pass muster?*

She spent time creating answers always hoping that when back in Blighty, she could scamper away unseen.

She heard passengers being advised about their imminent arrival and wanted to shout a drink for the chap who asked one question.

'Where are we landing, officer?'

'RAF Lyneham, sir, in Wiltshire about ten miles from Swindon.'

Louise's unseen grin revealed her teeth. Wiltshire gave her heart a pang. Her mother had re-married and moved there. Any thought of knocking on her stepfather's magnificent front door at—what time is it now in England?—lasted a second, two at the most. No, her sole task, her soul task was to reach London and unmask the SOE mole.

What if the mole is dead? What if they've been rumbled and fled to Bavaria? What if all this stowaway adventure has been in vain?

RAF Lyneham, Wiltshire

In the rear of the plane, Louise's bottom told her about touchdown. The Dakota stopped and everyone except Louise moved. Passengers disembarked and then the ground crew came to remove the cargo. *Here we go*, thought Louise; *Act One Beginners on stage please.*

The boxes which created Louise's hideaway were manhandled. She could hear and then see the men doing their job. Any moment now she'd be discovered. In the dim light, the last box disappeared with one squashed SOE agent left exposed in the rear of the fuselage.

She didn't know the last and enthusiastic ground crew chap had a date that night as he hurried to grab the final box. He didn't see Louise, leaving her alone. Her elation was tempered by the agony of cramp as she tried to stand. Leaning against the side of the fuselage, she limped to the door, paused in the open space and stared at a dark sky and an even darker airport. She crouched then dropped to the ground. Her landing made a noise and a voice responded.

'Hey! You there!' The same ground crew officer who failed to spot the stowaway hurried towards Louise. He saw the person up close. 'Excuse me, Miss, but what are you doing here?'

Louise drew herself up to her full five foot seven and a half inches and used her Hockey Sticks Sports Mistress voice from Roedean. 'Miss? It's WAAF Flight Officer Patience Capable to you, sonny.'

In the dark, the young chap with flat feet and thick spectacles, stood shocked and corrected. He saluted. Louise waved a sort of salute in return and became less brusque. 'Carry on,' she said and set off not having a clue where.

Welcome home, Plum, old girl.

Chapter 30

Home Guard, Swindon

She remembered the officer on the aeroplane saying RAF Lyneham was about 10 miles from Swindon. She knew Swindon was a railway town and would certainly have trains running up to London. But at what time? Would a wartime timetable allow for traffic after midnight? If for military purposes, yes. But where is Swindon?

She made out the dimly lit buildings of RAF Lyneham and walked away from them. She remembered her SOE lectures on airport security and how to avoid it. Any patrol may well include a dog, and unless she found a stream, her chances of escaping undetected were shrinking faster than the contents of Ronnie Culpepper's codpiece.

She saw dim lighting and assumed it to be a village in the far distance. She headed in that direction. Surely there'd be a perimeter fence at the airport, even search lights and an anti-aircraft battery. She saw only blackness and heard only her footsteps.

She walked on grass, her mind buzzing. *I've crossed the Pyrenees with old folk and children. Surely a walk in Wiltshire is a breeze.*

The darkness kept her hidden but meant she travelled blind. Still no perimeter fence sprang up to meet her. The lights in the distance didn't seem any closer. Surely she hadn't been walking in a circle. Then, in the still night air, came a cry of pain and voices.

What was that? Who is that? Do I investigate and reveal myself? Do I press on and remain dead to the world?

The cries of pain sounded genuine and the voices worried. Someone needed help and Louise set off. As she approached the sounds, she saw torches being used. From about 20 metres she called.

'Hello? Do you need any help?'

The voices and cries of pain died and two torches shone on her face. She kept moving but with a hand across her face. A voice let rip.

'Halt! Hände hoch!'

Louise spoke German although not as well as her brilliant French. She chose to reply in English.

'I heard your cry of pain and wondered if I could help.'

'She sounds English,' said another voice.

'Good evening. Yes, I'm English,' she replied reaching three men.

Another voice spoke. 'You've broken the curfew, Miss. You'll have to come with us.'

Louise loved that instruction. 'Yes, and I do apologise. I'm staying with friends up at the Manor House, and their beloved dog ran off after a rabbit, and I've been walking for miles trying to find the poor thing, that's the dog not the rabbit, and I think I'm lost. I don't suppose you've seen the dog or the rabbit? No, of course not, it's jolly dark.' She didn't miss a beat. 'Am I still in Wiltshire?'

All three men were falling for the charms of the attractive and beautifully spoken young woman. 'Yes, Miss,' they said as one.

She showed genuine concern and stepped forward. 'But one of you has taken a tumble.' She knelt beside the wounded in action old codger sitting on the ground and gently squeezed his ankle. His thoughts caught fire. *My God, I've died and gone to Heaven.*

'It's only a sprain, Miss, nothing to worry about.'

'Nonsense, you should be at home with your foot up, and a snifter of brandy. Have you got far to go?'

'Not far, Miss. I'm in the next village.' She offered a hand. 'Let me help you.'

The wounded gent hopped up with a spring in his step. One of his mates took the Mashie Niblick his fellow part-time soldier carried. Rifles were thin on the ground in this part of England, and the Home Guard made do with whatever came to hand. Besides, Jerry hates golf.

'Now, put your arm around me,' said Louise, and the two fit fellows wished they were the one with the sprained (slightly sprained) ankle. They were typical of many older men who react a certain way to a young attractive female. Forget lust, it's more a fading memory of what was once delight and pleasure, but will never come again.

'We should report back to platoon HQ,' said the first chap, and so off they went, three elderly members of the Home Guard, and the much younger and far prettier SOE agent recently returned from foreign climes. These chaps knew how to exit RAF Lyneham.

The officer in charge of the platoon of this merry band of retirees, by name Captain Harold Barking, was a former WW1 corporal, retired bookkeeper, and known as Captain Barking-Mad. He dozed in his office at the rear of the church hall waiting for the last of his security teams to return. The others were back at HQ waiting to be dismissed. The captain was rudely awoken which ignited his short-fused temper.

He stumbled from his office and suffered drop jaw when three of his men hobbled in with a woman, a female woman, locked in a sort of embrace with one of his men. The fact the woman appeared devilishly attractive only ramped up his confusion and frustration. Captain Barking addressed the arrivals.

'What is the meaning of this outrage? Who is this woman and why, Corporal Grimley, is she attached in such a manner to your person?'

The wounded soldier made a pathetic request. 'May I sit, Captain Barking? My ankle is giving me merry hell.'

A chair was produced and the injured hero collapsed thereon.

Louise took over. 'Good evening, Captain. Being a trained nurse, I offered my professional services to help a soldier in need. We thought it best to report immediately to you.'

The promoted-above-his-station Captain was enthralled by the beautiful and beautifully-spoken woman, the first to ever enter his platoon HQ, oh apart from a whist drive held to raise funds, when wives and sweethearts were invited, and encouraged to bring a plate.

'I see,' said Barking, struggling to run two sentences together.

'I have to commend you, Captain,' said Louise. 'Your men did a splendid job in protecting RAF Lyneham spotting me stumbling around in the dark hunting for a lost dog.' The gallant three were never going to contradict the bombshell from the Dark Moor.

Barking's next and immediate response would surely be to the interloper, "What were you really doing there, who the hell are you, and where is your identification?" but instead he came up with, 'Well, thank you Miss for … I'm sorry, I didn't catch your name.'

She thrust out her hand which he took in a limp, wet-fish grip. Louise slipped into aristocracy circles. 'I'm Lady Phyllis Nightingale-Hamilton, although all my pals call me Phylly.' She guffawed, laughing at herself. 'Actually my best chums call me Silly Phylly but we won't go into that.' More chuckles and Barking sensed his knees begin to surrender. He automatically bowed his head.

'My Lady, what an honour it is to welcome you to our humble platoon.'

'No, no, no, it is *my* honour to meet you, sir, and your outstanding and brave fighting men. Against the might of that wretched man—we all call him Herr *Horrible* Hitler—you and your boys are keeping us safe in our beds, and I salute you all.' Smiling, she saluted them.

Every gent wanted to applaud. Two actually started to do so. Harold again gave a restrained bow. 'Most kind, my Lady, and is there any service which we might provide for your good self?'

'Ah, yes, actually there is,' said Louise maintaining her over-the-top aristocratic character. 'I'm staying up at the Manor House but couldn't possibly barge in on His Lordship at this late hour. Could you by any chance point me in the direction of the nearest hostelry?'

'Hostelry, my Lady? Why I'm sure we could offer you a far better style of accommodation within our humble homes.' A surge of support greeted the commanding officer's comment. His men were never so keen to go along with the well-named Captain Barking.

'Oh, my goodness,' said Louise with genuine relief. 'How awfully kind you are. But is there anyone who could help me out?'

Every man, *every* man raised his hand, one chap raised two. 'I can, m'Lady,' became the common cry. They bragged about the size of their cottage, or the breakfast their missus could prepare in the morning, even the size and contents of their green house. 'I've won The Biggest Marrow prize for the last three years, m'Lady.'

They stopped and settled only when Louise raised her hand and spoke. 'Gentlemen, please, your generosity is overwhelming. How can I possibly choose only one?'

Harold wanted to snaffle the visitor for himself, although knew his wife would enact her petticoat government legislation, rule number 3.1 if he even *thought* about bringing a woman into their home. Rule 3.0 was frightening but 3.1, horrific. He regretted not pulling rank but reckoned his being generous might pay dividends down the track.

'I believe Private Walsingham would make the perfect host, my Lady.' A sigh of disappointment oozed from the others while old Wilf beamed.

'I would be delighted, sir, and my Lady,' he said hoping like hell his flies were buttoned up.

Harold explained. 'Private Walsingham is a widower with two daughters and two daughters-in-law, all at home, and each with their respective husband away fighting for King and country.'

'How brave you all are.' She smiled at the winning hotelier. 'Good evening, sir. I should be honoured to visit your fine establishment.'

And so Louise and the widower left with Harold escorting them to the door and giving the visitor his best salute. He didn't know whether to shake hands, bow, wave or salute. He saluted—twice.

And so Louise Beatrice Wellesley returned to England, avoided the authorities and found a bed for the night in a pretty Wiltshire village.

Next morning, after a slap-up breakfast, she needed to reach Swindon to catch a train to London. Both of Alf's daughters-in-law were Land Girls.

'We can give you a lift to the next village, m'Lady,' said Gladys. 'There's a bus from there to Swindon.'

'How super,' said Louise, and sat in the back of the cart with the horse taking her along narrow lanes before pulling in at the farm on which they worked.

'It's around the next bend, m'Lady,' said Maud, and Louise hopped down, waved and wandered off to catch a bus.

Getting on board a bus and train without a ticket would have been a problem for most citizens, but the highly-trained Louise Wellesley knew a technique or two to find her way through enemy lines, so overcoming drivers and conductors should prove easy.

In the end she didn't need the bus. While waiting at the stop, a woman pulled up in a battered old Morris and sang out, 'Want a lift?'

She turned out to be a real aristocrat, and Louise forgot her Lady Phyllis patter and came up with her being a Londoner down to see her flying ace boyfriend based at RAF Lyneham.

Being dropped at Swindon station suited her perfectly, and Louise waved to her lift before entering the station. A London train stood ready to depart. She walked to the end of the platform and observed.

With the coast clear, she slipped off the end of the platform, walked to the other side of the train and climbed up and into an empty carriage. With a little difficulty, she opened a window and dropped into the compartment. Oops. She failed to see two small boys sitting together in a corner. Their jaws dropped.

'Hello,' said Louise in her friendliest voice. She sat and smiled.

The children were instructed, under pain of an eternal sweets' ban, never to speak to strangers. The mother of said boys arrived and stared at Louise before staring at the boys.

'Good morning,' said Louise and the mother said nothing.

Wanting to avoid any accusations from witnesses, even those of tender years, Louise stood. 'Oops,' she said and moving, 'wrong compartment.' She left and moved to another carriage.

'Mummy,' said the older child. 'That lady climbed in the window.'

'Nonsense,' scowled his mother. 'Stop making up silly stories.'

It's true; there are parents who never believe their children.

London, England

As her train neared London, Louise planned her movements. When it arrived, she went to the Ladies, waited for the right moment then slipped out of the station. She actually bought a ticket for the Tube not wanting to be caught at the last moment. She alighted at Maida Vale, walked to Paddington Recreation Ground to recover her flat key beneath the third tree west of the 19th century pavilion, and made her way home. She ran a bath then collapsed on her bed.

What a trip. Become a nun, kill Gestapo thugs, watch a bishop fall to his death, climb a mountain range, cross a ridiculously flimsy bridge, twice, tackle would-be perverts and rapists, find a lost doll and avoid death by the luck of the draw.

The bath, she thought as the water sounded full.

She stripped and soaked until her skin decided to sing.

Despite being early afternoon she craved a plate of egg and chips. She dried, dressed and departed. The Maida Vale shops were close.

When will I contact family? How will I tackle the SOE traitor?

She bought eggs, potatoes, milk and bread, and wandered home. Her mind focused on her family.

How is my dear brother Edmund? She wanted to know but froze when her brother spoke.

'Plum?'

She spun around and stared at him.

Chapter 31

Maida Vale, London

It *was* her brother who spoke, her other brother, her older brother. Henry Wellesley, like his brother Edmund and father Charles, went to Cambridge and read Law. Henry married, some said well, Louise said appallingly, a woman whose father was a judge. Louise last saw Henry in 1939, when she told everyone she would be touring Australia performing Shakespeare, when in fact she set off for Paris as a sleeper for the Secret Intelligence Service.

Henry became a father last year but Auntie Louise knew nothing about her niece, or his war service, if any. She knew everything about brother Edmund and his battered body but about Henry, nothing.

Now he stood before her on the pavement in the Maida Vale Road. Louise thought it the most remarkable coincidence in British history.

But she forgot the surprise, and pushed aside her shock and desire for an explanation. Familial love took priority, and besides, it's true that absence does make the heart grow fonder. Passersby watched with interest as the couple hugged, kissed, laughed and cried.

These two siblings always enjoyed a close relationship. Both brothers teased their baby sister as she grew with Henry the team leader. Both brothers invented and promoted her nickname of Plum; pity about their spelling.

'What a wonderful surprise,' said Louise, after they settled.

'You haven't changed at all,' said Henry, lying. He thought she looked like a beautiful mature woman.

'What are you doing here?' she asked, her curiosity killing her. 'Do you live in London? Are you still practicing law? Oh, and congratulations on continuing the Wellesley line.'

He laughed. 'Too many questions, Plum. Let's have a cup of tea.'

She pointed. 'There's a café across the road.'

'What's wrong with your flat?'

They stared at one another and she knew he knew. 'I knew it couldn't be a coincidence.'

She took his arm and they walked to her flat.

'I've been here before when Eddie first bought it. He told me you moved in. I called and discovered you'd returned.'

'You discovered?' This intrigued her. *Is Henry in Intelligence?*

He grinned. 'I'll tell you later.'

'How is Edmund? Have you seen him?'

'He's getting better, slowly, but better.'

'And Mummy?'

'She's fine but Sir Anthony took a turn last week.'

Louise's spirits dived then she remembered. 'Oh, forgive me, Henry. I haven't asked about *your* family.'

He sensed she'd forgotten either or both the names of his wife and baby daughter so tactfully helped her out. 'Georgina and little Hester are both well. I think my daughter is the spitting image of my sister but whatever you do, never, repeat never tell my wife I said that.'

He grinned, she made tea and an interesting conversation began.

'I'll come straight out with it, Louise.' He worried her. He only called her Louise when something serious needed to be discussed. 'I've signed the Official Secrets Act and I'm guessing you have too.' She studied him and thought.

He's my brother, my own flesh and blood. I've known him all my life. He could not possibly be trying to trick me. It is beyond belief he is an enemy agent.

He understood her confusion and continued to explain what he knew, step by step. 'I know about your pretend visit to Australia and your real trip to Paris, about your ENSA performances, and your latest incarnation as a nun while working for the SOE.'

Louise finally spoke. 'And yet I know nothing about your war effort; not a thing.'

'When you disappeared in France last month, and people said you were probably dead, I knew my sister would not give up without a fight. I'd seen her trick our father into letting her go to Cambridge; a Wellesley girl defying tradition would never be a pushover.'

She began to weep in silence. He continued, quietly, methodically.

'If dead, I couldn't help her but if alive, ...

Louise wondered why he referred to her in the third person.

'Of course I'd be obliged to help and so I used all my contacts, and while nothing confirmed your demise, lots of snippets suggested you were alive. I figured there must be a reason why you hadn't announced your survival and arrival.' He pointed at her. 'Something is rotten in the state of Denmark, and young Plum wants to rescue the good name of the Bard.'

She smiled. 'Are you auditioning for the role of my hero?'

He smiled back. 'I called here a week ago and found nothing. Yesterday I called again and placed a tiny stick under the door.' Louise grimaced having forgotten part of her basic training. 'When I arrived an hour ago, the stick had moved. I wandered to the nearest shops in the Edgeware Road and Bob's your uncle.'

She hopped up, crossed to him and they embraced. It lasted a good time. She broke away. 'And can I ask *how* you know all this?'

He shrugged. She poured more tea. 'Does it matter? Your training taught you torture can't make you reveal what you don't know.'

She enjoyed his comment. 'Thank you, Henry. You've given my self-belief a real boost. I knew you'd be involved in doing your bit.' He smiled without moving his lips. They sipped tea. She reminisced.

'Can you imagine what Daddy would say if told one of his sons had been badly wounded in battle in a world war, and two of his children were working undercover to keep old England safe?'

'He wouldn't believe his darling daughter spent her days and nights killing Nazis.' Louise felt a pain in her chest remembering her father with great fondness. 'If I can help, Louise, please let me. My guess is you haven't told the world you're alive for a reason.'

'I haven't told anyone I'm alive.'

'My second guess is it's because you think being dead gives you the best chance to tackle something important.'

'You always were good at guessing, Henry, damn good.'

He wanted to help. 'Okay, it's your decision. Tell me everything, nothing or something. If I can help, I will.'

She paused. This issue dominated her life for weeks. The last two years taught her one thing; trust nobody and especially those who appear to be on your side.

He remained silent. The fact he didn't try to persuade her, helped her decide. She told him everything.

'I know there's a traitor in the SOE. In Lyon, I overheard an enemy agent speaking to a traitor in London. I shot and wounded the agent and before he could tell me the traitor's name, would you believe a bishop shot and murdered the agent. I know the London traitor exists. I don't know his or her name. So by pretending to be dead, I hope I can somehow trick my way into the SOE and find the mole.'

'*Somehow* seems pretty vague.'

Louise lost it. 'Oh, Henry, please, I'm at my wit's end. If I ask the bosses for help, I may blow the case. It could be one of them. Or they could deliberately or accidentally tip off the mole. There've been some disastrous cock-ups made from London.'

He nodded. 'Understood.' He paused wanting her to be calm and rational. 'How about you confide in someone in Intelligence, someone who knows their onions, with no axe to grind, is experienced and impeccably qualified?'

Louise sighed with her relief palpable. Now she saw light at the end of the tunnel.

'That sounds wonderful. Can you tell me his name?'

'It's a woman,' said Henry. 'I'll have her meet you tomorrow at 10am in Highgate Cemetery.'

'Where?'

'Highgate, north London, you went there as a kid, we all did.'

'No; where in Highgate, it's rather large.'

'Oh, sorry; let's make it Karl Marx's tomb.'

'You sound as if you do this all the time.'

'Not quite,' said Henry and removed a card. 'Here's my phone number for an emergency. Memorise it then destroy the card.'

'How will I know this woman?'

'She'll find you. Your code name will be Plum.'

She smiled at him and he winked. He gulped his tea, and headed for the door. 'I'll give your love to Eddie and Mummy.'

Louise panicked. 'What? Henry, wait! What will you tell them about me? I need to know if they ask.'

'You sent me a letter from your latest stunning ENSA performance. You're well, enjoying life and *still* unmarried.' He grinned. 'Now don't be late tomorrow.' He opened the door, kissed her, and headed down the stairs raising his voice. 'It's lovely to finally meet you, Mildred, and good luck with the FANY.'

She knew this red herring was for any nosy neighbours.

She slept well and rose early. Being able to choose her outfit became a treat. She found a near-perfect hiding place for the jewel given to her by Benjamin Roth. With folding money in her pocket, she set off to meet a woman she hoped would help her discover the SOE mole.

For a trained SOE agent, Louise's preparation scored a Fail as she alighted at Highgate Tube Station instead of the closer Archway, forcing her to hurry. Karl Marx's grave was in the East Cemetery. She got one thing right. Her training meant she wasn't searching for her contact but rather studying the graves.

Surreptitiously she checked her watch. *We're both late.* No contact to be seen. Mind you there's a sort of jungle in many parts of this cemetery making it easy to hide. Then from behind a tombstone, a voice could barely be heard. 'Plum,' is all it said. Louise knew how to react. She took her time wandering away from Comrade Marx, turned into a path and saw a woman reading a headstone. The woman turned her head and gave a lovely smile. Louise approached the woman who held out a gloved hand and said, 'Hello, I'm Jean.'

They shook hands. Louise reckoned her contact to be about 30, well dressed with immaculate blonde hair and sparkling eyes.

'Shall we walk and talk,' she said, and they strolled, a couple of tourists inspecting the graves in the massive cemetery.

'Your brother has told me a little of your situation,' said Jean. 'Is your best chance of success returning to the organisation in disguise?'

'It's my *only* chance and if I'm discovered, I'll blow it.'

'Henry told me you're an actress, so I guess you plan on becoming someone else.'

'Yes, but I've no idea who. I can think of characters but then what am I doing there, and my biggest problem is how do I even get in?'

'Someone in a menial role would be ideal. You want to be unimportant and as close to invisible as possible.'

Louise immediately liked Jean's thinking but needed specific details. A menial role sounded promising, and with the right costume and make-up, plus an accent, she might have a chance. But what is the menial task and how would she apply for the job? What job?

'Can you type?' asked Jean.

Louise saddened. 'No, but my Morse is excellent.'

'Can you make tea and deliver messages?'

'Definitely.'

'What about limping? Have you ever played a cripple on stage?'

Louise understood. 'I can, but wouldn't that draw attention to me when I'm trying to operate in the background?'

'The sympathy vote may help. Now, I know people in the SOE and will try and have you employed downstairs. Why don't you prepare a background story for your new character—your new family, where you come from, how you became poorly after your accident, et cetera, and I'll see what job you might be able to do. I have your address in Maida Vale. Let's meet tonight at 1900 hours. Will that suit?'

Louise tingled with excitement. This calm and no-fuss woman seemed to think Louise could pull it off thus lifting her spirits and self-belief. Now, there was a new character to create and a possible way to re-enter the SOE. Louise could investigate and unmask the traitor. Best of all, this progress was happening at speed.

'It sounds wonderful.'

'Good-oh,' said Jean. 'I'll bring the crumpets, you make the tea. Till 7,' she said and turned and disappeared through the greenery.

Louise gave a little hop of excitement; quite out of place in such a serious setting.

Heading home she made a couple of stops. Going into town to the Theatre Royal would solve her problems with props and costumes, but she wanted all this to remain hush hush. If word got around that the ENSA pantomime star was in town, her cover would be blown. She went to a couple of places and came away with a few quirky objects.

The tale she told an undertaker would, in peacetime, have had her shown the door, but Britain was at war. Her unusual request was granted and Miss Wellesley's next role took shape.

She had no support staff whatsoever. She became the writer, dresser, make-up artist, director and performer. All afternoon she honed her character. Her name, date and place of birth, her parents, siblings, schools, church and favourite food were committed to memory. She even picked a favourite film, and created a tale about the boy she loved and lost.

She tried on her recently acquired costumes, and added the appropriate accoutrements including spectacles. She swore off wigs after her old woman routine in France failed, and instead went for a change of colour and style. The clock headed towards 1900 hours.

The soft door knock gave her heart a start. She drew in a deep breath and opened the door. Jean from Highgate stood there with a small parcel in her hands and an expression of confusion on her face.

'I'm sorry,' she said. 'I thought I wanted Flat 4.'

'Bonsoir, Madame Jean,' said Louise in a French accent, and beckoned her visitor enter. Jean twigged and slowly shook her head.

She entered and stopped as Louise closed the door. 'I heard you were good and guessed your brother exaggerated his sister's talent, but that is remarkable.'

'Thank you,' said Louise in her normal voice and accent. 'Do go in.' Jean entered and Louise followed.

'Crumpets, as promised,' said Jean handing Louise a package.

'Lovely, thank you; please take a seat.'

Jean sat and Louise fussed in the kitchen then came back. 'Tea and crumpets now or would you like to meet the hopeful SOE employee?'

'I'd like to meet the new SOE employee,' said Jean, sitting back.

And so Louise performed for her visitor. She introduced herself and ran through the facts created about the new Louise. She spoke in English with a French accent and a voice slightly lower in pitch to her own. Jean stared and revelled in the quality of the presentation.

'My name is Holle, with an e, Fontaine. I was born in Antwerp, Belgium. With my mother always poorly, when my father died, I moved to England aged 8 to live with my English grandparents in Birmingham, which is why sometimes I sound like a Brummie.'

She used a Birmingham accent. Jean glowed. A French-speaking woman speaking English as a Brummie sounded fascinating.

'I went to school in England then, after I left school, I trained as a nurse, but a car accident meant I gave up because of the injury to my left leg. I walk with a slight limp and wear a special brace.'

She lifted the left leg of her trousers to reveal a metal and leather device strapped to her leg; prop courtesy of an undertaker.

'My brother lives in Belgium with his wife and family. I would like to return as my grandparents are dead. I live alone in a bedsit in

Shepherd's Bush. I work as a kitchenhand in a café, but would dearly like to help Great Britain so the land of my birth can be free.'

Still in character, she gave the briefest of curtsies and asked, 'Does Madame have any questions?'

Jean stood, clapped then opened her arms. 'Brilliant,' she said, 'absolutely brilliant.' The women hugged and Louise tingled.

'Right, young lady, let's have tea and I'll tell you my news.'

Louise limped to the kitchen. Butter would have been nice with the crumpets but old marmalade would have to do. Once they were sipping and swallowing, Jean delivered her news.

'I wasn't sure I would tell you tonight. But you're so well prepared I will. You have a job at the SOE and can start in the morning.'

'What?' gasped Louise. She liked this woman thinking her smart, polite and businesslike. But her news shocked the actress. 'Are you serious?' She stopped, thinking her question insulted her guest. 'Oh I'm so sorry; I didn't mean I doubted you.'

Jean laughed. 'Of course you didn't. It's thanks to the Old Girls' Network. Chaps are not the only ones who stick together. I know someone who knows someone who works in the kitchen in Baker Street. This lady, Merle, is a collector of waifs and strays.' She paused. 'That's you, Holle Fontaine.' Louise smiled. 'I told them I knew a young woman who wanted to help the war effort and is keen to start.'

'But what work will I do and where? The SOE has many locations.'

'You'll start downstairs at 64 Baker Street doing menial tasks; running errands, delivering mail, making tea.' She held up her cup. 'This is excellent by the way.'

Louise shook her head. 'I can't believe we are moving so quickly.'

'You'll need a security check with your new name on these documents.' Jean handed Louise an envelope. 'In there too is a hand-written letter of recommendation from my boss in the WAAF, so with Merle in the back office supporting any worthy cause, you should be fine.'

'Jean, I can't thank you enough.'

'To be safe, I'll be there and in uniform to impress any big-wigs.'

More head shaking from Louise. 'Three days ago I was stuck in Spain wondering if I'd ever see England again.'

'Alas, my help ends once you enter the SOE back office. From there, you're on your own, young lady.'

They both knew the seriousness of rooting out traitors. Failure didn't bear thinking about, and if Louise was rumbled, a cornered double agent wouldn't hesitate to kill the would-be spy-catcher.

'And you think my character's convincing?'

'I think you'd make any character convincing. But do you have a plan once you're safely settled as a Baker Street Irregular?'

Louise hesitated. 'I'm sorry?'

'Do you have a plan?' Louise still looked confused. Jean twigged. 'Some SOE people call themselves the Baker Street Irregulars.' Louise continued to be vague. 'Sherlock Holmes used children to help him solve cases, and he called them his Baker Street Irregulars.'

'Of course,' said Louise covering her embarrassment.

'So, have you settled on a plan?'

Louise winced. 'I'm afraid spying on my colleagues is not my forte. I've been so worried about getting home and then getting back in the SOE, I haven't thought much about the actual investigation.'

'Well, speaking of Sherlock Holmes, you could try a couple of his methods. He reckoned you should eliminate the impossible, and believed there is nothing so important as trifles.'

'I'll take your advice.' They paused. 'You've been a wonderful help, Jean. If, sorry *when* I discover the mole, it'll be largely thanks to you.'

Jean smiled. 'Get a good night's sleep, young Holle. I'll be outside the Baker Street Tube at 0800 hours. Don't be late. Till the morning.'

They hugged, Jean left and Louise tapped her head on her front door. She'd played many roles before and no matter how many rehearsals, always experienced nerves. But this role, this looked to be exceptional. She must deceive people who knew her well that she was someone else and, wait for it, find and capture or kill a traitor.

A good night's sleep? Ha! Fat chance.

Louise's brilliance with character creation, and her expertise with costumes, props, hair and make-up meant her new persona stood a good chance of fooling the SOE top brass. When you add the fact they all thought she died in the Dakota crash at Gibraltar, her chances of fooling her colleagues improved even more. But did she have a plan to find the traitor and if so, would it work?

Hello Holle.

Chapter 32

Near Antibes, France

The submarine surfaced. The night sky, crammed with clouds, made moonlight irrelevant. The French coast lay 200 metres away and the two SOE agents were at the pointy end of their mission. David Eden and Emile Rousseau endured the rigours of SOE training, and were ready to link up with dedicated anti-Vichy souls in Southern France.

The captain exchanged a light with the party ashore. 'All good, gentlemen,' he said to the agents. 'Good luck and God speed.'

The inflatable bobbed in the frisky ocean and, using a rope, the agents clambered aboard. It was paddle your own canoe time as the inflatable headed towards France.

Ashore, members of the local Resistance scrambled down the cliff onto the beach. Each knew their specific task. The craft rode the crest of a wave. Slipping into the sea and grabbing the inflatable, the agents ran through the waves being greeted by their new comrades.

Actually Eden was on his second trip so knew most of the locals. Hugs and handshakes complete, they headed for their safe house.

At this time everything seemed promising for those fighting the Vichy, Gestapo, and the odd Wehrmacht force in southern France. Sabotage attacks were not major but useful and small victories added up. But the greatest danger for Resistance fighters and SOE agents remained the traitor, the local who would betray anyone, often their own countrymen or women. And worse, some traitors were working from unusual places such as 64 Baker Street, London.

The new arrivals were led to a farmhouse far from neighbours. The isolation helped in two ways. Locals wouldn't see any strangers, and anyone approaching the property could be seen from a distance.

The farmer and his wife welcomed their visitors and provided the finest of rural French foods for the SOE agents.

Before long new arrivals appeared in dribs and drabs. They were all keen to work with the SOE wanting weapons, advice, and intelligence. There were Resistance fighters, passeurs, even a politician and a priest both of whom were keen to disrupt, destroy, and drive out the dreaded invader.

With so many attendees, the group moved to the barn. Eden spoke to the group in French. 'Thank you for your kind welcome. We have received your messages in London, and there will be weapon drops arranged soon, as well as other equipment and even more agents. We are on the verge of a real push against the enemy.' The locals purred.

In the fields surrounding the farmhouse, German soldiers with blackened faces crept towards the house. A dog, trained to bark at any new arrival, sensed intruders and bounded towards them roaring defiance. His barking ceased abruptly when two shots from a Walther P.38 with silencer killed him instantly.

His best mate, a female, barked and received the same treatment.

In the kitchen, the farmer's wife stopped kneading dough wondering why the dogs barked and then stopped as they did. She opened the back door and died, like her beloved dogs, instantly but in her case with a bullet in her heart.

Eden continued his speech which gave hope to all until everything changed. The night sky filled with dazzling lights. Those in the barn panicked. Terror brought fear. The exterior and then the interior of the barn flooded with bright light. Automatic weapons opened up killing men and animals. Calling it a blood bath was accurate.

Eden and Rousseau hit the floor of the barn. They survived as bullets smashed through and into everything.

'Which way?' yelled Eden, spitting straw.

'They're everywhere,' shouted his French comrade.

'In with the animals,' shouted Eden and set off crawling. The wretched beasts were in turmoil, their cries of panic, fear and pain went unheeded. The SOE agents used them as protection.

In fear of bullets, and now being trampled by terrified cows, Eden held his fire. If the enemy received fire, they would see his position and their superior numbers and weapons would saturate it with flying metal. A few of the locals, those injured but still alive, fired sporadically. But this one-sided battle would only end one way.

Rousseau lay on the straw struggling to use his radio. A cow whacked him with its tail. He transmitted. He sent his code word, his ID. Then he sent the word *Ambush,* and then the word *Dead.*

His final word accurately described his condition as bullets smashed the side of the barn against which animals were penned. This time a human protected an animal. A cow survived as Rousseau shielded the beast, taking fire to the Frenchman's torso and head.

Eden knew he faced a helpless task and didn't fancy dying clutching an unfired weapon. Trouble being he couldn't see the enemy. He could see gunfire flashes and fired at them.

He leapt out of the animal pen, snatched a rifle from beside a dead Resistance fighter, and flattened himself against bales of hay; concrete they were not. All firing stopped. Apart from the moaning from injured humans and the awful, distressful cries of the wounded beasts, an eerie silence settled on the farm.

The slaughter seemed over and Eden's fear now became hate; self-hate for being alive. He heard shouted orders, in French, but the voice contained a Germanic tone and accent.

Eden checked his revolver. There were three rounds left. He would kill before they killed him. Footsteps sounded and stopped. Someone was checking the carnage. Why? Prisoners are a burden. Kill them all.

The Englishman saw the intruders and flattened himself deeper into the straw. A Vichy officer sloshed petrol around the barn. A Gestapo agent, holding a gun, spotted something.

'Radio,' he cried and stepped towards it. A movement caught his attention and he turned to see Eden lying still with a face of death, but pointing his Enfield No. 2 revolver. Eden fired and the Gestapo agent fell, onto soft straw as it happened, but with a slug in his guts, the fall became the least of his worries. He suffered serious pain.

The Vichy officer saw what happened, dumped the can, dropped his lit cigarette and fled.

Eden swung, fired and missed. One shot left.

The cigarette ignited the petrol-soaked straw, the flames kicked up their heels, and soon the barn needed to escape. It couldn't. The SOE agents and their comrades were massacred. Eden stared hard at his enemy, the Gestapo officer. Their eyes met. The flames lost all control. They were closer to Fritz than Tommy. Both were about to die, with the loser having the last laugh.

Eden waited as the flames raced towards the Gestapo officer. His face screamed fear. Being burnt alive seemed appropriate for one of the black-coated warriors from Prinz-Albrecht-Straße in Berlin.

The screams from Fritz were loud and clear. His leather boots gave off a pungent smell. The last thing he saw was his sworn enemy, David Eden, raising his revolver and firing the last bullet into his own head. The fire did nothing to hurt David Eden. Fritz suffered mightily.

SOE HQ, Baker Street, London

Buckmaster worked long into the night; a normal routine for him. Tonight he felt dog tired when a radio operator entered.

'You must see this, sir.' Buckmaster needed to but didn't want to.

When Eden and Rousseau paddled away from the sub near Antibes, its captain radioed London, and Buckmaster knew his agents departed the sub safely. When they reached the safe house, Rousseau sent the pre-arranged signal, meaning they were at their correct location. But then, an hour later came Rousseau's last message.

'No,' cried Buckmaster, his scream of frustration grabbing attention elsewhere in the building. Vera Atkins and Jermain Attard arrived in haste.

The radio operator shared the message. The others felt sick.

'They planned to have everyone at that safe house,' said Atkins.

'Everyone,' whispered Buckmaster unable to believe the disaster.

'Does it mean they 'ave all been killed?' asked Jermain.

Buckmaster shook. 'This can't be true; it has to be a mistake.'

Atkins kept calm. 'If it's true, Maurice, we have a serious problem.'

Jermaine disagreed. 'Not necessarily. The agents could 'ave been seen landing on the beach and followed.'

Buckmaster wanted to vomit. For some time he pondered the possibility of a leak here at home. Now he was sure it was true. 'Someone in the SOE knows our moves and informs the enemy in France.'

'Or Berlin,' added Atkins.

'Or wherever,' shouted Buckmaster. 'My God, there is a traitor here in Baker Street.'

Chapter 33

The Special Operations Executive HQ, London

64 Baker Street became an important SOE building, but as their staff numbers grew to 13,000 plus, many more locations were established in and outside London. Next morning, Jean and Louise met at the entrance to the Baker Street Tube and headed across the busy street.

'Be prepared to play the long game, Holle,' said Jean. 'And, as sad as it sounds, be prepared to fail.' A limping Louise glanced at her companion. 'The traitor may be dead, may have left, or be too clever even for you.'

Louise worried. *So much for encouragement.*

They entered the building, explained their appointment with Mrs Merle McAdam, had their papers examined, and were escorted to the basement. The collector of waifs and strays was sorting tea-towels, and greeted the new arrivals in the, in *her* kitchen.

'Good morning ladies and welcome to the heart of the SOE.'

Most people being introduced to a female called Holle would naturally think Holly, which is exactly how Merle reacted. 'You're very welcome Holly and I'm sure you'll like working here. Let me take your coat.'

Jean spoke to Louise. 'I'll leave you, Holle. Good luck and I'll be in touch.' She gave Louise and Merle a warm smile. 'Bye.'

Jean left and Merle took over. 'Right then, Holly, let's give you a tour of our hidey-hole, and then get you settled in.'

Off they went visiting various rooms. Up a flight of stairs and along a corridor, they entered a typing pool where several women tapped away. 'Good morning, ladies. This is Holly. She'll be helping me although I'm sure if you need any messages taken, she's your girl.'

Louise smiled at the women, all of whom greeted the new girl. In the corridor, they bumped into a woman with a scarf over her hair and the biggest overall in England. She grasped a cleaning rag in both hands, and had an unlit roll-your-own cigarette between her lips.

'Morning Flo, this is Holly.'

'Hey?' asked Flo, the deaf as a post cleaner.

'Good morning,' said Louise in as loud a voice as she dared.

Merle took off with Louise following. They walked along the corridor when a door opened and a woman stepped out of an office. Tall, striking and dressed beautifully in a smart suit, Louise knew Vera Atkins well, had spent time in her office during Louise's early SOE days, and now Louise's stomach started to play war games. Her first test began.

'Good morning, Miss Atkins,' said Merle. 'This is a new girl, Holly Fontaine. Holly this is Miss Atkins.'

Vera examined Louise and something pinged in the back of her brain. 'Good morning, Holly. Welcome to the SOE.'

Louise took the say-as-little-as-possible approach and spoke in a soft and timid voice. 'Thank you, Miss Atkins.'

Vera picked up on her accent. 'Oh, you are French?'

'Belgian, Miss, but I 'ave lived 'ere since I was a little girl.'

Vera replied in French. 'And how is your French?'

Louise replied in kind and pretended to assume Vera was English. 'It is good, I hope, although in England I speak mainly in your tongue.'

Vera replied in English. 'Not in Romanian you don't. Now I hope your arrival brings us good luck, Mademoiselle. We heard terrible news last night. Do carry on.' She headed off expelling cigarette smoke. Merle and Louise exchanged glances and Merle shrugged.

'They tell me nothing but I hear gossip from time to time. My guess is an agent has been captured or killed in France.'

Louise thought. *If true, is the mole behind it?*

Merle led Louise back to her domain. 'With your accent I should have known you might speak French. The French section is always after good translators. You might be more use to the people upstairs. Anyway, let's get you familiar with our world.'

After learning the ropes of the lower levels at 64 Baker Street, Louise enjoyed a cup of tea with Merle. 'So tell me your life story,' said the elderly woman, and Louise, pretending to be Holle, did.

Merle's heart of gold beat faster, and with Holle's sad story of parents and grandparents dying, and her only sibling living under the Nazi jackboot across the Channel, the kindhearted Merle had to help.

'I'll tell the people upstairs about your French skills. As much as I'd like to keep you, I'm sure they can make better use of your talents.'

Wonderful warmth flowed through Louise's veins. The SOE gave her a job, she worked with the friendliest lady in London, and now had prospects of working in important translation work meaning she would be close to the bigwigs.

Then reality kicked in. She knew Rome wasn't built in a day, and patience would indeed be a virtue.

For the rest of her first day, she followed and helped Merle which became a worry for Louise. Merle performed dead boring tasks which offered Louise little opportunity to tackle her investigation. And she worked floors below where SOE messages were sent and received. True, Jean told her to play the long game, but Louise knew waiting for something to happen may never produce a result, and if the mole continued to perform treasonous acts, more agents and their allies and families were in danger of being captured, tortured and killed.

She wracked her brains and came up with precisely nothing.

Manchester Arms Public House, Baker Street

Known as the Green Pub, it became a regular watering hole for SOE staff after a hard day's work. They worked long hours under trying conditions, and a pint and a laugh were good for morale.

Louise survived her first day, but survival didn't help. To eliminate the impossible, she needed to find the possible. Who sent messages to France? Who received them? Who enjoyed access to confidential information? Stuck in the kitchen with the wonderful Merle would not a traitor find.

'You've done a wonderful job on your first day, Holly,' said Merle. 'Tomorrow I'll go and tell the folk upstairs about your French. Okay?'

'Thank you, Missus McAdam, you're most kind.'

'Not at all; now off you go and I'll see you in the morning.'

'Bye,' said Louise and headed for the door. As she went to open it, someone came through and they almost collided. Apologies all round.

'Sorry, love, I'm Dora from the Typing Pool. A few of the girls are going for a drink in the Arms. We thought you might like to join us.'

'Oh,' said Louise playing shy but feeling excited. 'Thank you; you're most kind.'

'You sound like a Frenchie.'

'I speak French but I am from Belgium.'

'Good for you. Now follow me.'

And so Louise met four of the women who worked in the typing pool. They wanted to know what she did before she arrived at Baker Street, and how she came to be employed in the SOE. But much more, they wanted to know if she had a boyfriend at home, and if said boyfriend had a brother. Two would be better and preferably single.

'As you must know, Holly,' said Lucille, there's a major shortage of fellas with a war on, so if you've got any going spare ...' She indicated with her head. 'Shove 'em over this way.'

The other women laughed and Louise joined in. As they laughed, a handsome gent, one Jermain Attard, approached.

'Oh no, here's trouble,' said Daphne.

'Bonsoir, ladies,' smiled the gent.

'Bonsoir, Monsieur,' said the four ladies from the typing pool with a hint of sensuality.

Dora warned him with false seriousness. 'You'd better watch out, Monsieur, our new girl 'ere speaks your lingo.'

He admired the blushing new team member. 'Ah,' said the smiling officer who kissed Louise's hand. He introduced himself and charmed his way through a few French compliments.

Louise explained in French. 'Not France, Monsieur, Belgium.'

'Well wherever, Mademoiselle, your French is excellent. Come and see me tomorrow; Room 42.'

He flashed a smile and the other women all made the same "Oooh" sound. Louise tried hard to blush more while inside her heart purred.

Maida Vale, London

She reached her flat hoping to find Jean or Henry loitering in the vicinity. Neither arrived. She had memorized Henry's number, she assumed a work number, but with little to report, stayed in and retired early.

Next morning she used her newly-acquired pass, and found Merle already hard at work. 'Well, you're a fast worker,' said her boss.

'Good morning,' replied Louise, thinking the comment referred to her punctual arrival.

'Monsieur Attard popped his head in not five minutes ago asking, "Where is the young woman from Belgium? Tell 'er to come to my room immediately".' Merle's pathetic French accent played with the word *immediately*.

'Goodness,' said Louise in shock as her heart went straight from walking to running. 'Did he tell you 'is room number?'

Merle forgot. 'He probably did but I'm getting forgetful. Ask when you get there.'

'I guess it is because I speak French,' said Louise, turning to leave. 'I will return as soon as possible.'

Working hard at breathing normally and limping lightly, she headed upstairs. No need to ask directions. She knew the upper floors well. She headed towards Room 42 then died.

Out from his office popped one Maurice Buckmaster, the man who interviewed, tested, advised, and sent her on various tasks; the man who informed her of her success in joining the SOE. She kept limping, definitely avoided eye contact, and kept going. She passed the senior officer but stopped when he spoke.

'Hey! Wait!' She froze and didn't turn because he came back to her and stared. 'Who are you and what are you doing here?'

'Miss Holle Fontaine, sir, I work with Missus McAdam in the kitchen but 'ave been requested to see Monsieur Attard in Room 42.'

Buckmaster showed surprise. 'Show me your ID.' No please involved. Louise played it by the book. Buckmaster seemed less interested in her papers than in her. He glanced at her ID, but scrutinized her face.' Her worries multiplied. 'I've seen you before.'

Louise played her obsequious card. 'I do not think so, sir.'

'Where did you live in Paris?'

'I am from Belgium, sir. I 'ave never been to Paris.'

Louise was sure Buckmaster knew who she was, but pretended not to before unmasking her. A door opened and Jermain Attard poked his head around the frame.

'There you are,' he smiled. 'I thought I 'eard your dulcet tones.'

Buckmaster hesitated, studied his colleague and then Louise. 'Carry on,' he said and walked away. She headed to Room 42.

Attard spoke entirely in French. He took a real interest in Louise. He found her limp appealing. He found *her* appealing. 'Take a seat, Mademoiselle.' She did. 'Why do you wear spectacles? You are much more attractive without them.'

'Because I am short-sighted, Monsieur, and I 'ope you have not asked me to your office to discuss my appearance.'

He smiled. 'But I am French, Mademoiselle. What did you expect?' She gave the weakest of smiles. He handed her a document in French. 'Please recite this to me in English.'

She did, perfectly; he took back the document, and spoke in English.

'You are exceptional, Mademoiselle. 'ow would you like to perform translation work for me?'

Louise worked hard not to seem enthusiastic when inside her heart fairly raced. From kitchen to SOE HQ in two days could not have been better. She continued to push the meek and mild line.

'If you think I am capable, Monsieur, I would be 'appy to be of service.'

'Good, you can start tomorrow. Report to me at 0800 hours.' He paused. 'I mean 8 o'clock in the morning. Comprendre?'

'Oui, Monsieur.' *I have a rough idea,* she thought, smiled to herself and left.

Chapter 34

The Special Operations Executive HQ, London

Royston Black tapped on his boss Buckmaster's door and entered. 'A word, old man,' said the visitor taking a seat without being asked. Buckmaster knew this wasn't a chat about golf.

'What's up?'

'Attard.' Black paused wanting to discover his colleague's response to the name.

'What about him?'

'I don't trust him.'

Buckmaster tossed his pencil on the desk, showing interest. 'What's happened?'

'I don't think I ever told you we were at the Sorbonne together, studying different subjects, but we mixed in the same social circles. We all thought him strange back then and now, what he says and does in here, well I don't think he's changed.'

Buckmaster worried. 'What sort of strange?'

Black shrugged. 'His views on politics and sex for starters.'

Buckmaster showed little interest. 'He's French so sex is a given, but what about his politics?'

'You know he's already chatting up the kitchen staff.'

Again Buckmaster was unimpressed. 'She speaks French.'

'His politics are weird. He hated Communists, and despised the army, the future De Gaulle and company. His main concern involved a return to the aristocracy.'

'What?' Buckmaster didn't believe Black. 'You're joking.'

'He claimed the revolution destroyed France. He wants to bring back the Monarchy, and death to the lower classes and all who rebel.'

Buckmaster sniffed. 'All very interesting, old man, but what's it got to do with the SOE, and finding missing agents?'

'Okay, nothing at first glance, but what if it's a foundation for his real ambition? What if the leaks from here are from someone who thinks democracy is not the best and only thing worth fighting for?'

Buckmaster pondered Black's comments.

'You're drawing a long bow there, old man. Haven't you got enough work to do? The man's eccentric, yes, but a traitor ...' Buckmaster shook his head. 'I can't see it.'

'Oakey dokey,' said Black heading for the door. Before opening it, he turned and asked a question. 'Do you have any objection to me digging a little deeper?'

His boss waved. 'Just don't let it interfere with your work.'

Louise returned to the kitchen and waited for Merle to start quizzing her. She didn't. *Surely she must want to know what happened.*

'I'm back,' said Louise. 'And I have news, Missus McAdam.'

'So do I,' said Merle stopping Louise in her tracks.

She paused, and as her boss didn't continue, Louise did. 'Monsieur Attard 'as asked me to 'elp with translation work.'

'Well, who's a busy little bee then?' said Merle with a tinge of anger. She'd offered to take in another stray, and help the lass get back on her feet, and instead of thanks and recognition, all Merle gets is everyone else pinching the person in question.

Louise didn't understand. 'I'm sorry, Madame, I don't follow.'

'Young Dora from the typing pool popped in and wants you to accompany her to the Museum; says you need to know the routine in case you get asked to do the job in the future.'

'The museum?' asked Louise confused. 'I don't understand.'

'Don't ask me, I only work here. Ask Dora in Typing.' Louise hesitated. 'Well off you go then, chop chop.' She picked up a small parcel. 'Oh, and here are the sandwiches.'

Louise didn't need to act to show a face of gratitude and confusion. She smiled at Merle, grabbed her coat, and the sandwiches, and left.

'Don't mind me,' said Merle the Miserable. 'I only work here.'

Louise and Dora waited on the Underground platform for the next train. Dora couldn't wait to hear Louise's news. Louise couldn't wait for more details on this, her latest assignment.

Dora spoke first. 'Well come on, Holly, what happened with the gorgeous Frenchman? And don't tell me he didn't turn on the charm because I won't believe you.'

Louise forced a half smile. 'Nothing 'appened. I was asked to translate a report, and then 'e said there might be more work for me in the future.'

'In the future? What's that when it's at home?'

'I 'ave to report at 8 o'clock tomorrow morning.'

'Whoa,' cried Dora. 'Who's a lucky girl then?'

'I think you're reading far too much into what is a simple translating job. You'll probably 'ave to type what I transcribe.'

Dora's wish for gossip hit the buffers.

Louise switched topics. 'So why are we taking the Tube?'

Dora explained about the SOE boffins making gadgets while working in the British Museum, the Natural History one. She tapped her bag. 'These are financial reports covering their budget. I have to take them every week to make sure they don't overspend. But if the girls in Typing are flat out, our boss, Miss Iron Drawers, said you should know the routine. And here we are.'

'And the sandwiches?'

'Oh, Merle makes them for the boffins.'

The train arrived and they headed off to South Kensington.

British Museum of Natural History

Louise visited the British Museum as a child. This visit she made as an SOE agent in disguise, trying to discover a traitor within the ranks of her colleagues. Dora didn't fit the traitor profile.

They entered the impressive Victorian building with its welcoming facade. An exhibit made Louise stop and stare. Dora, who'd seen them a hundred times with zero interest in science—she preferred scientists, male—gave Louise the hurry up.

'Come on, Holly, no time for day dreaming.'

Deeper into the museum they went until Dora took a turn and walked along a corridor. Louise tried to remember signposts within a building in case of an escape, and to remember possible hiding places, although she couldn't imagine a reason why she would want or need to hide in the British Museum.

Dora knocked on a large door. 'Always knock,' she said, 'and never enter without permission.'

'Why?' asked Louise when the sign on the door said *Records*.

'You don't ask questions, Holly; you follow orders,' said Dora who jumped when the door opened.

'Ah, the damsel from the Deep,' said a balding, short gent wearing a brightly-coloured bowtie to match his complexion. He studied Louise. '*Two* damsels,' he observed.

'This is Holly, Mister Henderson,' said Dora. Then with a twinkle in her eye said, 'She's a new addition to the SOE downstairs department where all the *real* work is done.'

'How do you do, Holly? Come in, come in.'

They did and Louise gasped. The exhibits were now in storage and in their place were benches surrounded by men, in army shirts and trousers, working on all manner of tasks—measuring, weighing, sawing, hammering, and designing. Untidy best described the place with tools, paint tins and spills aplenty scattered higgledy-piggledy. If some experiment worked, a rousing cheer was heard.

Dora gave Mr Henderson the papers and the sandwiches.

'Take your friend on a tour,' he said, and the women left.

Louise felt privileged and excited. This SOE operation was unknown to most of the military let alone millions of civilians. In different rooms, different projects were in various stages of development. Dora flirted with a couple of the men while Louise wandered around studying items, some of which reminded her of things she once used in training or in the field. Many were new to her.

She watched one man attempting to bend a piece of metal around a box. His hand slipped and a splinter pushed into his flesh. He swore then turned to see Louise behind him.

Wringing his hand, he apologised. 'I'm sorry, Miss. I didn't know you were there.'

'You 'ave a tricky job to perform I think,' smiled Louise, although inside she trembled. She hoped her French accent held firm.

He worried because of what he said, and watched the young woman who seemed none the wiser. He'd made a mistake. She discovered something vital, and began asking questions in her mind.

Before Louise could speak again, a man entered and called. 'Everyone go to Workshop 1. The Royals are here in five. Move!'

Louise and Dora were swept up in the mass movement. 'What's happening?' whispered Louise almost forgetting to limp.

'We're going to meet the King and Queen,' replied Dora. They entered Workshop Number 1 where all activity stopped.

'Line up in two rows facing inwards either side,' yelled Mr Henderson. Louise panicked. *But the Royals know me.*

Louise and Dora finished at the end of one line. The secret SOE agent worried more than ever. She'd fooled anyone who knew her at Baker Street. Could she now fool the King and Queen of England having met them in person after performing for their Majesties in *Cinderella?* As she moved closer to finding the traitor, would she be undone when a Royal said, 'Oh, hello Cinders'?

Mr Henderson barked further orders. 'Don't faint, fall over or feel you need to chat. Speak only when spoken to. Are we clear?' The half-hearted reply made him speak again, louder. 'Are we clear?'

Back came the whispered mass voices. 'Yes, clear.'

Silence filled the room. A few heads tried to glimpse the regal couple who were yet to enter. Then it happened.

King George V1 and Queen Elizabeth arrived with Hendo bowing and scraping all the way to his bootstraps. Down the first line went their Majesties. They chatted with selected persons who, later, would talk about the occasion forever. Turbulence began in Louise's waters.

The official party crossed to the second line, and moved ever closer to the typist and SOE sandwich carrier. Louise had confidence in her clothes, hair colour, specs and limp, believing she would survive.

Not my limp! I'm standing still.

Then the Windsors were upon them and Dora was the first to be quizzed. 'And what do you do?' asked the Queen.

'I'm in the Typing Pool, Your Majesty.'

The King stopped in front of Louise. A puzzled expression came over his face and he almost stuttered. 'Good morning,' he said. Louise froze. *He knows me.* The Queen turned back and smiled.

'Let me guess,' said Her Majesty, 'you work in the kitchen.'

Louise curtsied and remained with head bowed as the official party headed off to encourage others engaged in vital war work. As they left, polite applause sent them on their way.

Staff broke up, a hubbub bubbled, and Dora stared at Louise. The typist's eyeballs imitated organ stops. 'The Queen is psychic.'

Louise laughed off the claim, but wondered if they spotted Cinders and realised she must be working undercover. *What on Earth made me think that? The Royals meet huge numbers of their subjects.*

All the way back to Baker Street, Dora couldn't stop chatting. Louise had something else on her mind, and pondered what she saw and heard in the Museum. Did she have a lead on the mole?

That pub in Baker Street

Dora insisted on Louise joining the women in the Green Pub after work. Louise didn't fancy it, but felt fantastic when she did.

Dora rabbited on about the Royal visit. Louise spotted two men; her charming boss, the Frenchman Jermain Attard, and his drinking buddy, the boffin in the Museum who swore when he hurt his hand. His name was Harry Williams, a former movie special-effects man. Louise watched them without making it obvious. These two seemed good pals. They spoke with animation and on the quiet.

Louise wanted to leave. The typing gals were up for a chat, a drink, and even a visit to a show or a dance. The latter posed a problem because of a lack of half-decent chaps or rather any chaps full stop.

Louise pleaded a headache and left. Jermain saw her at the last moment and called, but she pretended not to hear him and fled.

In a dark and misty Baker Street, apologetic rain fell as Louise settled in a shop doorway. No problem with being spotted by street lights during the blackout. She pulled her hat and coat in close and waited. She prayed, well, hoped for a speedy arrival.

It happened when Williams and Attard came out of the pub, shook hands and went in opposite directions. Now her following skills were required. Tail that boffin.

He disappeared into the Tube, and Louise followed. Forget the limp. She needed all the fitness she could manage. Williams knew where he was going, and Louise waited in the tunnel entrance until he boarded the train. She then skipped to hop aboard another carriage and sat facing him behind a newspaper, carried for such a purpose.

She would have been on this train anyway. On the Bakerloo Line, they headed north towards Maida Vale.

Chapter 35

Kilburn, North London

Louise smiled. It would be too much of a coincidence to have her suspect live in Maida Vale. If so, she could finish her observation and stroll home for an early night. But no, he didn't exit at Louise's Tube station but rather the next one, Kilburn Park. She saw him move and waited till he passed her carriage, then hopped up and jumped out as the doors were closing.

She slipped in behind fellow passengers using them as cover to check on her target.

The weather remained lousy. Persistent rain and darkened streets helped anyone following anyone. The boffin walked north along the Kilburn High Road, head down, and the sooner home the better.

He turned left into Victoria Road. Few folk were out and Louise dropped further back to be safe. When she turned the corner, her quarry was ahead, and about to climb the steps to a front door of a three-storey attached block of flats. These peas-in-a-pod apartments stretched as far as the eye could see.

The man didn't use a key to enter the first door, but Louise reckoned he'd need a key to enter the ground floor flat, the two above and even the one in the basement.

She sheltered under a tree on the other side of the road and watched. Everyone covered their windows with curtains or blinds, but Louise saw a chink of light appear in the front room of the flat on the first floor. Did this reveal the relevant flat? And if so, what else? Nothing else and it might mean nothing at all. The tree gave her some shelter so she drew her coat closer and settled in to wait.

Not for long though as her target reappeared, skipped down the steps and headed back the way he came. Strange. She watched him turn into the Kilburn High Road. It was decision time. She crossed the road, climbed the steps, and opened the unlocked front door.

Inside on her left she saw a door to the ground floor flat with stairs to the upper floors straight ahead. She listened and heard nothing.

Up the stairs she went hoping noisy creaks were not in fashion. She reached the first landing. In front of her were more stairs heading skywards, but a hard left turn along a landing led to the front door of the flat where she reckoned the boffin paid a short visit.

She crept along the landing. Now the damn creaks kicked in. *Why here and not on the stairs?* Louise froze. Slowly, gingerly she moved towards the front door. She reached it taking long, deep breaths.

A thin strip of light peeked from under the door. Pressing her ear to said door, she listened. Louise heard nothing but then gasped as a familiar sound leaked out. Could it be someone sending Morse?

It *was* Morse. She picked up letters but the faint quality of sound made it difficult. Her heart kick started. Questions filled her mind.

I've followed a man I suspect to a house from which I've heard Morse code. Is this the cell of the SOE mole?

She needed advice, help more like. What would happen if she knocked on the door? *I need to know who is in this flat and what they're doing. But how can I discover those things?* The Morse sounds stopped. Louise didn't fancy going back into the street and waiting in the rain for fortune to favour her. It was bite the bullet time. She knocked.

It wasn't loud or demanding, more gentle and polite. The strip of light under the door vanished. She heard footsteps inside, and stepped back ready to defend herself when a voice gave her a fright.

'Hello, hello, and who have we got here?'

Louise turned to see the person at the top of the landing. Harry Williams stood holding a loaf of bread and a bottle of milk.

Before she could recover from his shock return, the door opened and a curious Mr Morse appeared in the darkened doorway.

'Grab her,' hissed Williams, and the occupant dragged Louise inside. With her unarmed combat skills, she knew how to escape the grasp, but Williams rushed forward and ruined a good pint of milk.

As the lights in the flat were put out, so too were Louise's. She collapsed and when she came to, her head throbbed, she had milk down the inside and outside of her coat, and her hands were tied tight behind her back.

'She's coming round,' said Mr Morse.

Williams pulled up a chair and sat facing Louise, slumped on the floor with her back against the settee. 'So then, what have you got to say for yourself, young lady?'

She lost her French accent and spoke in English as Louise Wellesley. 'I could ask you the same question, Mein Herr.'

Williams smiled. He liked her pluck but possessed a sociopath's supply of empathy, and a Nazi-inspired vision of a German victory. 'I'll leave my friend here to help you find eternal rest, but am curious as to how you know about my German ancestry and political beliefs.'

'If I tell you, will I die quickly?'

'You're not from the typing pool like that idiotic woman with you today. Am I correct?'

'You gave yourself away at the Museum.'

He understood and nodded. 'Ah, when I swore.'

'If you said *shit* I would have ignored you, but *scheisse*; now that word gave me a start.'

'Sprechen Sie Deutsch?' he asked.

'Ein bisschen,' she replied.

Mr Morse grew impatient. 'What's happening? I need to send another message.'

Louise tried a game of bluff. 'I know who gives you the intelligence from Baker Street.'

'Is that so?' said Williams, impressed.

'And how you are given the information.'

'I don't believe you.' She smiled at him. 'Well come on, tell me.'

'I saw you in the Green Pub tonight with your contact.'

She was testing him and it worked. He smiled at her. She noted his reaction which told her what she wanted to know. If only she could survive to tell the world what she now knew.

Williams snapped at his comrade. 'I'm late. Get rid of her.'

'How?' asked Morse.

Williams stopped at the door. 'Make it appear as a nasty rape and murder. Dump the body in a lane.' He smirked at Louise. 'Guten Abend, Fräulein,' he said and left.

Chapter 36

Kilburn, North London

Mr Morse needed to make a decision. Killing the woman would be easy, but getting her downstairs, into an alley, and interfered with would take a bit of doing. He reckoned gagging her, knocking her out again, and carrying her downstairs would be best.

He found cleaning rags and tied a gag. Louise found the taste revolting, like eating rotten fruit. She used the give-up routine; her head slumped on her chest. Morse decided she'd fainted. He grunted, crouched behind her, and lifted. With her back facing him, she slumped forward. Holding her up, he shuffled his way around her then, facing her, bent to throw her over his shoulder. For an SOE agent trained in hand to hand combat, Louise gratefully accepted this schoolboy error. In this case her hand to hand routine became knee to head. He bent, she thrust her knee and, for him, it was lights out.

Her brutal thrust caught the radio operator beneath his chin. His teeth severed the tip of his tongue, and the blood exploding in his mouth brought on the panic of drowning. It's hard to scream with massive pain and blood in your mouth. If you open your mouth to yell, you give out a torrent of blood and the tip of your tongue. In serious trouble, Herr Morse panicked.

Louise left him and searched the kitchen. She found a knife, and jammed it in a cutlery drawer, pushing the drawer shut with her hip. By leaning against the drawer, she moved her tied hands around and cut. She struggled but Morse struggled more.

She finally freed her hands, grabbed the knife, and put the radio operator out of his shocking distress.

Making as little sound as possible, she left the flat, ran to the Tube station and caught the next southbound train. She knew her destination, and wondered if she should call for help. Time became vitally important. She must strike while the traitor was hot.

The building lay dark and silent. She worked her way around the side and saw a sliver of light from a window with blinds. The nearby door received a gentle knocking. Footsteps sounded then a voice she didn't know.

'The Museum is closed.'

She spoke as Holle. 'Good evening. My name is 'olle Fontaine. I work at 64 Baker Street. When I delivered some papers today, I left my bag in the main workshop. Please, I will be only one minute.'

A boffin opened the door. 'I shouldn't do this but you have a kind face,' he said.

'Thank you so much,' said Louise and entered.

'There,' said the scientist, pointing.

She knew where to go and hoped like hell it would be worth it. Opening the door to the large workshop, she saw six men working on an unusual, exploding device. They all stopped and stared. The scientist who opened the door arrived.

'She's from Baker Street and left her bag behind.'

The lie got her inside and when she spotted Harry Williams she sensed elation. He didn't and hit the panic button. He moved about.

He pointed and shouted. 'Look out! She's a spy, a double agent. She wants to kill us all!'

The other scientists were shocked and froze. Williams grabbed the device they were developing, and raised it as if to throw. Now the others came alive, panicked and screamed, 'No! That's the model with nitroglycerine; you'll kill us all!'

Louise kept moving forward. She craved a firearm. Although unarmed, Williams decided his cover was blown and escape his best, his only option. He gently put down the device, turned and ran. His shock continued. He'd left the bound and bashed woman in Kilburn. Now she turns up in South Kensington alive and dangerous. She was good. He needed an escape route.

As she chased him, Louise thought grabbing an ancient bone as a weapon might not go down well with the authorities. They entered the Museum proper. Giant ancient shapes stared at her through the pitch black conditions. She could hear Williams but not see him.

He stopped moving which left her flying blind. As Louise, she lied with a calm tone. 'The Police, the Army and the SOE are all on their way, Mein Herr. Come quietly and you'll avoid any bloodshed.'

She stopped moving hoping Williams would give himself away.

'I know you aren't the only traitor. We want the source of the SOE leaks. Who is giving you the data?' More silence. 'I know how you receive the details. I saw the greaseproof paper on your workbench.'

He hated the woman whose clever skills brought him undone—the bitch. He slipped out of his shoes, ducked, and tip-toed around the edge of the room. His whereabouts were a mystery to her. He aimed for a window which he knew opened to a darkened lane.

He climbed onto the window ledge. Heavy curtains covered the glass. The top part of the window was a foot above his head. He reached up.

'If you surrender, Mein Herr, you will be treated with respect.'

He felt for the latch between the curtains. The window opened and made a slight sound. Other sounds from a London night were heard. Louise peered through the blackness in the direction of the sound. Harry's head and shoulders were out of the window. He needed one more push. He went for it and failed. His socks slipped on the glass, and then a loud scream with a strange crashing sound filled the room.

The other scientists arrived and a light came on. What a sight they discovered. Harry Williams, in pushing for a final escape, slipped and fell backwards landing on the frame of a Diplodocus carnegii. The giant dinosaur skeleton would, in time, be repaired; not so Harry. Skewered on a bone, he lay there, as dead as the exhibit.

Boffins gathered around paying as much attention to the damage to the skeleton as to their colleague's demise.

'Close this room and touch nothing.' The men stared at this slip of a girl giving orders as if she was some high-ranking officer. 'Do it,' she snapped, and they did. She headed for the exit. 'Nobody in or out.'

Louise ran into the London night desperate to find a taxi. A bus would do but she faced an emergency. She saw nothing and no-one so ran. It was more than 3 miles to Baker Street and she needed an immediate closure. A taxi headed towards her. She ran onto the road, waving and forcing it to stop. She confronted the driver.

'You got a death wish, lady?' asked the cabbie.

'64 Baker Street,' she puffed, opening the passenger door. 'This is an emergency. Please feel free to break the road rules.'

The cabbie liked her line of thinking and joined the game. In Baker Street, she jumped from the cab, thrusting too much money at the driver, before fleeing into the building.

SOE HQ, Baker Street

'Hey, hey, hey,' barked a retired military man, working as a security officer. 'Stop right there, young lady.' He stood defiant, blocking her.

Holle or Holly Fontaine vanished. Louise Wellesley entered the fray. 'I need to speak with Mister Buckmaster now. Is he here?'

'He's always here but you'll need to make an appointment.'

'This is an emergency. Please let me pass.'

He didn't like her attitude, this flibbertigibbet in a dress. Louise contemplated sitting the old boy on his tail but chose the subtle threat instead.

'When I make my report in person to the Prime Minister, I hope I can mention your excellent contribution in saving British lives. Now please, I must see Mister Buckmaster.'

The security guard wavered. 'I'll telephone. Wait there.' He rang and Buckmaster answered. 'Sorry to trouble you, sir, but there's a young woman in Reception says she wants to speak to you.'

'Who is she?'

The guard covered the mouthpiece. 'What's your name?'

Louise thought for few moments. 'Tell him it's Sister Claudine.'

The guard spoke to Buckmaster. 'Says her name is Sister Claudine.'

Buckmaster's face did a twist and scrunch combined. Incredible summed up his mindset. 'Who?'

'Sister Claudine, although she's wearing civvies, sir.'

'Tell him it's Louise Wellesley,' said Louise.

'Ah, she's given another name, sir; Louise Wellesley.'

Buckmaster covered the receiver, and announced the news to his colleagues. 'Sister Claudine's in Reception,' he gasped.

Vera Atkins, Jermain Attard and Royston Black copied their boss with faces to stop a clock.

'Put her on,' snapped Buckmaster to the guard who handed the phone to Louise.

'Good evening, sir,' she said.

He heard and recognised her voice. 'It *is* you. We were told you died in that plane disaster at Gibraltar.'

'Not true, sir, and I really must see you as a matter of urgency.'

'What? Oh, put the guard back on.' He was given the phone. 'Send her up here immediately,' barked Buckmaster.

Jermain headed for the door. 'I'll fetch her.' He left.

Buckmaster bellowed into the phone. 'No, keep her there.'

The guard gave birth to kittens. What in blue blazes is going on? He put down the phone.

'Well?' asked Louise losing patience and considering the trip-an-old-man routine.

'Ah, you're to remain here.'

'I don't believe you,' she said and took off. She outmaneuvered the former sergeant-major, and ran for the stairs. Halfway up she met Jermain Attard who stared in disbelief. This wasn't Louise Wellesley. This was the limping, French-speaking tea-lady from Belgium, the young woman he used as a translator and planned to seduce.

'Mademoiselle Wellesley?' he muttered in disbelief. This woman was exactly like Honey, no Holly, spelt Holle. He gasped when she spoke flawless English.

'Good evening, sir. I need to see Colonel Buckmaster to make my report. Is he available?'

The normally suave Frenchman struggled to believe her remarks, her appearance, and re-appearance, and muttered.

'Well, yes. Please follow me.'

Upstairs, Buckmaster paced the room. Atkins and Black exchanged glances. They worried their boss didn't always handle a crisis well, and this shaped as being a cracker. He thought aloud.

'How did she survive? Escape? Why haven't we heard about her time in France?'

'Relax, old man,' said Black. 'Look, I'll check our Parisian pal has found the visitor.'

Black was gone before anyone could say anything. Buckmaster turned to Atkins who shrugged. A minute later they heard voices and Black entered. 'She's here and all the way via Belgium.'

Louise and Jermain entered and the shocks continued. Buckmaster and Atkins stared in disbelief. They'd both met and spoken with her here for days. All four SOE leaders were stunned.

Buckmaster muttered a welcome and offered Louise a seat. She spoke to a rapt audience of four.

'As you can see, sir,' she said removing her spectacles, 'I've been back a few days and joined the SOE as a French-speaking Belgian.'

Her audience veered towards the drooling stage.

'I performed this charade because in Lyon, I found an Englishman working for the Germans with a link to the SOE in London. The reason we have lost so many agents in France is due to a mole right here in Baker Street.'

A pin drop would have been louder than an exploding grenade.

'I've infiltrated the cell in London, and two of its members are dead. The third, who works here in Baker Street, is yet to be exposed.'

She paused and Buckmaster finally spoke.

'Do you know their identity?'

Louise nodded. 'I do.' They couldn't tell if she really knew, was bluffing, or solving the mystery as she went along. She explained.

'Details of agents landing in France are passed from here to a German working in the British Museum of Natural History, and then to a flat in Kilburn where a radio operator sends messages directly to the enemy in France.' Her words seemed unbelievable but her performance was impeccably believable.

Buckmaster mumbled. 'We lost two agents and several Resistance fighters and helpers in one ambush two nights ago.' He struggled to ask. 'Were they betrayed by someone here at Baker Street?'

Louise paused. Her drama training taught her this tactic. The tension kept rising. She nodded. 'I can't be sure but I believe so.'

Vera Atkins wanted proof. 'But how is the data sent from here?'

'Sandwiches,' said Louise and her answer knocked her previous claims for six. All four SOE officers were transfixed. She explained.

'Details of agents and their drops are written in code on greaseproof paper which encloses the sandwiches. The food is taken from the kitchen downstairs to the Abwehr controlled German spy working in the British Museum. He takes the details to a radio operator in Kilburn who sends messages to France or Berlin, and our agents are intercepted, tortured and executed.'

Her tale seemed fantastic, *was* fantastic, and left the others speechless. Finally Buckmaster spoke.

'And there is a traitor working for the SOE, here in this building?'

Louise created another pause and again nodded. She knew the identity of the mole but needed proof. Her pause became her bluff. It worked. Royston Black leapt at the door, ripped it open and fled.

While Buckmaster fiddled as Rome burned, Louise and Attard took off in pursuit. Atkins addressed her boss. 'Good luck in explaining all this to Mister Churchill.' He swallowed.

Royston Black supported Oswald Mosley in the 30s, although as a silent believer. His anti-Semitic fanaticism fueled his desire to see a Nazi flag flying above Buckingham Palace. His best way to achieve his goal would be to subvert those who sought to subvert the Germans.

He would often go up to the roof of 64 Baker Street for a smoke, although smoking didn't cross his mind right now as he burst out onto the roof.

He wasn't so much angry he'd been discovered, although it made his blood boil, but rather he couldn't accept being hung for treason. Those smug Jew-loving English aristocrats would make him swing.

'That's far enough, Herr Schwarz,' called Louise.

He turned and glared at her. Attard arrived and called. 'Come on Royston, let's be civil and talk this over like English gentlemen.'

That added a touch of black comedy with a Frenchman describing himself as an English gentleman.

Black hated them all, the English, the French, the Jews and especially women. Now he added a new name to his Hate List, himself.

He spat in their direction then turned and leapt into the London night. The cobbled Mews below stood empty, thankfully, and no-one volunteered to "pick up" his remains.

Back in Buckmaster's office, Louise gave a potted history of her recent French journey, her life as a nun, as a Resistance fighter, and finally as a guide in crossing the Pyrenees. The trio of SOE officers listened in silence and in awe.

'Do we know if there is a new contact in France?' asked Atkins.

Louise shook her head. 'If there is, they won't be getting intelligence from that Baker Street source anymore.'

After their praise, Louise asked for her debrief to take place later as she rather fancied a hot bath and a good night's sleep. Buckmaster had a car take her home. She staggered upstairs to find a visitor.

'So, who's the star of the show then?' asked big brother Henry.

They embraced. He took her key and let them into the flat.

'You must tell me what you do, Henry. I suspect you are much higher up the chain than I imagined.'

He laughed and made tea as she described the last few hours. He called from the kitchen. 'I telephoned Jean. She's on her way.'

'I can't believe what's happened,' she called back, luxuriating in her settee. 'If that scientist making props for the SOE had sworn in English and not German, I might never have found the cell.'

Henry came into the sitting room. 'Harry Williams is the German Hans Walter who came here years ago and became a highly successful technical director in the movie business. Your wonderful SOE saw his expertise and recruited him without seriously examining his past.'

The door knock announced another visitor. Henry let Jean in, and she and Louise hugged for a long time.

They drank tea and shared the cake Jean brought. Louise went through all the details answering questions from both her guests.

'Royston Black would pop into the kitchen and ask Merle to make sandwiches for the chaps in the Museum. I saw him scribble on the greaseproof paper. SOE agent movements were written in code. Dora from the Typing Pool carried the sandwiches with no idea they contained agent drop details. All she saw on the greaseproof paper was the name, Harry Williams.'

'Hans Walter,' said Henry. 'We've been watching him for a while.'

'Greaseproof paper is a proven way to smuggle details,' said Jean. 'My father received information from a wrongly-convicted prisoner in Scotland who hid notes on greaseproof paper in his mouth.'

Louise hesitated wanting Jean to explain her last remark. She didn't so Louise spoke.'

'Did you say your father?'

'Yes, he told me the greaseproof paper story years ago.'

Louise struggled, feeling the odd one out.

'She doesn't know,' said Henry.

'Oh, I'm so sorry, said Jean, 'I thought you knew.'

'Knew what?' asked Louise. Henry told her.

'Jean is the daughter of Sir Arthur Conan Doyle.'

They studied Louise who needed time to absorb the news. *No wonder she kept telling me how bloody Sherlock Holmes operated.*

Laughter and cake were perfect to celebrate Louise's triumph. About a month ago she parachuted into France and pretended to be a nun. Now, home with mighty milestones achieved, she couldn't stifle a yawn, and Jean and Henry knew Louise needed sleep.

'I'll be going,' said Jean, and hugged Louise. 'Congratulations on your brilliant sleuthing. My father would have been thrilled.'

Jean left and Henry gave his baby sister a hug.

'What's the latest with Eddie?' she asked.

'He's getting better, slowly, and will continue to do so now he has two women waiting on him hand and foot.'

Louise frowned. '*Two* women?'

'Missus C of course and now Mummy's moved back to Farnham.'

Louise recoiled. 'What?'

Henry frowned. 'Oh damn, I should have told you. Bit of sad news old girl. Sir Anthony has fallen off the perch.'

'What? When? Why didn't you tell me?'

'Last week but after we met, you seemed so busy, and I didn't want to interrupt your tales of derring-do.' Louise went quiet. 'Turned 92 last May, he did. Good age. At the funeral, I decided to tell Mummy about Eddie being injured. I think it tipped her over the edge.'

'What?' Louise thought the worst.

'About returning home to live I mean. Between Missus Crossley and Mummy, Eddie's being spoilt rotten.'

'And so he should be. I hope you didn't tell them about me.'

'What, and break the Official Secrets Act? I'll leave that decision to you, Miss Wellesley.'

'Thanks and that settles it. I'm off to Surrey in the morning.'

Henry reacted. 'But don't you have to report to the SOE?'

'That's a job for you, big brother. Tell them I've been called away on urgent family business. I'll phone them next week.'

'You cheeky little ...' He laughed, hugged her, and left.

Excited, Louise ran a bath. *Interrupt tales of derring-do, indeed.* But her real excitement came from the prospect of a family reunion.

On the train down to Surrey, memories flourished. Her big worry centered on being honest with her mother and Edmund because Henry had maintained the ruse about Louise still touring as an actress. She decided to play it by ear.

Walking from the station, the many butterflies in the Wellesley garden numbered fewer than the ones in her stomach. As usual, she walked around to the back garden. A single bark from Horatio gave her a burst of happiness. Then a squeal and a cry made her spin around. Edmund sat in a wheelchair being pushed by their mother.

The reunion wallowed in warmth and love and tears. After lunch they relaxed in the garden and reminisced. Louise couldn't bring herself to tell the truth about her wartime activities—the ones involving the Gestapo, Wehrmacht soldiers, Vichy police, traitors, and others. Edmund had lost his gruesome appearance, and Victoria seemed at peace as a widow again, and this time in the family home.

Louise related the Windsor Castle pantomime tale with no mention of a certain after-show adventure. Victoria delighted in hearing about her brilliant daughter performing for royalty.

The front door knocker sounded and the Wellesleys wondered who it might be. Regular visitors always came to the kitchen door.

'I'll go,' said Louise and trotted off around the garden. She approached the front door and stopped at the steps. The caller turned and both resident and visitor gasped.

'Miss Wellesley,' he said. 'I heard you were acting in Australia.'

'Doctor Curzon,' she replied. 'I heard you were practising in Sussex.'

Time stood still as both were unsure what to say. He came down the steps. 'I've called to see how your brother is getting on.'

'How kind. We're in the garden.'

He stood close to her; close enough to touch her, and found his heart begin to race as it once did in Cambridge in 1937 when they first met. She remembered how she so wanted to kiss him.

She took his arm. 'Come with me,' said Louise and smiled at him.

Together they walked around to the back garden where Horatio was the first to welcome the happy couple.

The Detective Joanna Best Mysteries

www.cenfoxbooks.com

Joanna Best is the youngest homicide detective in town. Smart, feisty and gorgeous, she's brilliant at cracking cases and rubbing people up the wrong way. Some jealous colleagues are desperate to undermine her. Certain criminals want her dead. Juggling a career with Victoria Police, having three men madly in love with her, and a strange family, Jo Best's adventures will drag you in. Her second banana is an Australian born Chinese IT guru who makes computers sing. Her best pal is a female 60ish police surgeon, a forensic genius and chocoholic.

I could not put this series down. The characters, plots, settings, kept me reading. I really liked the word comedy phrasing. A couple of characters I wanted to smack. **Amazon**

Sherlock Holmes

The great man is soon to retire. On his last night at Baker Street, the loyal landlady drops a bombshell. Holmes is staggered. Mrs Hudson has done what!? Sherlock Holmes never panics—until now. Dr Watson arrives and is stunned. It's their greatest challenge. Sir Arthur Conan Doyle is furious. A famous author turned WW1 counter-intelligence spy is on the case. *The Strand Magazine* smells a scoop. Inspector Lestrade from Scotland Yard plans revenge, and at stake is the brilliant reputation of the world's most famous consulting detective. His only hope is to 'play the game'.

www.cenfoxbooks.com

A delightfully imaginative pastiche. Recommended. **Peter Blau BSI**
An extraordinary book, one of the most enjoyable pieces of Holmesian fiction I've read in a long time … a complex, ingenious and deliciously funny story of intersecting realities, and the conclusion is entirely satisfactory. I love it! **Roger Johnson**
Commissioning Editor: ***The Sherlock Holmes Journal***